An Undeniable Attraction

Drake turned Elizabeth toward him. She placed her forehead against his shoulder, unable to meet his eyes, afraid he could read her thoughts. But he wouldn't accept that. He traced his finger down her cheek, then lifted her chin.

"Look at me," he demanded.

She opened her eyes and saw the deep clouds that had built in his. Her heart raced. She held her breath.

"I think it's time we put this thing between us to rest," he said. Then, deliberately, slowly, he lowered his lips to hers.

Elizabeth closed her eyes again, fully absorbing the gentle touch of his lips against hers. Tiny sparks of kaleidoscopic sensation ripped through her as moist flesh met flesh. Her lips opened to taste him, her tongue ventured to explore him—rough and soft, sweet and masculine all at once. She heard a groan let loose from deep within him . . .

heartbeats

Susan Rae

BERKLEY SENSATION, NEW YORK

THE BERKLEY PUBLISHING GROUP
Published by the Penguin Group
Penguin Group (USA) Inc.
375 Hudson Street, New York, New York 10014, USA
Penguin Group (Canada), 90 Eglinton Avenue East, Suite 700, Toronto, Ontario M4P 2Y3, Canada
(a division of Pearson Penguin Canada Inc.)
Penguin Books Ltd., 80 Strand, London WC2R 0RL, England
Penguin Group Ireland, 25 St. Stephen's Green, Dublin 2, Ireland (a division of Penguin Books Ltd.)
Penguin Group (Australia), 250 Camberwell Road, Camberwell, Victoria 3124, Australia
(a division of Pearson Australia Group Pty. Ltd.)
Penguin Books India Pvt. Ltd., 11 Community Centre, Panchsheel Park, New Delhi—110 017, India
Penguin Group (NZ), Cnr. Airborne and Rosedale Roads, Albany, Auckland 1310, New Zealand
(a division of Pearson New Zealand Ltd.)
Penguin Books (South Africa) (Pty.) Ltd., 24 Sturdee Avenue, Rosebank, Johannesburg 2196,
South Africa

Penguin Books Ltd., Registered Offices: 80 Strand, London WC2R 0RL, England

This is a work of fiction. Names, characters, places, and incidents either are the product of the author's imagination or are used fictitiously, and any resemblance to actual persons, living or dead, business establishments, events, or locales is entirely coincidental. The publisher does not have any control over and does not assume any responsibility for author or third-party websites or their content.

HEARTBEATS

A Berkley Sensation Book / published by arrangement with the author

PRINTING HISTORY
Berkley Sensation edition / November 2005

Copyright © 2005 by Susan Rae Marotta.
Cover photo by Larry Williams/Corbis.
Cover design by Erica Tricarico.
Interior text design by Stacy Irwin.

ISBN: 0-425-20682-3

BERKLEY® SENSATION
Berkley Sensation Books are published by The Berkley Publishing Group,
a division of Penguin Group (USA) Inc.,
375 Hudson Street, New York, New York 10014.
BERKLEY SENSATION and the "B" design are trademarks belonging to Penguin Group (USA) Inc.

PRINTED IN THE UNITED STATES OF AMERICA

10 9 8 7 6 5 4 3 2 1

For Michael, Rae, and Rita—
You amaze me every day.
May you always continue to pursue your dreams.

And for George—
For taking this journey with me as I pursue mine.

In loving memory of my father,
William B. Shogren

one

She knew it was crazy that her hands should tremble on this occasion, considering she could thread a catheter to the heart as precisely and steadily now as the best in her field, but Dr. Elizabeth Iverson never felt comfortable in the limelight.

"I know many of you share my story in one way or another," Elizabeth said, her gaze moving from table to table, guest to guest, as she scanned the seven hundred or so university alumni seated in the Grand Ballroom of Chicago's Palmer House Hilton, "or know someone who has benefited from the fund. I grew up on a farm about forty-five miles northwest of here. When I was little girl, I always dreamed of becoming a doctor. My Barbie dolls didn't wear clothes; they wore bandages and tourniquets, and I was always pretending to try the latest medical procedure on some poor, unsuspecting farm animal—with some very interesting results, as you can imagine." Now well into her speech, she raised a playful eyebrow and was rewarded with mild laughter.

"Back then, though, college seemed financially out of the question. That's why what we're doing here tonight is so important. We're helping to fuel dreams. For me, it's not about the glamour of being a doctor. As a cardiologist, it's about looking into a patient's eyes and seeing that spark of hope shine back when she's just learned she has another lease on life. To me, that's priceless."

Her attention moved to the guests at the back of the room. "With our silent auction tonight, we'll help more students turn their dreams into realities. With the money you'll so generously donate, I know . . ."

Elizabeth's lips froze in mid-sentence. Her words caught in her throat as her heart did a major flip-flop. She recognized him instantly. There was no mistaking the identity of the man who stood in the entrance to the ballroom, nametag in hand, as if he had just arrived. She stood, motionless, staring, unaware of the murmurs of uneasiness arising from the gathering. She watched, mesmerized, as his lips curved into that slow, Mona Lisa smile of his and his chin lifted in acknowledgment of her awareness of him. Although quite a distance away, Elizabeth could easily make out the slight cleft in his chin, the sexy, firm line of his jaw—and those deep-set eyes, which she knew were the most amazing shade of midnight blue.

"Dr. Iverson, are you all right?" the alumni president asked at her side.

Suddenly the awkward coughing of the guests, the clinking of glasses, the shuffling of chairs reached her senses. Embarrassed and frustrated by her reaction to him, she broke contact with those eyes and grabbed for her water glass as if reaching for a lifeline. When she looked up again, he was gone. The twinge of disappointment she felt at that surprised her, but she forced it to the back of her mind as she turned her attention once more to the gathering.

"I'm sorry, where was I? Yes, the dreams . . ."

Elizabeth made her way back to her table. Glancing at the empty chair beside hers, she noted that Julie Parks, her former college roommate and best friend, still hadn't arrived. Evening bag in hand, she hurried from the room and headed for the ladies' lounge.

Her knees wobbled as she leaned against the vanity for support. Turning on the tap, she splashed cold water onto her face, trying to shock the blood into returning to her cheeks. Why was he here? she wondered. Why now, when everything was finally going so smoothly for her? Why did Drake McGuire have to show up now like a ghost haunting her from her past?

But if he was a ghost, he was the most handsome ghost she'd ever seen. She gazed into the mirror, into her own amber eyes, remembering. . . . It had been over six years since they'd been together, and he looked older, naturally, and even more put together. She smiled. Yes, he was one solid hunk of a man and he looked downright delicious in that sleek suit of his—delicious like the sleek vanilla mousse with chocolate swirls they'd had for dessert—yes, *definitely* the chocolate swirls—melting in your mouth.

Jeez, get a grip, she scolded herself. Another woman entered the lounge. Elizabeth reached for her evening bag, trying to look like she wasn't falling apart at the seams. She reapplied mascara and lipstick, repairing the damage done to her face, then contemplated her own pale reflection. Did she look older? Of course she did. More sophisticated? Maybe. But the surface of her skin was still smooth—she'd avoided the cynical lines around her mouth that some doctors developed during the long hours of residency. Her complexion was still fair—well, actually somewhat ghostly now, although her color was starting to return.

But her naturally curly auburn hair was another story. No matter how hard she tried to tame it, it had a will of its own. She made a face, then tucked an errant curl back up into the knot at the top of her head.

Finally, she smoothed the sequined dress she'd picked up in a shop on Michigan Avenue barely two hours ago—there'd been no time to stop at her apartment to change into the dress she planned to wear to the banquet. She smiled at the way the shimmering sheath hugged her form, glad she had ignored her conscience for once and splurged. If Drake McGuire was still out there, she'd give him an eyeful, but definitely not the time of day. There was too much at stake for that.

She really should not have been so shocked to see him. It was an alumni dinner, after all, she reasoned, despite the niggling suspicion that inched into her heart. He was here to support the scholarship fund, she told herself, although a little voice inside her head argued that she'd never known him to attend their university's alumni functions in the past. She shook her head, trying to erase the doubts from her mind.

It was Julie asking about him earlier today that had set her nerves astir.

She frowned and reached for her cell phone. She punched in her number at home and waited. Julie was getting out of a rough relationship—her third marriage in nine years. Only this breakup wasn't going as smoothly as the others had. Elizabeth had convinced Julie to stay with her for a few days while she sorted it out. They were supposed to meet at the apartment that afternoon, then travel downtown together. But plans changed at the last minute when Elizabeth was called back to the Heartland Cardiac Center for a consultation. They decided to meet up at the banquet instead.

But Julie wasn't at the banquet, and she wasn't at Elizabeth's apartment, either, or at least she wasn't answering the phone. Elizabeth heard her own voice on the answering machine. She left a message, then snapped the phone shut and slipped it back into her evening bag. She would give Julie a few more minutes before letting herself get more concerned. It wouldn't be the first time her friend didn't show up when or where she was supposed to.

Sighing, she opened the door and stepped out into the hallway, praying that she would make it back to her table before she had a chance to come face-to-face with Drake. But she barely made it into the golden-hued State Ballroom, the reception area for the banquet, when Drake blocked her path. Like a true lawman, he had staked her out.

"Dr. Elizabeth Iverson," he said, his lips curving into his signature smooth smile. "It has a nice ring to it, doesn't it?"

The sound of his voice, deep and casually sensual, even with that touch of cynicism, made her heart take off again. Now that she was over her initial shock, it also sent the blood rising to her cheeks, warming them in a most annoying way. She forced her most confident smile to her lips. *Fake it until you believe it,* she told herself. The words were her mantra.

"Special Agent Drake McGuire," she said. "It's good of you to come. I'm glad that you support the fund."

"Yes," he said, his dark blue eyes sparkling with amusement. "We must support the old alma mater." He held up a glass, offering it to her. "Gin and tonic, with a twist of lemon, just the way you like it, as I remember."

"Thank you." She accepted the drink, then nodded toward his, trying to avoid meeting his eyes. "And yours, Gentleman Jack, on the rocks."

"I like the color; it reminds me of someone." He held the glass up very near to her face and studied the honey-colored contents of his glass, then her eyes. Finally he brought the glass to his lips and took a slow sip.

"Besides," he said, after he swallowed, "it eases the soul."

"And your soul needs easing?" she teased, her pulse throbbing in her throat. She needed to keep the tone light until she could make her escape.

But he wasn't going to let her get away with it.

"Hmmm . . ." His gaze raked down boldly over her form. She felt her blood simmering, threatening to boil over as his gaze caressed her curves, moving down past her waist, over her hips, then down the long sheath of her legs before slowly sliding back up. He lingered at her breasts where their rounded crests swelled above the low-cut scooped neckline, then returned to study her face.

"I didn't think my soul needed easing until tonight," he said, his voice oddly tight, "when I saw you up on that podium. That dress becomes you."

Elizabeth's skin sizzled with sexual tension. She sipped her drink, welcoming the iced liquid, trying to concentrate on anything but him.

"How long has it been?" he continued. "Five, six years?" But she could tell by his tone that he knew exactly how long it had been. "You left me high and dry, Elizabeth."

Strains of music from the jazz band hired for the evening spilled out to them from the Grand Ballroom. "You make it sound like there was something to leave," she said. "As I recall, we spent a weekend together. A rather nice weekend, but that was all it was."

He laughed. "Nice? Is that how you'd describe it? Funny, that's not at all the word I would use." His blue eyes flamed darker with something more than cynicism, something dangerous. "I remember a lot of heat, and it wasn't from the warm Atlanta day. Hot-lanta was on fire that spring, as I remember."

The heat of his gaze and her own memories of their time together sent tremors of awareness rippling through her body. Part of her wanted to slap him for bringing that out in her, but the rest of her reveled in the sensations. And he knew it.

"I need to return to the banquet," she said smartly. "Thanks again for the drink." She pushed the still half-full glass into his hands.

His smile deepened. She tried to ignore it as she turned to reenter the ballroom.

Somehow, he still managed to get in the last word.

"This isn't over yet, Doc," she heard him say as she stepped back under the glittering light of the Grand Ballroom's crystal chandeliers.

Drake watched her slim hips sway ever so slightly as she retreated. His hand itched to curve over her nicely rounded buttocks, even as he cursed himself for letting her have that effect on him. The meeting hadn't gone anything like he planned, but when she looked up at him with those seemingly innocent eyes of hers, he couldn't resist stirring the fires he knew dwelled within her. When she smiled at him with those heart-shaped lips, the memory of how she had once cried out his name in passion burned his soul.

For a five-foot-five neatly wrapped package she packed a hell of a wallop.

"Damn!" he cursed. He downed his own drink, then slammed both glasses onto a table and headed for the elevators.

two

Elizabeth parked her car and stepped out onto the sidewalk. Overhead, the leaves rustled in the quickening breeze. She glanced up at the windows of her second-floor apartment as she grabbed her evening bag and briefcase and locked the car. She had moved to this building—a three-flat on a quiet, tree-lined street a few blocks north of Wrigley Field—during her residency. She hoped to give her daughter, Allison, then a toddler, a safer place to live. Only a couple of blocks from the elevated train, it had allowed her an easy commute downtown to the university hospital. But the building was rundown, past its prime, as so many of the three-flats in the area were. Now that she had secured a good position that paid well, Elizabeth considered moving, but her flat had another convenience that was difficult to give up—a wonderful landlady who didn't mind babysitting when she was on call. Mary Parisi had been a lifesaver during her hectic years of residency and subsequent fellowship. Although lately, Elizabeth got the odd sense that Mary disapproved of all the hours she put in, as if the long hours required for her profession were not compatible with good mothering. Mary hadn't said anything, but . . .

Allison was at her grandmother's tonight.

Elizabeth didn't see any light coming through her windows and she wondered again just where Julie was. After another fifteen minutes at the banquet, she had called the apartment again, and then Julie's cell phone. With no success on either line, she made her excuses and left.

The shrill bark of a dog coming from somewhere down the street sent a shiver snaking up her spine. Glancing down the sidewalk, she had the uneasy feeling that someone was watching her.

"You're being paranoid," she told herself. Still, she hurried toward the building and up the porch steps. She unlocked the front door and crossed the common foyer, aware of the blare of the TV coming through the door of the main floor apartment. She wondered if Mary was becoming hard of hearing. She made a mental note to check into it as she started up the old, worn wooden staircase, knowing that Mary's hearing loss could have a significant effect on Allison's safety.

At the landing, she tried her own door, then frowned in annoyance. What would have possessed Julie to go out and leave the apartment door unlocked? No neighborhood was totally safe, even with an outside security door. And they had new tenants in the garden apartment that she hadn't had a chance to meet yet. She pushed the door open and stepped inside. The glow from the streetlights spilled in through the lace curtains at the front of the apartment. It caught her eye as it danced eerily with the tree shadows upon the ceiling. Turning her gaze to the right, down the dark hallway, she spotted a sliver of light coming from the bathroom.

"Julie?"

She waited for an answer, but none came. Instead, the steady dripping of water from the bathroom faucet met her ears. Mary obviously hadn't had a plumber up yet to fix the leaky faucet like she'd promised. Elizabeth took another step inside and flicked on the light switch, aware of the click of the apartment door as it closed behind her. A quick scan of the living room revealed Julie's evening gown draped across the sofa. The plastic dry cleaning bag still covered it.

"Julie?" Elizabeth called again, louder this time. She glanced to the left, where Allison's door stood ajar. Sensing nothing there, she turned toward the hallway, debating whether to continue on or call the police. Now she was really being paranoid, she chided herself. Julie probably just changed her mind about attending the banquet and decided to go out somewhere else, or—her husband had shown up.

Elizabeth set her briefcase down. She took her cell phone out of her evening bag and flipped it open, just in case, then started down the hallway. At the bathroom she paused. Glancing around the partially opened door, she discovered Julie's makeup scattered on the counter along with her own toiletries. A damp towel lay on the floor. She pushed the door open further, but the bathroom was clearly unoccupied.

She took another step toward the bedroom, then stopped as a dark spot on the beige carpet caught her eye. She bent down, stretching her fingers out to touch it. The familiar texture of the moisture that wicked against her fingertips left her feeling somewhat dazed. She turned her fingers to the light although her mind already knew what her eyes would tell her. The sticky substance was blood—spent blood—already drying with time.

Elizabeth's heart hammered in her chest. Further examination of the carpet revealed a trail of blood leading toward the bedroom. She willed her nerves to calm while she conjured up a thousand rational explanations for the blood. As she turned the corner and switched on the bedroom light, her worst fears were confirmed.

Julie lay facedown on the floor beside the bed. The towel that had been wrapped around her head had gone askew, her blond hair falling into the pool of blood that darkened the rug around her. The back of Elizabeth's own ivory robe glared back at her a bright red, drying darker at the edges of the stain. Deep gashes in the robe gave evidence of where Julie's blood had poured out. Elizabeth was instantly aware that no blood flowed now.

She blinked, trying to clear the horrid vision from her eyes even as she raced toward her friend. Suppressing the scream that threatened to choke the air from her lungs, she knelt and pressed her fingertips against Julie's neck. Finding no discernable pulse, her heart refused to believe what her head already knew. She shoved Julie onto her back and attempted to breathe life into her body, mindless of the blood that caked her lips. Palms open, she shoved against her friend's chest and began CPR. After a few reps she stopped to punch 911 into her cell phone.

"This is Dr. Elizabeth Iverson!" she shouted when the dispatcher answered. "I need an ambulance STAT! I have a multiple stab-wound victim—a thirty-two-year-old female."

She gave her address, then let the phone drop to her side while she continued to perform CPR—and prayed for a miracle.

* * *

Drake scanned the street from the shadowed interior of his car parked two doors down from Elizabeth's apartment. Then he glanced up once more at the light streaming from her windows. He had walked up to the building when he arrived a half-hour earlier and checked the mailboxes to make sure he had the right address. Then he'd retreated to the car to wait.

He didn't like the way he left things at the Palmer House. He still felt there was unfinished business between them. Hell, maybe he was nuts, or maybe he just wanted to get another look at her before permanently deleting her from his memory. He'd watched her pull up, noticed how she hesitated before entering the building, wondered if he should walk up to her right then and try to talk to her again, or if he should just get the hell out of town.

Drake figured he'd give her a few more minutes, then head up to the apartment, still unsure of what he wanted to say to her. Her flippant attitude toward him earlier had irritated him. True, their little tryst was a lifetime ago—he'd been to hell and back since then—but he could never get Elizabeth out of his head. When he saw her tonight, six years ago suddenly seemed like only yesterday. She left him so abruptly then. He didn't have the chance to say goodbye. At the time, he reasoned, it was probably just as well. He was crazy to think that Elizabeth Iverson could ever be a part of his life.

But damn, they were good together.

He pressed his hand against the door handle, then paused as he heard the blare of a siren approaching from behind. Glancing in the rearview mirror, he saw a rescue squad speeding toward him. Its flashing lights reflected garishly off the windows of the homes that lined the street. As it passed his car, a police squad screamed around the corner up ahead and raced toward him from the other direction. Both braked in front of Elizabeth's building.

A sense of dread seized him, followed instantly by the familiar rush of adrenaline as he grabbed his gun from the glove box and shoved it beneath his belt. He stepped out, eyes trained on the building, then jumped back as another squad car blared past, just missing him, and screeched to a halt behind the first. Deciding it was no time to be circumspect, he ran across the street. When he reached the front yard, Chicago's finest were already approaching the building with their guns drawn.

"Police! Open up!" an officer shouted, banging on the glass front door.

Drake ran toward him, his heart pounding violently. "What's going on here?" he yelled.

A second officer straight-armed him, holding him back.

"Sir, do you live here?" The cop gave him a quick once-over, taking in his suit and tie.

"No, but I—"

"Then stand aside."

"Hey, Sal," the officer at the door yelled back, "can they get hold of that lady yet?"

With his hand still on Drake's chest, the officer spoke into his shoulder mike, then replied a moment later, "She's not responding."

"Hell, we gotta get into this building! Shoot the lock off."

"Who's not responding?" Drake asked, shoving at the cop's hand.

"Sir, I asked you to step aside," Sal warned, then nodded at two of the officers in the yard. "Gus, go around and see if you can get in through the back. Kick the damn door in if you have to, but be careful. Nick, you cover him. The perp could still be in there, for all we know."

Drake had had enough. He reached into his suit coat and pulled out his ID. He needed info *now*.

"I'm FBI!" he shouted at Sal. "Now tell me what the hell is going on here!" The street that had been so quiet minutes before was now in chaos. Neighbors funneled out of their homes, trying to get a better look at the scene as another squad car approached. The paramedics waited impatiently beside their van, a gurney already wheeled out, ready to rush in as soon as the cops gave the okay.

Sal glanced at Drake's ID. His eyes narrowed, then his attention was drawn back toward the entryway where the shadowy figure of a woman appeared behind the glass door.

"Open the door, ma'am," the first officer ordered.

The lady fumbled with the lock, then the door flew open as the officer pushed through into the hall. Sal seemed to forget about Drake as he followed his partner inside.

But as the officers started up the staircase, two steps at a time with Drake at their heels, Sal shouted over his shoulder. "Thirty-two-year-old woman—multiple stab wounds."

Drake's steps faltered. A cold sweat iced his back and he was sure his heart stopped, if only for a second. Shoving his foreboding aside, he drew his own gun and pushed on up the stairs.

"Who's he?" the first cop asked as they paused on the landing.

Sal shrugged his shoulders. "FBI."

"Great!" But the look on the cop's face showed he clearly didn't think so. He stood to the side and began pounding on the door. "Police! Open up!"

A muffled shout sounded from inside. "In here! Hurry!" Elizabeth's voice? Drake couldn't tell.

Sal tried the door, then threw it open. The first cop went in and quickly scanned the living room, then motioned for Sal to follow. Sal stepped in and headed left to make sure the front of the apartment was clear.

Drake wasn't waiting. Leading with his weapon, he shoved through the door, then sprinted down the hallway to his right, stopping briefly to check the kitchen and bath.

"Hey!" the first officer shouted, but Drake paid no attention. The officer followed.

"In here!" the woman cried from around the next doorway. This time he was sure it was Elizabeth.

He paused to peer around the corner and scan the room. He nodded to the cop, who raced passed him and checked out the closet. Finally he allowed himself to look down toward her voice.

His stomach turned at the ghastly sight that met his eyes.

"Elizabeth . . ." he breathed.

She was bent over the victim, administering CPR, her hands covered with blood. Her hair had come undone, the wild curls falling in ringlets against her dress, its shimmer dulled now by blood as she knelt trying to save the victim.

Part of him registered relief that it wasn't Elizabeth lying on the floor; the rest of him reeled in anger at the horror of the scene. He'd seen plenty of homicides, but he never got used to them.

"Elizabeth . . ." he called again.

She glanced up, her eyes widening when they met his, then quickly dismissed him as she turned her attention back to the victim. Her brief glance was enough, though, for him to see the pain that blanched her face.

His heart did another flip-flop. "Are you hurt?" he asked.

She shook her head violently. "Where are the paramedics!"

The first officer called out. "Sal, we're clear. Send them up."

Drake was no doctor, but he could tell by the amount of blood on the carpet that it was too late for the paramedics. He stepped toward Elizabeth, careful to walk around the puddled blood. Shoving his gun back behind his waistband, he knelt beside her, laying a hand against her shoulder.

"Elizabeth, it's too late," he said gently.

"No!" she cried, shrugging against his hand. "It can't be! I can't let her die!" She leaned over and once more attempted to breathe life into the victim.

"I'm afraid he's right, ma'am," Sal said as he stood back, waiting in the doorway. Elizabeth paid no attention to him, but continued her compressions on the victim's chest. Drake's jaw tensed. He had seen this before, this stubbornness to deny death. Hell, he'd been there himself. All the animosity he felt toward her earlier that night drained from him. He wanted to pull her back into himself and protect her from the horror.

An uneasy silence filled the room, punctuated by Elizabeth's gasps into the victim every fifth compression as they waited for the paramedics to make it up the stairs.

When they arrived, Drake sensed Elizabeth stiffen. He tightened his grip on her shoulder as her hands suddenly stilled. When a paramedic tried to put his fingers on the victim's neck to check for a pulse, Elizabeth leaned across the body and blocked him with her arm.

"No!" she warned him. "Don't touch her!"

"Ma'am, we have to . . ."

"She's gone," she breathed out.

There was a moment of silence, then the paramedic replied, "Sorry, ma'am, but we need to check for ourselves and transport."

"I'm a doctor," Elizabeth seethed, her head tilting angrily, daring him to argue with her. "I can pronounce death." She swiped at a tear with the back of her hand, unwittingly smearing more blood across her cheek.

"With all due respect . . ."

Drake nodded to the paramedic. "Let it go."

"And who are you?"

"Special Agent Drake McGuire, FBI."

The paramedic looked at the police officer for direction. The officer sighed, then nodded. "Sorry, boys, nothing for you here now. Sal, call the coroner, and get the investigation team up here."

Drake shoved his gun beneath his waistband and grasped Elizabeth's other shoulder. He tried to gentle her toward him, but she still resisted.

"It's Julie," she whispered so only he could hear. "Julie Parks, my college roommate."

Stunned, Drake took his first good look at the victim's features—the blond hair, the long patrician nose and high forehead. Her eyes were closed, but recognition sparked at the corners of his mind. He had met Julie briefly—at the same party where he first met Elizabeth.

three

"I'm sorry," he whispered.

Through the numbness, Elizabeth felt Drake's hands, strong and reassuring, against her shoulders. A sob built in her throat, but she swallowed it down and willed her professionalism to take over. She forced herself to scan Julie's body. The back of Julie's hands were cut, as if she'd tried to fend off her attacker from behind, and a deep knife wound sliced across the top of her shoulder. Elizabeth reached to examine the wound more thoroughly.

"Ma'am, I can't let you do that," the officer told her, stepping forward now. "I can't let you contaminate the crime scene any more than it already is."

Crime scene. The words echoed through her mind.

"Elizabeth, let's go," Drake said. "The coroner will take over from here."

She let him lift her this time, let him pull her up against himself, then her knees caved. His arms tightened around her. She turned into him, grasping his lapels for support.

"I need air," she whispered.

She let Drake guide her from the room to the back porch. Suddenly afraid all the rich food she consumed at the banquet was about to come rushing back up, she hurried to the low wall and leaned over the edge, gulping in air, trying to regain control of her body, trying to block the reality of the last fifteen minutes from her mind.

"Sit," he ordered.

Elizabeth didn't argue. She sank into the chair that he brought over. Waves of heat and cold surged through her, making her skin feel icy-hot. Drake knelt in front of her, took the edge of a damp towel and wiped gently at her cheek, then dabbed at the contours of her lips. He lifted her curls and slid the towel against her neck. Even in her state of semi-shock, she was aware of his touch, of his fingers gently gliding over her skin—and the tiny shocks of electricity they sparked. Her skin grew hotter, but not even Drake's touch could erase the chill she still felt from the scene in her apartment. She closed her eyes, chiding herself. She was a doctor. She should be able to handle this. . . .

"Hey, it's nothing to be ashamed of," Drake said. The tightness in his voice drew her eyes open. Once again, he seemed to know what she was thinking. She looked up at him and felt the connection that fired between them. He, too, had seen his share of death and violence. But the difference, she reminded herself, is that in his role as an FBI agent he was often the shooter, taking a life. She was supposed to save lives.

For now, though, she ignored that distinction as she gazed into his eyes and drank in the comfort of his nearness.

"If you're okay now, I think I'll take a look inside before the detectives get here."

She nodded. She could use a few moments alone to get her jumbled senses in order.

"I need to ask you a few questions before the detective gets here, for my report," the officer said. "You look cold, though. Could you use a blanket or something?" The officer in charge found Elizabeth still sitting out on the porch, the wet towel now pressed against her forehead.

Elizabeth glanced down at her dress, aware for the first time of the bloodstains. She didn't know where her wrap had gone. It must have fallen from her shoulders when she was attending Julie.

"Who would do this to Julie?" she asked, trying to keep her lower lip from trembling.

"I don't know, ma'am, but we aim to find out. So, you're a doctor. Can I have your name?"

"Yes, Elizabeth Iverson. I'm a cardiologist."

"And the victim's name?"

"Julie—Julie Parks."

"And how did you know the victim, ma'am?"

"I wish you'd stop calling her the victim."

"Sorry, how did you know her?"

As Elizabeth explained her connection to Julie, she became acutely aware of Drake's presence behind the police officer. She was also aware of how intently he gazed at her while she answered the officer's questions.

"So you live here?" the officer asked.

"Yes."

"And Miss Parks?"

"It's Mrs. Parks, and no, she doesn't live here. She's going through a divorce. She was staying with me for a few days."

"Where were you this evening?"

"At an alumni event downtown. We were supposed to meet there."

"That's where you were before you came home and discovered the body?"

"Yes."

"Who else lives here? What about the woman downstairs?"

"That's my landlady, Mary Parisi. She lives in the first-floor apartment with her son, Donny."

"Well, I'll check and see if they heard anything. Anyone else live here with you?"

Elizabeth felt her heart skip a beat. "Oh my God!" she breathed. "Allison!" *What if Allison had been here!*

"Excuse me, what did you say?" the officer asked.

"Allison, my daughter. She's with my mother, at our farm up north. She could have been here!" She remembered the twinge of guilt she'd felt at shipping Allison off to her mother's for the weekend so she and Julie could have some girl time. They were supposed to drive up on Sunday and pick her up.

"Well, we can be thankful that she wasn't," the officer said, a note of sympathy in his voice.

Elizabeth felt Drake's gaze deepen on her. She dared not look at him. She knew he must have seen Allison's room when he checked the place out.

The officer closed his notebook. "Well, that's enough for now, but I'm going to have to ask you to stick around.

I'm sure the detective will have more questions for you. I'll have the crime techs find something for you to slip on—we're going to need those clothes for evidence," he said, pointing to her gown. "And, ma'am, you might want to call your mother. The TV cameras are already out there. I don't think you want her to see it on the news."

Elizabeth nodded. She glanced at her watch—it was well past ten. Her mother would be sound asleep by now, but Elizabeth knew she couldn't risk Allison seeing their apartment building surrounded by police cars on TV in the morning. She glanced at Drake, remembering how persistent and disturbing newscasters could be. She'd have to wake her mother.

The call to her mother had not been easy. Sharon Iverson wanted Elizabeth to come home right away. But Julie was dead, and Elizabeth needed to help in any way she could to find the killer, even if it meant sitting here, exhausted, while the detective bombarded her with what seemed like the same questions over and over again.

Drake sat across from her. Under the detective's grilling and Drake's unflinching assessment of her, she couldn't help but feel guilty—as if she had something to do with Julie's murder. She knew the thought was crazy, but it still plagued her. She couldn't help but feel some blame because Julie had been attacked in her apartment. She was beginning to wonder if this night would ever end.

"So, you can't think of anyone who might have wanted to harm your friend?" Detective O'Reilly asked again.

Elizabeth shook her head. "Just what I told you. She has a couple of ex-husbands, but I don't think she's had any contact with them. I know she's going through a divorce and she and her current husband have been having some sticking points, but I can't imagine he would resort to this."

"Did she ever mention that he struck her?"

"No."

"Well, there's no sign of forced entry—she either had to know the guy and let him in, or she left the door unlocked. Did she have a key to the apartment? Could she have given it to someone?"

"I don't think so. I know she arrived around two this afternoon. I gave her the code to the garage so she could park her car in there. I hide an apartment key in an old trunk just inside the garage door. She used that to get in. I don't think she had time to get it copied."

"And no one else has a key to the apartment? Any of your old boyfriends?"

Elizabeth frowned. "I've never given a key to anyone, except my mother," she said evenly. "I have my daughter to consider." Then she added, "Of course Mrs. Parisi, my landlady, has a key."

"Yes, well, we'll check it out. Now, you say you didn't make it home earlier this evening because you were called back to work at the last minute. What time was that?"

She cocked her head and rubbed at her temple. The events of the day were jumbled in her mind. She tried to sort them out. "I left the center for the first time just before six."

"The center—that's the Heartland Cardiac Center, down on Clark Street? You work there?"

Elizabeth nodded.

"You treat some pretty fancy clients there, don't you?"

Elizabeth didn't like his snide tone; as a matter of fact she was beginning to not like him at all. "We treat a variety of patients, but yes, many celebrities and more wealthy clients choose to undergo procedures with us."

"Yeah, I was in there once. Had to question some guy whose home was robbed while he was under the knife. Looks like the Ritz."

Elizabeth noticed Drake's eyebrow raise at the mention of where she worked. She hated the fact that it made her feel slightly defensive. "We believe in attention to detail," she explained to the detective, "and making our clients as comfortable as possible. They appreciate it that way."

"I bet they do. So what time did you leave for good, to go downtown?"

"It was six fifty-five to be exact. I remember looking at my watch and deciding I didn't have time to come back to the apartment and change. I was going to miss the cocktail hour already as it was. I called Julie and we decided to meet up at the Palmer House instead."

"And Mrs. Parks was all right when you spoke to her then? You didn't hear anyone else in the apartment?"

"No. Julie sounded like her usual, happy-go-lucky self, looking forward to the night out." She shuddered as a fresh chill ran though her. She realized it was the last time she would ever talk to her.

"Well, we'll check that out, too. It could have been another random act of violence, or it could have been someone she met recently." He turned to Drake and cocked a bushy red eyebrow at him.

"So, McGuire, it's been awhile, hasn't it? I'd heard you'd gone into the bureau."

"Yes," Drake answered, but didn't move his gaze from Elizabeth. She glanced up at him, then at O'Reilly. "You two know each other?" she asked.

Drake nodded, but he didn't offer any explanations.

"We were rookies together," O'Reilly said. "On the department. McGuire was always rushing in a couple steps ahead of us back then, too."

Elizabeth studied Detective Patrick O'Reilly more closely. She couldn't help but compare him to Drake, who had obviously stayed fit and trim since his rookie days. O'Reilly, on the other hand, looked like he had about five, maybe ten years before he became a serious candidate for a heart attack. Drake's biceps bulged slightly against the arms of his suit coat, whereas O'Reilly's stomach was jutting out against the buttons of his faded sport coat. There was more than a hint of animosity in O'Reilly's green eyes as he unleashed his questions now on Drake.

"And what brought you to the scene so promptly this time, McGuire?"

Drake's eyes narrowed as he shot a look at O'Reilly. "I'm a friend."

"But you didn't arrive with Dr. Iverson?"

"No, a few minutes after."

"I see. And did you know the victim?"

"Barely." His gaze flicked back toward Elizabeth. "Listen, O'Reilly, we can answer the rest of your questions tomorrow. Right now, I'd like to get Elizabeth someplace where she can get some sleep."

O'Reilly's cheeks puffed slightly. He seemed about to argue, but changed his mind as he looked over at her and smiled smugly. "I guess that's enough for now. Just leave an address where you'll be, and a phone number. And I don't have to tell you, McGuire, not to leave town for a while."

"Got it." Drake gave him his cell phone number and the name of a hotel not far from there.

Elizabeth shook her head. "I can't—"

"No arguments," Drake said. It was clear by his look and the deep intensity of his tone that he was in no mood to discuss it. "You're not staying in this apartment tonight. Pack some things, and we're out of here, if that's all right with you, Detective?"

O'Reilly raised his eyebrow again as he glanced form Elizabeth to Drake. "Sounds reasonable," was all he said.

The headache that had been building for the last couple of hours began to throb against Elizabeth's temples. She grimaced. The last thing she needed in her current state was to be in close proximity to Drake.

Suddenly, though, it all seemed out of her hands.

four

Drake tried to relax as he stared up at the ceiling of the darkened hotel suite, hands laced behind his head, his body stretched out along the living room sofa. It had been quiet for at least thirty minutes. He hoped Elizabeth was finally sleeping.

God knew he wasn't.

He wondered just what the hell he had gotten himself into. He'd been in town less than one day. His family didn't even know he was here—he hadn't planned on telling them. In fact, he hadn't planned anything. He made the drive up from New Orleans on a lark, a crazy, split-second decision after receiving an alumni brochure announcing the banquet. He almost missed the notice in the month's stack of mail, mostly junk, that he picked up from the post office after returning from his last assignment. He was a bit surprised to receive the brochure, seeing as he'd been out of touch with his alma mater for a few years. He figured some overzealous fundraising committee member must have tracked him down. Elizabeth was listed as a featured speaker. Her name jumped out at him, rousing his curiosity. *Well, what the hell,* he thought. He packed a bag, tossed it into the back of his car, and took off, figuring the long drive might do him good. He had nothing else to do for the next four weeks. His section chief had made it perfectly clear that he was to take a long vacation—or else.

But Drake had been unprepared for his reaction to Elizabeth. He thought after all this time he was over the physical roller coaster she had put him on. Seeing her on that podium, all surefire and shimmering, tore at his gut. He felt like it had been rubbed raw, especially after their little tête-à-tête. She was prettier than ever and just as fickle—running hot and cold all at the same time.

But as unprepared as he'd been for that, he was even further unprepared for the icy dread he felt when he thought *she* was the victim.

And now O'Reilly was on the case. The corners of Drake's mouth turned down into a frown. He'd have to see what he could do about that. Maybe his cousins, who were well connected with the Chicago Police Department, could pull some strings, get a couple more detectives on the case, detectives that had half a chance of finding the real perp.

O'Reilly had always been slow on the uptake. Drake wondered how the guy had ever made detective—he could barely add two and two. And Drake had a gut feeling that O'Reilly was missing the boat on this one. He'd failed to ask Elizabeth if there was someone out there who might want to get rid of her. It was *her* apartment. It would be easy to mistake Julie for Elizabeth in the dark bedroom, especially with Julie wearing Elizabeth's robe and a towel wrapped around her head.

The murderer could have been someone who fully expected Elizabeth to be in the apartment—someone who knew her and had an ax to grind, or some other sick pervert who kept watch over her, stalking her, until he was able to seize his opportunity to strike.

"Oh, hell!"

Drake closed his eyes and willed sleep to come. He had a thousand questions to ask Elizabeth and a lot of checking to do on his own, but it would have to wait another couple of hours until the sun came up.

Elizabeth opened her eyes, trying to get her bearings. Her unfamiliar surroundings gave evidence that last night was not the nightmare she hoped it was, but cold reality. Sunlight played against the edges of the room-darkening drapes. She glanced at the glowing face of the bedside clock. It was half-past twelve. She'd slept over eight hours.

As Elizabeth made her way to the bathroom, she heard the murmur from the TV in the next room. Drake was obviously still here. She splashed water onto her face and tried to push last night's horror out of her mind. Instead, as she started to dress, she let her mind wander to the last time she and Drake had shared a hotel room. Correction, the *only* time she and Drake had shared a hotel room.

It was in Atlanta, in the spring term of her final year of medical school. Elizabeth was attending a conference on infectious diseases. In need of a break, she sat at a table in the hotel bar nursing a drink and going over some seminar notes when she suddenly felt someone staring at her. Looking up, she spotted Drake. There was no mistaking his dark looks. She often wondered where he got them with a name like McGuire. He looked more Italian than Irish. The direct, sensual look he gave her sent her heart skipping, and made her lips burn with the memory of the kiss they'd shared five years earlier at a New Year's Eve frat party when at the stroke of midnight her boyfriend, Kevin, was not to be found. Drake came to her rescue. He smiled that slow half smile of his, then whisked her into his arms and kissed her speechless.

Afterward, he held her close while they swayed to the lilting refrain of "Auld Lang Syne." His warm breath caressed her cheek, his hand gently stroked her back, and her heart beat so violently against her ribs that she knew he must have felt it, too. When the song ended he continued to hold her close. "You looked like you needed that," he whispered into her ear.

Then Kevin showed up and she quickly excused herself to slide into her boyfriend's arms for the next dance. She was perfectly aware, though, a short while later, when Drake left the room. Aware, also, that she didn't even know his name.

She saw him only a couple of times on campus after that. Intrigued by that half smile of his, Elizabeth did a little checking and discovered that Drake McGuire was graduating in May and heading off to the Police Academy. Only a college junior herself, she had one more year to hit the books hard and then hopefully she was headed for medical school. She figured it was best to keep her distance from Mr. Drake McGuire—and keep her plans on track.

But five years later, in Atlanta, they met again. By that

time Elizabeth was engaged to be married to Kevin. The date was set for the first Saturday in August. Kevin was on track to finish his last year of law school, and had already received a placement with a top Chicago law firm. She was set to begin her residency in internal medicine at the university hospital in the fall. Their life together was well planned, scheduled, and under control—just the way Elizabeth liked it. She and Kevin truly were the perfect couple, both very dedicated to their professions, both respectful of each other's work, and disciplined in the time they spent together.

Then came Atlanta—those deep blue eyes awakened yearnings within Elizabeth that she'd managed to suppress since their New Year's kiss. Drake's quiet smile, a mere turn of the lips which curved slowly, knowingly, sent off a thousand sparks in her belly. They shared a drink together, then dinner, then took a walk in the hotel gardens. The scent of azaleas whispered on the soft night air. He kissed her and she realized just how long she had been waiting to taste those lips again—how long she had wondered if what she experienced that New Year's Eve was just her imagination, a simple reaction to Drake's impulsiveness, or something much more. But Drake's kiss unleashed an even more powerful explosion within her. He kissed her again, then again, and suddenly Elizabeth couldn't get enough of him. His kisses fed a deep need, answering something that until that moment she had refused to believe was missing in her relationship with Kevin. When Drake led her up to his hotel room, she didn't protest. When he kissed her again and slowly started unzipping the back of her dress, she didn't protest. When he gentled her onto the bed, she still didn't protest, but unbuttoned his shirt, slipped her hands around his bare skin, and pulled him into her. She reasoned that even if for one night, this was her chance to experience all he could give her.

But one night had turned into two. His touch, his kisses, transformed her into someone she didn't know she could be. They made love most of the night, then again the next morning, then dressed, rented a boat, and went out on the river to make love again in the cabin while the boat swayed on the waves. That night they danced under the stars, then returned to his room for more passionate love-making. Neither one of them spoke about tomorrow, only reveled and marveled in the moment and the discovery of each other.

She hadn't realized how precious their time was.

Sunday morning, when she awoke, he was gone, with a note on her pillow saying he would return later in the day. She flipped on the TV to laze away the morning in bed. A newscast caught her eye. She sat up and increased the volume as an FBI jacket flashed across the screen. The one thing she did know about Drake was that he was nearing his second anniversary with the bureau. Her heart raced as she listened to the newscaster. FBI agents had seized over twenty kilos of cocaine from a warehouse in the downtown area. "The early-morning raid was a result of an ongoing investigation by the combined DEA and FBI task force, according to a police source," the announcer explained. "Two members of a drug ring reputed to be linked to organized crime were killed in an exchange of gunfire. An FBI agent was also fatally shot and another seriously wounded."

Elizabeth went numb. The screen showed paramedics wheeling the wounded agent into an ambulance. She caught a glimpse of Drake's dark hair before someone pushed the camera out of the way. The screen flipped back to the newscaster. "The FBI agent was transported to a downtown hospital, where he is listed in stable condition."

Panic seized her. She wondered what she had been thinking. Drake's life was too chaotic, too violent. She could not have a relationship with someone whose profession put him in the line of fire. After only two days with him, the thought of losing him to such violence was more than she could bear. She couldn't allow herself to become any more attached. Jolted back to her senses, Elizabeth dressed quickly and left the room. She needed to get back to Chicago and her scheduled life as soon as possible. What she and Drake shared was a fantasy.

But she couldn't help herself from calling the hospital before she got on the plane, just to make sure he was all right. The nurse told her his wound, although serious, was not life-threatening. He would survive.

Elizabeth hadn't seen him since, until last night.

And now he was just on the other side of the door.

Drake looked up from his laptop when she walked into the room and turned off the TV.

"Coffee?" he asked. "There are rolls and yogurt, too, although I'm about ready to have some lunch sent up."

"You shouldn't have let me sleep so long," she said, avoiding his eyes.

He'd been tempted to wake her a couple of times, but didn't trust himself to enter her room.

Elizabeth took the cup he handed her and walked over to the sofa, ignoring the chair across the table from him. He smiled to himself.

"It's a good thing you called your mother last night," he

said, reaching for another roll. "It was all over the news this morning."

She took a sip of coffee. "I should call Julie's parents."

"The police have already informed them."

She glanced at him, her gaze questioning. He saw by the guarded look in her eyes that she wasn't as put together as he'd first thought.

"O'Reilly called," he explained. "He wants us down at district headquarters this afternoon to give our statements. Nothing to worry about, just a formality."

She nodded. "I still need to call Julie's parents. She was staying with me. I feel responsible."

"You're nothing of the kind," he said with more force than he would have liked. "Oh, hell!" He stood and turned away from her, running a frustrated hand through his hair. He couldn't let her get to him. "Look, I understand you need to call them," he explained, turning back to her, "but don't do it because you feel responsible for Julie's death. You can't control everything, Elizabeth. Sometimes shit just happens."

His mind raced back to Atlanta, when his partner had died and he had felt responsible. It took him years to get over that, until he finally began to believe what everyone else told him, that he did everything he could in the raid—it just went down badly. They were ambushed. His fist clenched at the memory. He lost more than his partner that day; he lost Elizabeth. When he tried to call her from the hospital, it was too late. She had already checked out of the hotel. Later the nurse told him his sister called and that she wished him well. He didn't have a sister. His gut told him it was Elizabeth's way of saying goodbye. She had run scared. At first he was pissed as hell. Then he reasoned that it was just as well—life as an FBI agent tracking down international drug cartels wasn't for anyone with attachments. And Elizabeth would have been one hell of an attachment.

Right now, though, he could tell she was ticked-off, big time, at his last statement. She stood and set her cup very deliberately on the table. "Thank you for your help," she said, her tone terse. "But I'll gather my things and catch a cab. I can get down to headquarters myself. Did O'Reilly happen to mention how long I'd be out of my apartment?"

Anger frayed the corners of his reserve as he stared at her. She was less than an arm's length from him. He wanted to reach out to her, but held back. "Don't do this, Elizabeth," he said, his voice vibrating with his tension. "We started this together, and we'll see it through together. O'Reilly's an idiot. You may need my help with this one."

"I don't need . . ." she began, then her voice trailed off and she looked away, but not before he saw the intense pain flick across her face. She took a deep breath, then turned toward him again. He could see the effort it was taking for her to stay in control. "I'm sure the Chicago PD is competent enough to find Julie's . . . to find the murderer," she said firmly.

He shrugged. "Possibly, if they put the right detectives on the job. But I've already made some inquiries. It seems Julie's husband, Stephan Parks, financial wizard and philanderer, was out last night at an expensive restaurant in St. Louis with his latest conquest. He had many witnesses."

Elizabeth's eyes widened. "How did you find all that out?"

"You can do amazing things with the Internet and access to some critical data bases," he said. Drake waved his hand, indicating his laptop. "And an agent in St. Louis owed me a few favors. Seems Mr. Parks was still holed up this morning at the family homestead with the lovely woman."

"Then he's off the list."

"Possibly, although there is a question of work for hire. I assume there was a lot of money involved in the divorce?"

Elizabeth nodded. "They were having trouble reaching a settlement."

"It wouldn't be the first time someone was hired to murder a difficult wife."

He saw her shudder and tried to ignore it. There was one more thing she needed to face.

"Of course, there is one other possibility."

"What's that?" She slanted her gaze at him.

He put his hands in his pockets and met her amber eyes head on. He would give anything right now to be out on Lake Michigan in one of the dozen or so sailboats that dotted its sparkling waters this Saturday afternoon instead of having to ask his next question.

"Is there anyone you can think of who might want to harm you?"

"What?"

"Think, Elizabeth, is there anyone now, or in your past, who might want to do you bodily harm?"

"You mean who might want to *kill* me?"

"Yes."

"That's absurd. Who would want to kill me?"

"That's what I'm asking."

"I think you've been an FBI agent far too long. You've turned cynical. I'm a doctor. I haven't done anything to make anyone get that angry at me."

"What about your ex-husband?"

"My what? I don't have an ex-husband."

"Well, none that I could find, anyway."

Her jaw dropped. She glanced at his laptop, then back up at him. Her voice was breathless when she replied. "You've been checking up on me."

"I needed to cover all the angles."

Elizabeth felt dazed. She needed to get out of there— fast. She took a step around him and headed toward the bedroom to retrieve her shoulder bag.

"What about the father of your child?" he asked pointedly.

The air left her lungs. Her step faltered, and then she realized she couldn't let him see how affected she was by his question. There was too much to lose. Slowly she turned and forced herself to meet his gaze. His blue eyes seemed to grow darker. She tried to still the panic that made her heart race.

"Allison's father wanted nothing to do with her," she said evenly, praying that he wouldn't see through her half-truths. "He wasn't ready for children. I decided to raise her on my own."

"Wasn't that rather difficult?"

"My family helped me. My sister stayed with me for a time, then I moved into the brownstone with the Parisis. Mary has been very good to Allison."

Drake's eyes narrowed and his features softened. For a moment Elizabeth thought she saw a touch of admiration flash across his face. She lowered her eyes and bit her bottom lip. The last thing she deserved from him was admiration.

Suddenly the tension in the room cleared. He grabbed his suit coat from the back of his chair and flipped his laptop shut. "I think its time we get on down to headquarters."

Elizabeth was thankful for the temporary reprieve.

She'd avoided the fire—this time. Part of her desperately wished that Drake didn't feel the need to help in the investigation, but unfortunately, she shared his doubts about Detective O'Reilly. Julie was her best friend and Drake was FBI, and damn good at his job if her instincts were correct. The sooner Julie's killer was brought to justice, the better. Then Drake would leave town and Elizabeth could get on with her own life.

five

Elizabeth phoned Julie's parents on the way to district headquarters. She tried to keep her voice from breaking as she offered her condolences. Julie's parents were planning a service for her on Monday, in Orland Park, the Chicago suburb where Julie grew up. Elizabeth assured them that she would attend.

Hanging up, she kept her face turned away from Drake as she stared out of the passenger window at the beautiful autumn day. Pedestrians strolled the sidewalk, smiles lighting their faces as they enjoyed the fair weather. Tears formed in Elizabeth's eyes. She wanted to scream at the unfairness of it all. Julie should still be numbered among them. Anger seethed within her at the fact that someone had taken her friend's life so violently.

At district headquarters she and Drake were led into separate rooms. Elizabeth gave her statement to a woman who introduced herself as Detective Andi DeLuca. Elizabeth could add nothing more to what she told O'Reilly the night before.

Elizabeth couldn't sit still while she waited to sign her statement. She paced the room, pausing at the doorway to look out across the hallway into the window of another interrogation room. O'Reilly was grilling Drake again. Suddenly Drake rose and slapped his hand down on the table. Moments later he stormed out of the room.

Elizabeth watched as Detective DeLuca stepped in front of him to block his escape. The detective touched his shoulder, urging him to calm down. Drake rubbed his hand across his face, then took a deep breath. The familiar way the woman rubbed his shoulder sent a twinge of jealousy surging through Elizabeth. It both surprised and annoyed her. She studied DeLuca more closely. She looked to be in her late twenties, with short brown hair and quick, intelligent brown eyes. She wore a V-necked satin blouse and a slim skirt, which was just short enough to show off shapely legs. The outfit was professional, yet chic. It was clear by the way DeLuca talked to Drake that they shared some kind of history. Suddenly they both glanced toward her. Elizabeth quickly looked away and sat down again.

Seconds later Drake strode into the room. Although he tried to hide it, she sensed the cold anger that boiled beneath the surface of his features.

"How are you holding up?" he asked, his voice tight.

She smiled. "Better than you, I think. I take it you know Detective DeLuca, too?" She tried to make her voice sound light.

He nodded, folded his arms across his chest, and leaned back against the wall. "I worked with her for a few months. She was my partner. She just told me she's been put on the case along with O'Reilly. That's a good thing. She's a good detective."

Elizabeth noted the touch of fondness that cracked through his tone as he talked about Andi DeLuca. "So, she was your partner." She gave him a sideways glance. "Just exactly how close were you?"

"Do I detect a hint of jealousy, Dr. Iverson?" A light sparked in his eyes and a slow smile curved his lips.

Self-consciously she reached up and smoothed a curl that didn't need smoothing. "Not at all. I was just wondering. I don't think just any woman would be capable of calming you down like that."

"No, not just any woman." His smile deepened. "Don't get so worked up, Iverson. Andi's married to my cousin."

"Hey, I . . ."

"It's okay," he said. "My cousins hold important positions on the force. I pulled some strings this morning to make sure this case would be handled properly."

"Oh . . ." She was surprised to feel how relieved she was at the news. "What did O'Reilly say, then, that set you off?"

The light disappeared from his eyes. He unclasped his arms and rubbed a hand against his jaw. "It's not important. As soon as our statements are done, we can leave."

"Not so fast, McGuire," O'Reilly cautioned as he stepped into the room, followed by Detective Deluca. "You still haven't answered my questions."

Drake glanced briefly at Elizabeth, then back to O'Reilly. "You've got all the answers you're going to get from me."

DeLuca put a hand on Drake's shoulder. "Sit down, Drake. I'm afraid you're going to have to answer these."

He shook his head. "You can't good-cop bad-cop me, Andi. I know all the tricks."

"This isn't a trick." She tapped the notebook she held in her hand. "These are legitimate questions, and it would make it easier on all of us if you just answered them now and got them out of the way."

Standing beside him, Elizabeth sensed the tension that drew his muscles taught again. She could swear that at any moment he was going to haul off and punch O'Reilly in the face.

Finally he sighed and sat down. "Okay," he said. "Let's get this done."

DeLuca motioned for Elizabeth to sit. Then DeLuca and O'Reilly took chairs across the table. O'Reilly opened a folder.

"I've got eyewitnesses that put you at the scene a good twenty minutes before the call came in," O'Reilly said. "Can you explain that one?"

"What eyewitnesses?" Drake asked.

"That's not important now. Just answer the question."

Drake ignored O'Reilly and looked pointedly at Andi.

"A lady in the building across the street," Andi told him. "And the young man who lives in the downstairs apartment."

"Donny?" Elizabeth asked.

"Yes, ma'am," O'Reilly piped up importantly. "We showed him your boyfriend's picture here and he identi-fied it."

"What did you do that for!" Drake's voice rose in anger.

Elizabeth shook her head. "Detective, Donny is mentally challenged. He's a great kid, but he gets confused sometimes. He must have been mistaken."

"Nope, I don't believe he was, with all due respect. Granted, he doesn't seem like he's all there upstairs, but he recognized your boyfriend's picture, all right."

"I'm telling you, O'Reilly, you're barking up the wrong tree!"

"Drake, please—" DeLuca urged.

Drake stared long and hard at her for a few moments, then finally replied. "Fine. If you must know, I was waiting for Elizabeth to come home."

"And you didn't see anything suspicious while you waited?" DeLuca asked.

"Not a damn thing."

"Why were you waiting for Dr. Iverson?" O'Reilly asked.

"I told you, we're friends."

"When's the last time you saw each other?"

"Earlier that night, at the alumni dinner."

"And before that?"

Drake glanced at Elizabeth. She could tell that he was not happy with the direction the detective was taking. He held her gaze as he answered and their shared memories collided.

"I don't think that's any of your business."

"I'm afraid it is," DeLuca told him.

"A few years ago."

"How close were you then?" O'Reilly asked.

Drake stood, pushed his chair aside. "Okay, O'Reilly, that's enough. I think it's time you got off your soapbox and started looking for the real killer."

"One more question." O'Reilly was relentless. "What was your name doing in Julie Parks's address book?"

Elizabeth gasped. Julie was the only one who knew the truth about her history with Drake. She hadn't even told her family about what really happened. Her brows furrowed as she wondered just what Julie had been up to. Glancing up at Drake, Elizabeth discovered a surprised expression etching his eyes.

"Damned if I know!" he told O'Reilly.

"So, why do you think Julie had my name in her address book?" Drake asked later as they sat in a restaurant down the street from district headquarters. "Seems I'm suddenly up to my ears in this murder."

Elizabeth shook her head. "I haven't the faintest idea," she replied, but to be honest, she had her suspicions—and she didn't like them.

"I'm not a particularly easy guy to track down," Drake went on. "I keep it that way. Not even my cousins know where I've been assigned lately."

She sipped her water and tried to avoid Drake's direct gaze. He must be hell on suspects, she thought. No wonder he was so good at his job.

"Julie could be very persistent when she wanted something," Elizabeth finally said. "In some ways she was like a spoiled child, always demanding her way. But she was also a very good friend. She would do anything for me, even if she was often misguided."

"And what was she trying to do for you this time, Elizabeth?"

She took a sip of her drink, trying to collect her thoughts—brandy this time, to calm her nerves.

"I'm waiting."

Elizabeth smoothed her napkin, trying to decide just how much to tell him. When she finally looked up into his eyes, she felt a sudden urge to pour her heart out. She wanted to tell him everything, then cry into his shoulder over how difficult these years had been without him. But she knew she couldn't do that—not yet. She smiled stiffly, trying to diffuse the tension. She would tell him only part of the truth.

"All right. Although I'm not completely sure, I have a good idea why Julie was interested in you. You have to understand her, she is—was—an incurable romantic." Her voice broke slightly at the insertion of the past tense but she continued on. "Unfortunately, I think that's why she kept getting divorced. She was looking for the perfect man. When she thought she had him, she married him, then when things weren't perfect, she divorced him and started her search all over again."

"I don't see what all this has to do with me," Drake said, taking a swig of his own drink.

"I'm getting to that. Julie felt there was a perfect man out there for me, too," Elizabeth continued. "I haven't been seeing many men." She didn't feel the need to tell him that it was virtually none. "Julie would call and we'd talk and she'd ask me about my love life and then she would scold me, telling me that I worked too hard and that I needed to get out and have some fun."

"Why doesn't that surprise me?" His lips twisted into a sardonic smile. "Although it certainly isn't because of your looks."

Elizabeth cheeks warmed, foolishly, at the backhanded compliment. "I told her about us."

Drake was silent for a moment, then said, "We were an *us* only very briefly."

"I know. But Julie got it into her head that you were the one for me. I told you she was an incurable romantic. I think she was trying to play cupid."

"She sent the alumni brochure I received."

"No doubt."

"It was addressed in care of the Atlanta field office. They forwarded it to me from there. I'm surprised I got it at all. And I'm really surprised that she would think I would act on it. You must have told her quite a bit about our weekend together."

Elizabeth felt his eyes searching her face. She looked away, toward the window and the street outside.

"Well, that clears up a lot," he said. "Now, where do we go from here?"

The question seemed more rhetorical than anything else, so she chose not to answer it. The waitress arrived with their meals, and Elizabeth turned her attention to trying to swallow her food.

It explains a lot, and nothing at all, Drake thought as he took a huge bite out of his sandwich. It wasn't an overzealous committee member who sent him the brochure, but Julie Parks. There was something else here that Elizabeth wasn't telling him, but he couldn't put his finger on it yet. She was even more uptight than he remembered.

Drake pushed his plate aside. "I think I need to talk to Donny Parisi. Find out for myself exactly what he saw. For all we know, he may have seen the real killer and O'Reilly just didn't get around to asking him about it."

"I think you may be judging O'Reilly too harshly."

"Yeah, maybe you're right. But I'd still like to interrogate the kid myself."

"Then I'm going with you." She pushed her own hardly touched plate aside.

"I'm not sure that's a good idea."

"You don't know Donny. He gets excited very easily. It will probably go better if I'm there with you."

"That's not what I meant. I'm not sure it's a good idea for you to go to the building just yet."

"I recover quickly. And anyway, I'd like to talk to Mary. I'm sure she's very upset."

"Let's go then." He put some money on the table and led her to the door.

six

"Yes?" Mary Parisi asked when she answered the door. Then when she saw Elizabeth, she exclaimed. "Oh, dear God! You must have been frightened half out of your mind! What a horrible thing to happen, and right in your own apartment! I shudder every time I think of it!" she said, hugging Elizabeth.

Drake quickly assessed Mrs. Parisi—mid to late fifties, stylish short hair, dyed, judging by the gray roots peeking out at her temples, decent figure. There were some lines around her eyes and lips, but mostly good skin tone, probably not a smoker. She was dressed in blue Capri pants and a bright pink turtleneck.

Elizabeth's face pinched at the memory. "Yes, it's still hard to believe. I've been worried about you and Donny. How is he taking it?"

"He's disturbed," said Mrs. Parisi, releasing Elizabeth

and placing her hand against the top of her chest, clearly still disturbed herself by the violent event. "All the excitement was too much for him. There were TV cameras all over the front lawn until a few hours ago, and all those policemen and sirens last night. It's not good for him. Now he won't come out of his room."

Elizabeth turned to Drake. "Mary, this is Drake McGuire. He's an FBI agent and he'd like to talk to Donny if that's okay with you."

Mrs. Parisi's attitude changed abruptly. "I don't know," she murmured. "He's pretty upset."

"I promise, I'll try not to upset him further. The important thing is to find out who did this, and I think your son may have some answers for us." Drake smiled his best good-cop smile.

Mrs. Parisi didn't budge. She stood in front of the doorway to the apartment, guarding it like a lioness guarding her cub. Then her glance grew even more suspicious. She pointed a finger at him. "Hey, I know who you are. You're the one Donny says was around here last night, before the murder. I recognize you from the picture that detective showed me."

A muscle tensed in his jaw. "I think you mean before the cops showed up," he said evenly. "Mrs. Parisi, I need you to believe that I had nothing to do with the killing. My only goal here is to find out who did this, and to make sure he doesn't come back and do it again."

"You think he would come back?"

"It's not likely, but until we know the motive, we can't be sure. Now, if your son saw me, there's a strong possibility that he might have seen the killer, too. I need to talk to him."

"That detective, what was his name . . . ?"

"O'Reilly?" Elizabeth prompted.

"Yes, O'Reilly. He already asked him a lot of questions."

Drake nodded. "I know, but I've found that people often remember more after they've had some time to calm down and absorb what happened. If I talk to him now, he might be able to help us."

"It'll be okay, I promise," Elizabeth said, reassuring her.

"Well, I guess if he could help—" Mrs. Parisi slowly extended her arm to invite them inside, but her gaze was still wary. "But only for a few minutes."

The Parisi apartment was set up differently from Elizabeth's. Whereas Elizabeth's living room extended all the way to the front of her apartment, this living room was cut in half. A wall partition ran across its width, forming a bedroom in front—Donny's room. As Drake entered, he noticed it was actually a combination sitting room and bedroom. Donny's computer console sat in the alcove. He sat there now, playing a computer game. Drake noted that from Donny's position behind the console, he had a great view of the street.

"Donny, this nice man would like to talk to you," Mrs. Parisi said, placing a hand on Donny's shoulder.

"No!" Donny said forcefully, continuing to play his computer game.

"Donny, dear, please look at me. This is important." But Donny just shook his head. Drake was aware of the tension in the young man. It was evident in the way he held himself, muscles taut as he hunched over the controls, squeezing angrily at the buttons.

"Let me try," Elizabeth offered. She walked up and stood beside him, placed a gentle hand on his shoulder. "Hey, Donny. Looks like you're doing great. How many points do you have now?"

Donny didn't answer.

Undaunted, she continued. "I bet you're pretty bummed out by what happened last night. I know I am. Listen, Drake is my friend. I promise he won't hurt you."

Donny shook his head again. "Go away! You're mean!"

Elizabeth knelt and spoke to him gently. By the way she approached Donny, Drake figured she must have a heck of a good bedside manner. "Now, Donny, you know you don't mean that," she said firmly, logically, but nicely. "We just want to talk to you."

Donny's hands stilled on the controls. After a few moments he slowly turned his head and eyed Drake suspiciously, very much like his mother had done earlier. One look at his features told Drake that Donny had Down's syndrome. He guessed his age to be somewhere around twenty.

"Go away!" Donny shouted, then turned back to his game.

"Donny," Elizabeth said firmly. "We're not going away. We want to help your mother. We need you to answer a couple of questions."

"You're mean," he said again. "You were mean to Allison. Bad things happen when people are mean!"

Elizabeth stood and sighed. She looked to Mrs. Parisi for help. "I'm afraid he's back to that again," she said. "That happened such a long time ago, and I explained it to him then."

"He has a long memory," Mrs. Parisi said. "Look, Donny, you know Dr. Iverson isn't mean. This man is with the FBI. They are the good guys. You remember, you•see them on TV catching the bad guys. He's going to help find out what happened to that nice lady upstairs. You want that, don't you?"

At that Donny slapped his hands down on the keyboard in frustration, then stood and stalked over to plop himself onto his bed. Folding his arms across his chest, he turned toward the picture window to stare outside, effectively shutting them out.

"Donny," Drake prodded gently. "I really am one of the good guys."

He held his breath as he watched the emotions play across Donny's face. Donny looked back at him, seemed to size him up, then looked out the window again. Just when Drake thought they were getting nowhere, he spoke up.

"The yellow-haired lady was mean."

"What did you say?" Mrs. Parisi asked.

"The yellow-haired lady was mean!" he shouted.

"The yellow-haired lady?" Elizabeth frowned. "Julie has blond hair, but she would never—"

"You mean the lady upstairs?" Mrs. Parisi cut her off. "The one that was visiting Dr. Iverson? She was mean to you? When was she mean to you?"

Mrs. Parisi's instincts for protecting her child were kicking in. Drake knew he needed to take over this conversation, quick. He slid the computer chair over and sat beside Donny. "Hey, Donny, want to see my badge?" He took out his ID folder and flipped it open. Surprisingly, Donny slowly turned his head and looked at it. "Go ahead, touch it," Drake offered. "It's real."

Donny reached out and touched the metal shield, then looked at the picture. But when he looked back at Drake, running his gaze over his suit, Drake could see fear settle behind his eyes. He turned to look out the window again.

Drake figured he needed to try another tack. "I bet you can see a lot from here. I bet you saw lots of stuff last night. You saw me, didn't you? You saw me walk up, come up to the door, and check out the mailboxes. Then you saw me walk back down to my car."

Donny didn't answer, just continued to stare out the window.

"I bet you saw some other things last night, too, before the cops came. Probably even before I got here. Did you see someone else last night, Donny?"

Donny shook his head. "No, go away. You're mean."

"Donny, Mr. McGuire is not mean," Mrs. Parisi scolded him, but at that Donny put his hands over his ears.

"No, no!" he shouted. He stood and shoved Drake aside, then went back to the computer and immersed himself in his game again.

"I'm afraid when he's like this you'll get nothing more out of him. He can be very stubborn when he wants to be. He just closes off. He's really a good kid, though, honest." Sadness deepened the lines around Mrs. Parisi's eyes.

Drake stood. "Maybe we should leave him be for a while. Can I talk to you, Mrs. Parisi?"

She hesitated briefly. "Well, I guess that would be okay. Come into the kitchen. I bought a cake yesterday and I just made a fresh pot of coffee. You can help me eat the cake so it doesn't all go to my hips."

Bright and welcoming, Mrs. Parisi's kitchen reminded Drake of the kitchen at his aunt's house not too far from here where he'd grown up. The walls were painted lemon yellow, with white cabinets and ocean blue tiles on the splashboard. Cheerful white-and-yellow curtains hung at the window over the sink. Mrs. Parisi sliced generous pieces of chocolate cake, then poured them all cups of hot, fresh-brewed coffee. Still, as she moved efficiently around her kitchen, there was a nervousness about her. He bet she was sharp as a tack most of the time and didn't miss a thing. For some reason, though, Drake could tell, she didn't especially like talking to him. And she wasn't doing a good job hiding it.

"I'm sorry Donny's so stubborn," she said, sitting down at the table to join them.

"Don't worry about it," Drake told her. "I'm sure he'll open up eventually."

Mrs. Parisi shook her head. "Don't count on it. He can close up tighter than a clam when he wants to."

"He seemed particularly fearful of me. Is there a reason for that? Is he always afraid of strangers?"

Mrs. Parisi smiled crookedly. "No. Actually he's pretty open to most people, but he has a problem with good-looking Italian types in suits. You probably remind him of his dad. Dan was probably just a few years older than you when Donny was born. He was a great guy, until Donny came along. He was ashamed of him. Donny didn't fit into his image of successful businessman and father. I could tell he didn't want to be seen with him, especially around his associates. He always found an excuse not to be with us. It got worse than that, though. One day I came home from shopping and Donny had a bloody lip and a bruise on the side of his face. That was enough for me. I kicked the sonuvabitch out and divorced him. I got the building and a nice settlement. Donny and I have been doing just fine on our own ever since."

Drake could hear the bitterness in her tone.

"No, it's nothing against you, Mr. McGuire," she went on, "but, like I told you before, Donny has a long memory."

"I can't believe he brought up that incident with Allison," Elizabeth added. "It was over a year ago," she explained. "I bought Allison her first bike. She was so excited. I ran upstairs to grab some money so she could ride it when we went to the store. I told her to stay in the yard until I came back down. Two minutes later she was gone. I found her halfway down the block, just as pleased with herself as she could be for riding her bike that far. My daughter can be very headstrong. I panicked. I brought her back and yelled at her, forbidding her to ride it again for a week. Donny saw me. He wouldn't talk to me for a month after that. He's very protective of Allison."

"I see," Drake said, but he didn't like the picture the two of them were painting. He wondered just how far Donny would go to protect Allison. "Mrs. Parisi, was there any time yesterday when Donny could have been with Julie? Any time she could have done something mean to him, or something he construed as mean? He's very adamant about it."

Mrs. Parisi shook her head. "I didn't even know she was here. Donny and I were out yesterday afternoon. We always go to a movie on Friday and then to the store to do our food shopping. It's the only day he doesn't go to his work program." She glanced accusingly at Elizabeth. "I'm surprised you didn't tell me your friend was coming."

"I'm sorry. I just didn't think of it. I knew you'd be out, so I made other arrangements to let her in."

"Oh," Mrs. Parisi replied, but Drake could tell she didn't quite believe Elizabeth's story. He wondered about that, too. If Elizabeth and Mrs. Parisi were close, then it would seem natural for Elizabeth to tell her that Julie would be staying with her for a few days.

"So you're sure Donny wasn't alone with Julie at any time?" he asked again.

"Just what are you asking me?" Mrs. Parisi's gaze turned suspicious once more.

"Was there any time yesterday that Donny could have been alone with Julie? A time when Julie might have done something mean to him?"

"Julie wasn't like that!" Elizabeth insisted. "She didn't have a mean bone in her body."

"And you do?"

"No, I—"

"Exactly."

She glared at him, obviously frustrated by his pointed logic.

"Listen," he said, trying to explain, "it could have been something that he misinterpreted, just like when you yelled at Allison."

He turned back to Mrs. Parisi. "Was he alone at any time with Julie?"

"I don't see how. He was here in the apartment with me the whole evening, except for a few minutes when he went out to sweep the hall and the stairs after dinner. He likes to help me out. I give him odd jobs to do around here. We're a team, you know."

Drake leaned forward. "And what time was that?"

"Around seven, seven-thirty I think—maybe later."

"Did he act any differently when he came back in?"

"No," she said, but he was sure by the way she suddenly closed off that she remembered something. "He just went into his room like he always does and started playing his video game."

"Are you sure?"

Beside him, Elizabeth stood and gave him a reproving glance. "I think it's time to go, Drake. We've taken up enough of Mary's time."

"Yes, I do need to start Donny's dinner," Mrs. Parisi said, obviously thankful for a way out of the questioning. "He hasn't eaten a thing all day," she added, then stood and gave Elizabeth a quick hug. "If you need anything, please call me. It's just so awful about your friend. And if you need me to baby-sit Allison, anytime, just let me know. You know how much I love that little girl of yours."

"Thank you. I'm hoping to get back into the apartment in a couple of days, get our lives back in order."

"Do you think that's wise?"

"It's sad to say, but I don't know what else to do."

Drake put a smile on his face. He tried to hide his annoyance with Elizabeth for ending his interrogation so abruptly. Normally he wouldn't let her get away with it, but he figured he'd given Mrs. Parisi enough to think about for now.

"Thank you for your time," he told her. "The coffee was delicious. If you think of anything else, please call me." He stood, took one of his cards out of his pocket, and jotted down his cell phone number on the back. "As you know, the Chicago Police have assigned detectives to the case, but I'd like to help out, too. I want to do everything I can to keep both you and your son safe."

seven

Elizabeth wondered how her life had been turned upside down in such a short time. A mere twenty hours ago everything was on track. Now her best friend was dead and the one man she really didn't want in her life was smack-dab in the middle of it.

She turned toward Drake, her anger refueling. But before she could give voice to her ire, he grabbed her arm and pulled her with him.

"Outside," he said crisply.

At his touch, she felt a shock go through her, which only fed more fuel to the fire. This was definitely *not* the time for him to have this effect on her. Out on the porch, with the heavy door closed behind them, she pulled free. "How dare you question Mary like that!" she said hotly, rubbing her arm, not because he'd hurt her, but because it still tingled where he'd held her.

For a moment she thought lightning would flash from his eyes, then he put up a hand. "Hold that thought. I want to take a look around while it's still daylight."

Before she could object, Drake bounded down the steps and disappeared around the side of the building. Trembling with frustration, Elizabeth looked up and down the street. Suddenly she felt conspicuous and vulnerable. Her car was still parked at the curb. She realized that Julie's red Jaguar was still in the garage in the alley. No doubt Julie's husband, Stephan, would pick it up in a day or two.

As she stared at her own shiny red car, another thought occurred to her—had someone caught a glimpse of Julie's car in the garage and thought it was hers? Could Drake be right? Was *she* the intended victim?

She hugged her arms to herself. The sun was lowering, giving a chill to the late afternoon. She needed to call Allison, but knew she should hold off for at least another hour—she didn't want to upset her daughter by breaking their routine. Every night when they were apart, Elizabeth called Allison just before she went to bed, and the two of them chattered over the day's adventures. Elizabeth brought her lips together in a thin line and headed for Drake's car. She'd wait until he finished his inspection, then like it or not, he would hear what she had to say.

But once more he cut her off before she could get the words out. "Not here," he said when he returned. "I don't want Donny to see us arguing." He put the car in gear and they took off down the street.

Elizabeth was still fuming as she followed Drake through the crowd inside a nearby pub. In all the turmoil of the last twenty-four hours she had forgotten that the Cubs were in town. Drake had to bribe a group of die-hard fans to give up their corner table in the rear of the bar.

"I asked Andi to meet us here," Drake said, reminding her of the problem at hand. Elizabeth frowned. She didn't need Andi here when she told Drake to butt out of her life, which is exactly what she intended to do, just as soon as her beer arrived and she could down a couple of gulps to fortify herself. She didn't need Drake protecting her. She didn't want him here.

By the set of his jaw and the way he avoided her eye, she could tell he was still ticked at her, too. Well, he had no reason to be mad at her. She certainly hadn't asked him to step in and be her white knight. She looked away, trying to ignore the way her heart did that little jig every time she looked at him. She tried to gather her thoughts as she looked around the pub. A shout went up from the crowd. She glanced up at the TV. The Cubs had just hit a home run. Elizabeth smiled wryly, recalling the last time she'd seen a game at Wrigley Field. She'd gone with her father, during a summer break from college. She remembered how much she enjoyed it. Dad died while she was in medical school. Since that game, she'd been too busy raising Allison and trying to get through her training to spend a relaxing afternoon at the ballpark.

As soon as her beer came, Elizabeth lifted it to her lips, thankful for the bitter taste as it slid down her throat. After one more long swig, she set the mug down and looked up at Drake. He had already finished his Guinness.

"Don't ever do that to me again," he said, leaning his head toward her so she could hear him above the noise from the crowd.

"Do what?" she countered, keeping her voice level, not backing away from him.

"Don't ever interfere with my interrogation again. I understand why you did it, so I'll let it go this time. But don't do it again."

"You've got to be kidding! I think I need to remind you that I never asked you to investigate, and I certainly didn't know you were going to *interrogate* Mary Parisi. How dare you do that to her? She has enough problems taking care of Donny on her own—she doesn't need you adding to them."

"Listen, Elizabeth, whether you or Mrs. Parisi want to admit it, Donny knows something. And she knows he knows something. I could see it in her eyes—she's afraid. She's questioning what happened last night in her own mind. And now she's protecting Donny."

"What would you expect? You were accusing her only son of murder."

"I did nothing of the kind. But it isn't out of the realm of possibility. You said yourself that he's very protective. Who knows what he might have done if he thought Julie was a threat to your daughter. She was staying in your apartment."

Elizabeth's eyes narrowed. "I know. I *know* he couldn't possibly do anything so evil." But she shivered as the image of Julie's body lying facedown on the carpet in a pool of blood popped into her mind. For a brief moment she saw Donny in the vision. He was standing over Julie with a bloody knife in his hand.

She sat back and swiped at a curl that had fallen over her forehead, as if trying to wipe the image from her mind. "No," she said. "I know it's not possible. Donny could never do something like that!"

"Maybe not. But at this point we need to explore every angle. And right now I believe Donny is the key to this whole thing. I feel it in my gut. Sometimes, Elizabeth, you have to go with your gut."

Elizabeth turned her head and eyed him defiantly. She remembered a time when she had gone with her gut and it had turned her whole world upside down. Another shout went up in the crowd. The Cubs scored again. It gave her an excuse to look away, avoiding the tension that sparked between them, which was almost a palpable, breathing entity.

"Here's Andi," he said a minute later.

Drake signaled the waitress to bring them another round, then held up his fingers to change the order when he noticed Andi was not alone. A man walked beside her, helping her navigate toward the table.

"Hey, Drake, God, it's good to see you," the man said. "Why didn't you tell us you were in town. Man, Mama is not happy with you. She was spitting fire when she found out you were here and you didn't check in. I hate to say it, but that woman knows more swear words than some of the thugs I've picked up on the street."

Gazing up at the man, Elizabeth was stunned by his similarities to Drake, and his differences. He had the same dark hair and deep-set blue eyes, but he was a good few inches shorter than Drake and he was smiling—something Drake hadn't done much of in the past twenty-four hours.

But now Drake laughed, the scowl finally leaving his face. His laugh was deep and resonant and brought back instant memories, a quick flashback to another time. It sounded so good on him that Elizabeth felt a moment of sadness. She had a feeling he didn't laugh often.

Drake rose and clapped the man on the shoulder. "Yeah, how I miss the melodious tones of Mama DeLuca spitting fire," he said. "Hi again, Andi," he said and gave her a quick kiss on the cheek. Then he pulled out one of the chairs he'd managed to save for the two of them and winked. "So, Joey, how's it going, being married to this hellion? She must be what's keeping you in such great shape."

"Don't you know it," Joey said, giving his wife's backside a friendly, possessive pat before she could sit down. Andi smiled, cast him a knowing glance, then grabbed his hand and held it in hers as she took the seat Drake offered. Elizabeth witnessed the look that passed between them and felt a jealous twinge. It was obvious these two were still crazy about each other.

"And you must be Dr. Iverson," Joey said as he held out his hand.

"Dr. Elizabeth Iverson, meet Lieutenant Joey DeLuca, my cousin and scourge of North Side homicide," Drake said.

Joey laughed. "Don't let him tell you that. I run a tight ship, that's all. I was sorry to hear about your friend. Why don't we get those beers, then we'll put our heads together and figure this one out." He sat down and joined them at the table. "Just so you know, you've got the best here," he said, nodding toward Drake. "It was no surprise to us when the FBI snatched him up. Only trouble is, he doesn't get home much anymore, do you, Drake? Frankly, we don't hear much from him at all. It makes Mama a bit crazy, especially with most of us on the force," Joey explained. "At least with us here in Chicago, she knows what's happening with us. But with Drake, we never know where he is or what he's up to, although I hear you just finished a tough assignment in the Virgin Islands," he said, turning toward Drake again. "I guess congratulations are in order. You nailed that bigwig drug cartel guy—what was his name? Salgado, right?"

"Yeah, that's one of his aliases," Drake said, lowering his head as if embarrassed that Joey brought up the subject.

"The FBI was on this guy's case for the last ten years," Joey went on, paying no attention to Drake's discomfort. "It took Drake to finally bring him in. We're real proud of you, Cousin."

"I had help," Drake said, his voice deadpan. "I didn't go in alone, you know that."

Andi laughed. "Don't let him kid you. He's one heck of an agent." Then her eyes narrowed as she examined him more closely. "We also heard you were hurt."

Elizabeth's heart thumped. He'd been hurt—again. Of course, chances were that he would be, given his profession. She'd known that, but she now found herself wondering just how many times he'd been in the line of fire, and how many times he'd been caught.

Drake shook his head. "It was nothing."

"That's not what I heard," Joey persisted. "I heard the guy panicked when he realized he was dealing with U.S. agents. He took off running toward his plane and you gave chase. He was halfway up the gangway when you caught him, after you'd taken a bullet."

"How the hell did you get all that?" Drake asked, his tone clearly irritated.

Joey smiled. "Hey, I have my sources, too. I gotta say though, I was surprised you didn't blow his head off right then and there when you had the chance."

"Don't think I wasn't tempted."

"Sounds like you took a heck of a chance, Drake," Andi observed.

"Yeah, well, that's my job." He looked at Elizabeth. For a few scant seconds his emotions lay naked in front of her. Years of determination and cynicism flickered across his face. She realized, ironically, that the last six years had been just as hard, if not harder, on him. Curiosity surged through her. She wondered what his life was like, living on the edge, then she caught herself and smiled ruefully— *curiosity killed the cat.* And like Andi said, he took chances, too many, as far as she was concerned.

Drake ran his hand over his face, trying to bring his mind back to the present. Adrenaline pumped through him as he remembered his last assignment. Someone must have tipped Salgado off at the last second, just as the team was going in.

Salgado's goons fired from the other side of the airplane, hitting him, but he still managed to catch Salgado and throw him to the ground. He remembered the rage that flared through him as he held his gun to Salgado's temple. The slime had been running an international drug ring for over a decade. He was the head of a multibillion dollar industry that included corruption, gambling, and money laundering. There was also evidence that he had ties to terrorist organizations.

Drake had been a half second from blowing Salgado's head off when another agent caught him and yanked him back.

Afterward, a sense of loathing had crept over him—a dozen more thugs waited out there in the wings to take Salgado's place. Fighting drug trafficking and organized crime was a never-ending battle. His leg still throbbed occasionally where the bullet had knifed through his upper thigh, barely missing an artery. The pain reminded him of that other time, in Atlanta. Glancing at Elizabeth, he discovered her looking hard at him, her amber eyes playing into him. He knew, instinctively, she was wondering about his exploits. Hell, let her wonder, it was way too late now. Truth was, losing her had hurt just as much, if not more. He looked away and once more tried to concentrate on Andi's voice.

"Forensics found eight stab wounds," Andi was saying. "Five were superficial, probably due to Mrs. Parks's attempts to defend herself, but two hit their mark. One went up beneath the ribs into her lung, the other into her lower back, nicking a kidney. It was as if the killer knew exactly where to cut. They figure it took her a good hour to bleed out, as near as they could tell, about a half hour or so before you found her, Elizabeth. According to your statement, that was just before ten. They can't give the exact time of death."

Drake glanced at Elizabeth. She was taking it well, but then clinical discussion was right up her alley.

"So far they haven't lifted any fingerprints other than yours, your daughter's, and Julie's. Oh, and Mrs. Parisi's, your landlady, and that boy's, the one downstairs—Donny, right? And we have no murder weapon. Even stranger, no footprints, only smears on the rug. With all that blood, you would think the killer would have left shoeprints as he ran out. There's also no forced entry, and no sexual assault."

"I saw a trail of blood near the bathroom," Elizabeth interjected.

"I know. And it stops there. I'm not sure what to make of that since it was clear she was attacked in the bedroom. Any ideas, Drake?"

"The killer took the weapon with him. Sounds like he

concealed it at that point, wrapped it in something to stop the dripping, perhaps a towel."

"But you didn't notice anything missing, did you Dr. Iverson?" Joey asked.

"No, I told Detective O'Reilly that. No jewelry, or money, not even a towel."

"Or knives, as the report states," Andi said. "So we can rule out robbery as a motive. And we can assume the killer brought the weapon with him. That makes it premeditated."

"What's your take, Drake?" Joey asked.

Elizabeth made a face. "Your crack FBI agent thinks the handicapped kid downstairs did it."

Drake gave her a hard stare before turning his attention to Andi again. "*I think* that your assumption is most likely correct, Andi. I had another look around there today and saw no signs of forced entry or footprints in the yard. It would appear to be an inside job, by someone Julie knew, or someone who said they knew Elizabeth in order to get Julie to let them in. But, the rest of the evidence contradicts that. Julie was surprised from behind, after she came out of the shower into the bedroom, so it would appear that someone was already in the apartment, waiting for her, stalking her. I'd say some psychopath, but it has the stench of a professional job, too, with no fingerprints or footprints. It was likely the perp wore gloves, and something to disguise his footprints."

"That would seem to fit," Andi stated.

"I've taken the liberty of running a check on her husband," Drake went on. "He has an airtight alibi, but this could be a case of killing for hire."

"Yeah, we've thought of that one, too. That's why we're going to need you to come up with anyone you can think of who had any connection to Julie," Andi told Elizabeth.

"We're asking her parents, too. And there's one more thing; we also need a list of your associates, anyone who might have a grudge against you. We're not entirely sure Julie was the intended target."

Drake felt Elizabeth's eyes trained on him.

"It's not as far-fetched as you want to believe," he said.

Andi agreed. "You'd be surprised what can make people frenzied enough to commit murder. One thing that doesn't jibe with all this is that there was passion in most of those wounds. It contradicts the professional hit theory."

Joey looked across at Elizabeth and smiled reassuringly. "That's why we'd like someone to look out for you until we figure this out. I could put a man from the department on it, but, if Drake's up to the job, I'm sure he'd be just as good, probably better."

"Thanks for your vote of approval," Drake said sarcastically.

Joey smiled. "No problem."

Elizabeth's eyes widened. "I wanted to move back into my apartment soon, bring my daughter home."

"I wouldn't advise that," Joey said. "Someone breached your apartment, they could do it again. It might not be safe for you or your daughter."

She frowned and swirled the remaining beer in her mug. Drake was fully aware that she was less than pleased with the idea of having him as a bodyguard. More shouting went up from the crowd. The other team had just scored, and the tying run was on base. The fans weren't going to get off easy after all. They were in for a long, tense fight. He glanced back at Elizabeth. Yep, they were in for a fight, all right.

eight

"Just drive." Elizabeth wasn't in the mood to talk. To say she was less than thrilled with their odd arrangement, now endorsed by the Chicago Police Department, would be a huge understatement.

"I'm sorry about all of this," Drake said a short time later. "I know it's hard to take."

Joey and Andi thought it best that Drake stay with Elizabeth in the hotel suite for a couple of days until they had time to track down the few leads they had. She supposed she should be thankful to have a crack FBI agent looking after her, but the fact that he was cute and sexy and dangerous as hell scared her to death. She definitely didn't appreciate the way her thinking got messed up whenever she was near him. She should have insisted on someone else—anyone but Drake, especially when it was more important than ever to stay clearheaded. And, on top of everything else, Drake was bossy. Nothing irritated her more in a man.

Elizabeth stayed in Drake's black Monte Carlo while he went into his hotel to retrieve his suitcase. She brushed her hand on the soft charcoal leather seat. The car fit him to a T. It was dark, sleek—and dangerous. Holding on to that last thought, she punched in her number at the Heartland Cardiac Center on her cell phone. She had ten messages, six of which were from news reporters, trying to get her personal story regarding the murder. Three were from people she'd worked with at the university hospital who had recognized her apartment on TV and wished her well. The last message was from Dr. Carl Benson, head of the Heartland Center and her boss. He wanted her to know how stunned he was to hear about her friend's murder, how sorry he was for her, and that she shouldn't worry about coming in to work on Monday. He understood how upset she must be. He would call later in the week to see how she was doing.

Elizabeth bit her lip in annoyance. She saw no reason why she shouldn't go to work Monday. Doing routine tasks always settled her, and the sooner she and Allison got back into their routine, the better off they'd be. Allison had started kindergarten this year, and Elizabeth didn't want her missing too much school. She left a message for Dr. Benson, telling him that she planned to come in on Monday. Of course, she'd have to take off in the afternoon to attend Julie's funeral.

Then Elizabeth called her mother. She brought her up to date on the investigation, which to her mind wasn't going well at all, then asked her to put Allison on the phone. Tears welled in her eyes as she listened to Allison chatter on about her day. Elizabeth imagined her pint-sized daughter sitting at the counter, strawberry-blond hair sticking out every which way from her ponytail, eating a chocolate ice-cream cone and not caring one wit that she got half of it on her face while she talked. With her impish, impulsive nature, Allison definitely did not take after Elizabeth.

"We saw the cows today, Mommy," Allison said gleefully. "And Jeremy went in and poked one with a stick. I told him that wasn't right. His dad came out and told us to get lost and we ran to the corn maze. It's really cool. There's ghosts and spiders in there—but they're not real. It's kind of funny, but kind of spooky, too. When are you coming to get me, Mommy?"

Elizabeth smiled through her tears. It always amazed her how Allison could flit through twenty different subjects in a matter of seconds.

"Tomorrow, sweetheart," she said.

She'd drive up in the morning—Drake would have to allow her that much. She needed to explain to Allison what had happened to Julie, just in case she saw a news report on television. She knew her mother couldn't keep Allison away from the TV forever. At five and a half, Allison was a very precocious child who would know the score. But Elizabeth knew there was a more important reason for driving up to the farm than explaining it all to Allison—she needed a hug from her daughter.

"I'll be there by noon tomorrow," she said. "I promise."

"Are you sure?" Allison asked. Elizabeth heard the pouty demand in her young voice. She winced, remembering all the promises she'd had to break over the last few years when she either stayed late at the hospital or was on call. It was precisely for that reason she'd taken the position at Heartland, to gain more control over her hours. She owed that to Allison, although she had to admit, the kid had been super about her mother's demanding career.

"I promise you, sweetheart," she assured her. "I *will* be there tomorrow. Maybe you can show me the maze, then." Although for Elizabeth, visiting the corn maze would not be on her preferred list of things to do.

"Okay, Mom," Allison said, but a resigned sigh accompanied the words. It broke Elizabeth's heart. A kid shouldn't need to sigh like that.

"I love you super big," she told her. "Now sleep tight and don't let the bedbugs bite!"

"I love you super big, too, Mommy. Grandma says I have to go now. Bye!" There was a click as Allison hung up the phone, but not before Elizabeth heard the joy return to her daughter's voice. Allison was pretty darn resilient.

Elizabeth needed some time alone, away from Drake. When they finally returned to their hotel suite, she excused herself to retreat to her bedroom under the ruse that she was going to work on that list the DeLucas wanted. Her nerves were too frayed to look into Drake's blue eyes, and she couldn't bear to watch his hand rub across his jaw in that familiar way, darkened now with a day's growth of beard. Drake's nearness, coupled with her longing to hold her daughter, jumbled Elizabeth's senses. He nodded to her as she went into the bedroom, his eyes registering concern. Well, she must look like hell, she reasoned. The last two days had been worse than the seventy-two hours straight she had often put in as a hospital intern.

When Elizabeth awoke the next morning, it was with a renewed sense of hope. That's what a good night's sleep can do for you, she thought, smiling. She learned in medical school that one of the most important skills a doctor could master was how to turn everything off when you had a chance for some shut-eye.

She heard the shower running in the bathroom and glanced at the bedside clock. 7:00 A.M. Drake was an early riser. Her stomach growled. The only thing she'd eaten yesterday was maybe a quarter of her sandwich at the restaurant and a couple of bites of Mary Parisi's cake. Famished, she realized she would have to venture out into the living room for coffee. Knowing Drake, he had probably ordered some up already.

Dressed in her nightgown, Elizabeth cracked open the door and peered out, just to make sure the coast was clear. Verifying that the door from the living room to the bathroom was closed, she tiptoed into the room. The aroma of fresh-brewed coffee drew her to the table where a steaming carafe sat, along with a basket of blueberry muffins and two cartons of yogurt. The man was an angel, she mused— well, maybe not.

Biting into a muffin, she relished the sweet taste of the blueberries against her palate, then ravenously took another bite and poured herself a cup of coffee. She was about to take her stash into the bedroom when the bathroom door flew open. Drake stepped out, a towel wrapped dangerously low around his loins. He stopped in midstride. His eyes locked onto hers. He appeared as shocked as she to find her standing there.

Elizabeth stood there, transfixed, staring at him for a full ten seconds with her coffee cup in one hand, the muffin and napkin in the other. He stood stock-still, too, while water dripped from his forehead and into his eyes. His hair was matted forward. The dripping water drew Elizabeth's gaze downward. Her eyes traveled to his chest where a patch of dark hair glistened across his pectoral muscles, then down along the line that led to the six-pack of hard muscles that molded his abdomen. Her gaze traveled lower, to the edge of the towel where his hand was clamped around its ends, barely holding it in place at the top of his right hipbone. The knowledge of what lay beneath that towel brought a burn to her cheeks.

Quickly she drew her gaze back up to his chest, noting the scar to the lower left of his collarbone. An old scar, she judged, grown white with time. She wondered where the new scar was—the scar from the bullet he'd taken in the Virgin Islands. In his back? Beneath the towel? Now that was a scary thought. What a tragic loss to womanhood if he was damaged goods.

Elizabeth, get a grip! she scolded herself. Then another thought assailed her. She realized that if he had been hit there, beneath the towel, he might have come very close to death. There were umpteen blood vessels and arteries in the lower abdomen. Tearing through any one of them could be fatal. The possibility of that brought her eyes sliding quickly back up to his with a touch of panic that unnerved her.

But his eyes did not meet hers, for they were enjoying their own delicious feast. Her pulse hummed in her ears as she felt his gaze travel down over her clinging gown, down to her breasts where her traitorous nipples perked up at his look, then on to her waist, her hips, and finally to that place where her legs came together. Molten liquid surged up through her, as if a firebrand had been placed there. Thank God her nightgown wasn't transparent as well as clinging! Although she had the distinct feeling Drake could see right through the material anyway. She knew she should move, but found she couldn't. It was as if she was being held under some ancient power. Finally his gaze moved up again, pausing at her swollen breasts once more, before returning to her face.

"Oh!" she said. The mixture of surprise and passion she saw in his eyes threatened to make the coffee cup slide from her hand. Her heart thudded wildly against her ribs. She swallowed hard, trying to get control of herself. His eyes narrowed on her.

"I forgot my shaving kit," he explained, then tore his gaze from hers and crossed to the sofa to rummage through his suitcase with one hand while the other stayed clamped to the towel.

"Yes," she responded inanely, still unable to get her feet to move. She eyed his strong legs where the towel barely covered his thighs, noted the muscles that rippled along his back when he turned away. Noted, also, that there was no fresh scar on his back.

He turned to her again and she finally managed to tear her eyes away from him, embarrassed now that he had discovered her examining him.

"I'll just take this into the bedroom," she said and quickly made her escape.

Drake let out a long, deep breath. *That was just about more than I can take!* he told himself. Seeing her standing there in that flimsy nightgown with her curls spilling down around her shoulders and her sophisticated doctor's face all bright with the promise of the morning had almost undone him. He'd grown hard as he took in every inch of her. He grew harder now, just remembering it.

Maybe she was right. Maybe this arrangement wasn't the best thing for the two of them.

"Oh, hell . . ." he muttered, then strode back into the bathroom and slammed the door.

"Why are you doing this?" Elizabeth asked as Drake drove onto the Kennedy Expressway, headed toward Richmond, her hometown. He insisted on driving her out to the farm. She thought of all the reasons why he shouldn't, but in the end realized there was one really good reason why he should. In her heart, she knew she couldn't deny that reason. She finally agreed to let him drive her out, provided he agreed that they would pick up her car on the way back. She needed some independence. She was nervous now, already regretting her decision to let him accompany her.

"This is the quickest way I know," he explained tightly, sliding into the northbound traffic.

Elizabeth tried to ignore the tension in his voice. They'd been barely civil to each other over the last couple of hours. "No, I mean, why are you staying here? Why did you offer to be my bodyguard? You certainly don't owe me anything."

His hands tightened on the wheel. "Yeah, good question, isn't it? Let's just say it's in my blood. I can't pass up an investigative challenge. And you're right, *Sis,* I don't owe you a damn thing, do I?" He turned his head and gave her a scathing glance.

So, she thought, he knew she had checked up on him at the hospital in Atlanta.

"Tell me about the Virgin Islands," she said, trying to steer the conversation in another direction. "How did you get hurt?"

He laughed at that. "I got the distinct impression you didn't want to know anything about my work. You made that pretty clear when you took off in Atlanta. What was I, Doc, just a nice little diversion for you? When things got tough, you lit out quicker than a criminal with a get-out-of-jail-free card."

"Fine, don't tell me. I just thought it might be a way to pass the time. And in case you've forgotten, it was just one weekend of hot sex, that's all! You can't plan a lifetime on that." Elizabeth slanted her head away from him.

"Right. My mistake. Like I said, you were just using me for a hot time in Atlanta. I can deal with that. At least the truth is finally out there. But don't kid yourself, Elizabeth. I'm pretty quick on the uptake, and from what I've observed in the last two days, its obvious you spend so much time trying to make your life run so neat and smooth that you're losing yourself. It's a damn shame, because both you and I know there's a hell of a lot more to you than that." He gave her another fierce glance, then flicked on his turn signal and zipped his Monte Carlo around the car in front of them.

"Great," she said. "Now that you're done analyzing me, you can turn around and take me back to get my car. I've changed my mind, I don't want to spend the day with you."

"I'm afraid I can't do that."

"Suit yourself, but don't expect me to be civil." He was definitely wrong about one thing, she thought as she reached into the backseat for her briefcase—her life hadn't been smooth sailing. In fact it had been damn hard. She fumed as she took out the case files she'd taken from work Friday. She might as well get some work done if they weren't going to talk.

* * *

Drake loosened his grip on the wheel and tried to relax. Why the hell *did* he stay? Hell if he knew, except she had looked so vulnerable and fragile the other night. He remembered the look on Elizabeth's face when she realized what might have happened if her daughter had been in the apartment. Yeah, that was it, he was a sucker for a mom with a kid. He realized he subconsciously made a vow then and there to help find Julie's killer, and to protect Elizabeth. A child needed a mother.

But she wasn't making it easy for him. Her perfume filled the car, teasing his senses, and further irritating him. He supposed he should give her some credit. It seemed she'd done an excellent job raising Allison all on her own. Allison's father was an ass for not wanting the little girl in his life.

Then another thought hit him, jabbing him right between the eyes. Just how many hot, sexy weekends had Elizabeth had? And with just how many partners? The last he'd known, she had a steady boyfriend through college that lasted into medical school. He'd assumed in Atlanta that she was rid of him. His hands tightened on the wheel again. Perhaps this trip *was* a mistake.

After a few minutes the silence in the car grew unnerving. He switched on the radio. Rod Stewart's voice rasped out "Maggie May." He smiled wryly. Somehow the tune fit. He cranked up the volume, not caring whether Elizabeth minded or not.

Elizabeth rubbed her temples. She'd been listening to Drake's choice of music, or rather enduring it, for the last forty-five minutes, but she wouldn't give him the satisfaction of asking him to turn it down. She didn't need to give him directions, for he seemed to know exactly where he was going. Most likely he checked up on that, too, finding out where she lived as a child. With a slight quiver of trepidation, she wondered what else he found out. Realizing they were approaching Richmond, she shoved her files back into her briefcase.

As if aware of her thoughts, Drake finally turned the music down. Small concession.

"Where do we go from here?" he asked.

Elizabeth wasn't sure if he meant which way to get to the farm, or in their relationship, but she did notice the anger was all but gone from his voice. Well, if the music had calmed him down, great, but it certainly hadn't settled her nerves.

She chose to answer the first meaning. "Head into town, down the main drag, and take a left at the stoplight. The farm is about five miles west."

"Got it."

As they drew nearer to their destination, Elizabeth found herself growing more nervous and agitated despite the beautiful day. She glanced out at the oak trees that lined the road. Their leaves were dotted with the first splashes of oranges and russets. The sky above them was a deep, vibrant blue. Days like this, with temperatures in the high seventies and low humidity, were a rarity in northern Illinois. When they came, she cherished them.

Drake turned onto the lane leading up to the farm, but instead of continuing, he pulled over and turned off the radio.

"Why are you stopping?" she asked. Her stomach was in a nervous flutter.

Instead of answering immediately, he leaned back against the seat and released his hands on the wheel, letting them fall against his thighs. He continued to look ahead, as if studying something in the gravel in front of them.

Her heart beat in double time to the seconds while she waited. Finally he sighed. "Look, Elizabeth, I'm sorry," he said. "We got off on the wrong foot today. It's not what I wanted."

"No, it's okay," she replied.

"No, it's not." He turned toward her and she could see the effort it was taking for him to apologize. "You've had a rotten couple of days and you're going to see your daughter. You should enjoy the day as much as you can." He lifted his hand and reached over to touch hers where it rested against her briefcase. She almost flinched. This wasn't going well at all. She found him much easier to deal with when he was mad at her.

"I think we should talk about it, clear the air," he went on. "I had no reason to expect anything of you in Atlanta, and I certainly shouldn't be taking it out on you now. You were right to leave; I knew eventually you would have to. I guess I just didn't expect it so quickly."

Then he smiled that slow smile of his, the one that did awful melting things to her insides. This was nuts, she told herself. She was nuts—and much too old for this kind of schoolgirl reaction.

"Fact is," he added, "the one thing I was looking forward to when I came out of surgery was seeing you."

He rubbed the back of Elizabeth's hand with his thumb, sending tiny electric impulses shooting through her system. She was a doctor—she knew there was no scientific reason for the way he made her feel. Well, that wasn't entirely true. Adrenaline makes nerve endings more sensitive and increases dopamine levels in the brain, which in turn releases neurotransmitters that send even more chemicals surging through the blood, which make the nerve endings even more sensitive, which . . .

Oh stop! she scolded herself. *Get a grip!*

He released her hand slowly. She looked up again, swimming in those deep pools of blue. Drake's smile turned boyishly contrite—only, she reminded herself, this was no little boy sitting next to her.

"Look, why don't we declare a truce," he said. "I think it will be easier for both of us if we're not fighting. Agreed?"

She nodded and tried to sound like the adult she was. "Agreed," she said, but her hand still tingled where he'd held her.

"Fine." He turned back to the steering wheel, put the car in gear, and they continued on. The flutters in her stomach grew into full-fledged earthquakes. *The man apologizes. Great.* Guilt knifed through her, deeper and more painful than ever.

nine

"Mommy!" Allison cried. Elizabeth's daughter swung perilously high, back and forth on a wooden swing that hung from ropes tied to an old oak tree. As soon as she spotted Elizabeth, the girl scraped the soles of her scuffed gym shoes violently into the dirt, trying to stop the swing as fast as she could.

Sharon Iverson knelt in the garden, tearing out the last of the tomato plants. She stood as Elizabeth stepped out of the car. Elizabeth nodded, answering the question of concern in her mother's eyes. Then she turned her attention to her daughter.

"Careful!" she shouted. She stepped forward, her heart in her throat as Allison jumped while the swing was still high in the air, too impatient to wait for it to come to a full stop. But Allison, as usual, paid no attention to her. She ran full force toward Elizabeth, who waited with arms open to capture her.

"Come here, my beautiful daughter!" Elizabeth yelled as Allison jumped into her arms. Elizabeth pulled her tight, lifting and swinging her. She buried her face deep into her daughter's neck and reveled in the fresh scents of lavender and jasmine, the only evidence of the bath the girl had taken that morning. Dirt was already caked on Allison's jeans and her face was smudged, attesting to the help she must have given her grandmother in the garden. Tears came to Elizabeth's eyes. Her daughter was a healthy scent of soap, shampoo, and dirt all rolled into one—just the elixir she needed.

"Mommy!" Allison protested as Elizabeth held her even tighter. "You're hurting me!" Elizabeth loosened her grip and pulled her head back to look at her daughter's face. She kissed one smudged cheek, then the other.

"Are you my best girl?" she asked.

"Oh, Mommy," Allison said, laughing. "You know I'm your *only* girl!"

Elizabeth laughed with her. "Right you are, my precocious little toad." She kissed her strawberry-blond head again, then, aware of Drake coming up beside them, she set Allison on the ground and turned her to face him. She held Allison in front of her, her hands firmly placed on Allison's shoulders.

"Allison, I want you to meet Mr. McGuire."

Allison cocked her head to look up at him. Elizabeth noted that she barely came to Drake's waist. She followed her daughter's gaze to Drake's eyes and held her breath, searching for any signs of recognition. Surely he would notice the blue eyes, although they were a shade or two lighter than his.

But she saw no change in his expression, just the broad smile he wore to greet her daughter, who right now was holding her little hand out, very businesslike, for him to shake. "Nice to meet you, Mr. Mc . . . uh . . ."

"McGuire," Elizabeth prompted.

"Yeah, Mr. McGuire."

Drake laughed, a full deep laugh. Elizabeth breathed a sigh of relief. She'd just bought more time.

Chicken, she scolded herself.

"It's nice to meet you, too," Drake said, enfolding Allison's small hand in his. "How about if you just call me Drake. Mr. McGuire sounds so formal, don't you think?"

Allison giggled, then looked up at Elizabeth for permission.

"I think that would be okay," Elizabeth said.

"Awesome. So, Drake," Allison said, pulling her hand back and placing it on her hip. She gave him a critical eye. "I hope you're hungry. Grandma made a ton of pancakes, but she won't let me have any yet. She made me wait for Mommy. I had Frosted Flakes this morning. Do you like Frosted Flakes? She made ham and a cake, too. Do you like cows? We have cows in the barn now. Jeremy's dad raises them. Grandma let's him use the barn. Jeremy's my friend. Grandma calls it brunch."

"I see," Drake said when Allison paused for air. He smiled at Elizabeth. "However do you survive?"

She shrugged. "I just go with the flow."

He looked back to Allison. "In answer to your first question, yes, I'm starved. And yes, I do like Frosted Flakes— ate them all the time when I was a kid; and I think cows are cool."

Allison laughed and grabbed his hand, pulling away from Elizabeth. "Then come onnnn!" she said. "I'm hungry!" She started to pull him across the yard, then stopped suddenly and looked back.

"Mommy, are you commming?"

Elizabeth's heart was in her throat. Seeing the two of them going off together had sent a shock through her system.

"Yes, right behind you," she said, but it took her an extra second or so to get her emotions under control before she followed them up the steps.

Elizabeth couldn't help watching the two of them closely during brunch. Drake seemed genuinely delighted by her daughter, laughing when she said something particularly funny. Elizabeth's lips twisted down into a slight frown when she realized the little minx was practically flirting with him, not that Allison had a clue yet what flirting was. Eventually, though, Elizabeth found herself smiling inwardly at the way the two of them got along, and at the huge appetites Allison and Drake obviously shared.

The tantalizing aroma of the feast brought Elizabeth's appetite storming back. She was surprisingly hungry, which seemed to please her mother greatly. Sharon pulled out all the stops for this meal, filling them with ham, pancakes, biscuits, and fruit. And as if they could eat anything more, there was the promise of apple cake for later. But what seemed to delight the woman even more was the fact that Elizabeth had finally brought a man home. Elizabeth explained when they went into the kitchen for more pancakes and juice that Drake was only acting as her bodyguard. Her mother gave her a strange, knowing look in response.

Drake was very gracious to Sharon Iverson and she couldn't have been any nicer to him. Elizabeth watched as her mother sliced more ham and placed it on Drake's plate. She frowned. To someone passing by the dining room window, they would look like one big happy family. She wasn't sure she liked that picture. Suddenly feeling stuffed, she set her napkin on her plate and stood.

"How about we go for that walk now, Allison?"

"Yes!" Allison piped up eagerly. "We can take Drake and show him the cows and the corn maze."

Elizabeth made a face, but she didn't want to disappoint her daughter. "Sure, that would be great, but clear your plate first."

"Okay, Mommy."

Elizabeth gathered her own plate and her mother's and walked toward the kitchen.

"Corn maze?" Drake asked, a dark eyebrow raised.

"Ben Frazier, Jeremy's dad, rents the fields from me, and the barn, too, for that matter," Sharon explained. "He and his wife have been a godsend since my husband passed away. I'm sure I wouldn't be able to hold on to the farm without their help, although Elizabeth and her sister Janey have been able to help me out a little lately. Jack, Elizabeth's dad, and I didn't have any sons. It's a shame, but nowadays I'm not sure they would have stuck with farming any more than my daughters wanted to. I've had some offers from land developers, but I hate to sell it."

As her mother gushed on, it dawned on Elizabeth just how much alike her mother and Allison were in their penchant for covering a hundred subjects in a brief period of time. She wished her mother wasn't so forthcoming. Drake didn't need to know their whole history. He was just passing through.

"Anyway," Sharon went on, "Ben's cut a maze into one of the fields and every fall he charges admission for the local kids and their parents to find their way through it. He gives me a percentage of the profits. It's become quite popular, especially since he hires some of the older kids to, shall we say, populate the maze." She winked. "Ghosts, you know," she added in a whisper behind her hand. "Allison has been driving me crazy about it, but I won't let her go alone. I'm afraid Elizabeth doesn't share Allison's zeal for the maze. She's always been a bit claustrophobic."

Elizabeth caught Drake's eye as she leaned against the doorjamb waiting for Allison to return from the kitchen. Drake's eyes glimmered with amusement at her predicament. She sent him her own lethal gaze. *Don't be so cocky,* it said, but she couldn't keep a smile from turning up the corners of her lips.

Maze aside, she realized she was actually looking forward to having him accompany them on their walk. Well, she wasn't a total shrew. And she certainly hadn't forgotten the way he looked that morning in that towel, or rather, practically *not* in that towel. She found herself staring down at his chest, remembering the curling hair and muscles that lay beneath the rust-colored Henley shirt he wore above his khaki slacks. He'd dressed casually today. It made him somehow more approachable. When Elizabeth looked back up, she blushed. Once more she'd been caught examining him.

"I'll meet you outside," she said quickly and made a hasty retreat. *You'd think my brain had been left out to bake in the sun with the feed corn,* she scolded herself as she remembered how she freaked out only minutes before at the sight of him and Allison together.

* * *

"Your daughter is quite the little urchin," Drake said, plucking a leaf from a cornstalk as they walked along the neatly planted rows toward the maze. They'd already visited the cows. Allison was thrilled that Drake had shown, in her opinion, extreme bravery when he went up to pet them. "City people don't normally do that!" she had exclaimed.

Drake had smiled. "I'm not always in the city," he explained.

Allison was skipping ahead now. Elizabeth smiled as she watched her ponytail bob up and down.

"She doesn't take after you or Sharon, does she?" he observed. "As far as looks go, I mean. Although she's just as pretty as her mother, in her own way." He smiled sideways at her.

"No, I'm afraid she doesn't take after us," she said, choosing to ignore the compliment, although it did make her feel warm inside. Sharon Iverson had brown hair, and more delicate features, not the strawberry-blond of Allison's. Nor did she have that determined, stubborn chin. As for her own hair, Elizabeth thought, it was at least three shades darker than Allison's.

"She must favor her father," Drake added nonchalantly.

Elizabeth stumbled over a small mound in the path. Drake caught her arm, steadying her.

"More than you know," she replied. Of course, she was thinking more of Allison's impulsive nature, as well as those taunting blue eyes and that stubborn chin. "You seem quite comfortable with children," she said, trying to gain her equilibrium as they walked on. She needed to steer the conversation away from her daughter's lineage, quick.

"Survival instinct. I grew up in a house full of kids. My aunt and uncle were good Italian Catholics who didn't believe in birth control—until the sixth kid came along and my aunt had had enough. When they took me in, I was number seven. My cousins stayed in the area, for the most part. When we get together at the house, they bring all their kids with them and it turns into quite a zoo."

Elizabeth glanced sideways at him. "DeLuca—Italian, that makes sense. I always thought you looked more Italian than Irish. Where did the name McGuire come from?"

"From my dad." His gaze traveled up, again, to where Allison skipped along the path. "He was Irish. He had glorious red hair, as did my grandmother. Our Celtic roots run way back."

A cloud passed over his eyes as he looked upon Allison. Elizabeth held her breath, but it passed quickly.

"My mother was pure Italian, though," he went on. "What a mix that was." He smiled and Elizabeth was amazed, again, by the warmth his smile brought to his features. "I remember when they used to fight. You'd swear they would raise the proverbial roof. Ah, but when they made up, 'now *thar* was a pretty sight,' as my dad used to say. There was love all around. Mostly, I remember the love."

"What happened to them?"

He paused, then turned to gaze down at her. His brows came together and his eyes narrowed, as if he were trying to shut off the distant pain.

"I'm sorry," she said quickly, "I shouldn't have asked."

He shook his head. "No, it's all right. It happened a long time ago." He continued to look down on her, but he wasn't really seeing her. She swallowed convulsively. "They were killed in an accident when I was seven," he said, "coming home from the theater. They were driving south on Lake

Shore Drive when a car full of punks high on cocaine slammed head-on into their vehicle. The driver of the car was too stoned to realize he was going the wrong way on a divided highway. My parents were killed instantly."

Elizabeth studied him, imagining the child he had been—small, bereaved, lonely with the loss of his mother and father. "My father died a few years ago," she said softly. "As horrible as it was, I can't imagine how much worse it would have been had he died when I was seven— and you lost both parents."

He nodded, his eyes narrowing more, but he didn't speak. She sensed that at that moment, he couldn't.

The mother in her reached up and fingered a lock of his hair where it lay across his forehead. Gently she swiped it back, then brought her hand down to lay against his cheek.

He placed his hand over hers, his eyes opening wider now. For a brief moment she glimpsed into his soul. Pain melded there with a deeper need, and Elizabeth's knees went weak. Once more she was reminded that he was no small boy. Slowly he moved her hand from his cheek to his lips and kissed her palm, then lowered it between them, effectively pulling her closer.

"I've told that story to very few people," he said, his voice husky.

Elizabeth swallowed hard again. An overwhelming need to kiss him filled her. Heat emanated between them while passion flamed in his eyes. The heady scent of his aftershave and his own male virility mingled with the perfume of the corn drying in the sun and made her head swim.

They were interrupted by Allison's shout.

"Mommy, come on!"

Drake squeezed her hand tighter, as if unwilling to let go just yet.

"Mommy!" Allison insisted. She ran back to tug on Elizabeth's sweater.

Finally Drake released her. She turned toward Allison.

"Yes," she said, somewhat breathless. "We're coming."

She took Allison's hand with the same one that had just held Drake's. Walking with her down the path, she willed her heart to stop its hammering, fully aware that Drake was slow to follow.

"I think I'll let you go in with Drake," Elizabeth told Allison when they reached the maze.

Allison put her hands on her hips. "You're not afraid, are you, Mommy?" she asked accusingly. "You know the ghosts and spiders and goblins are all fake. They're just people made up to look like them."

"And you are such a smart little girl to know that!" Elizabeth told her.

"It's okay, Allison, I'll take you in," Drake offered, coming up beside them. "We'll have great fun trying to find our way out. Your mom can wait out here for us. We'll show her just how smart we are when we get through it in lickity-split time."

Allison giggled at his choice of words.

"Then she can buy us some of that cotton candy over there." He pointed to a stand set up a few feet from the entrance to the corn maze.

"Well, I guess it's okay," Allison said, scrunching up her face.

Thank you, Elizabeth mouthed over Allison's head.

"You owe me later," he replied, his eyes lighting with mischief.

* · * *

Drake glanced over at Elizabeth. They'd been traveling for over forty minutes now, and she hadn't said a word.

He couldn't blame her. They had had a great day at the farm until the last hour or so. After supper Elizabeth sat down with her daughter and tried to explain why she couldn't bring her home just yet. She also had to tell Allison about Julie. The two must have been close because the little girl kept calling her *Aunt* Julie. The kid was understandably upset, although Elizabeth had been careful to omit the details. *Man, that little girl is tough,* Drake thought as he remembered how she nodded, as if understanding far more than her years should allow. He thought he might almost start crying himself at the way she took it. Elizabeth had looked up at him, then, as if for strength.

"Drake is a big FBI guy," she told Allison. "He's going to help find the man who did this."

Allison looked up at him, too, with her great big saucer blue eyes, and nodded, as if she fully expected him to do just that.

"Let's just forget about all this for now," Elizabeth told her. "I'll take you to bed and read you a story before I go. And I'll be back here before you know it. Now give Grandma a kiss good night."

The little girl kissed her grandma, then turned toward Drake. She sidled up to him and hugged him, placing a kiss on his cheek. "I know you'll help my mommy," she said. Drake's arms went around her and he gave her a little squeeze. When he released her, his gaze caught Elizabeth's, and he was hit with the sense of sadness in her eyes and more than a touch of fear. It was no wonder. She was probably scared half out of her wits at how close she and her daughter had come to death.

When Elizabeth took Allison into the bedroom, Sharon Iverson turned to him and clasped his hand with both of hers. "Keep her safe," she'd told him.

Well, it was a heck of a burden, one he could not now shake, even if he had been thinking of leaving. There was no way he could deny little Allison. The girl stole his heart in one day.

And as for her mother . . .

The Chopin sonata that had been filling the silence ended. Drake turned down the radio. "So, do you want to tell me about the maze?" he teased.

A smile touched the corner of her lip, but she kept her gaze averted out the window as she answered. "It's really quite silly and childish."

"I promise not to laugh."

She glanced at him, her eyes narrowing, then sighed and looked back out the window at the city skyline, which was looming closer with every mile they traveled.

"When I was young," she began, "not much older than Allison, a group of us kids played together often, including some boys from a neighboring farm. These boys were quite mischievous. One day they thought it would be great fun to play hide-and-seek in the cornfield. I wasn't thrilled with the idea, but I didn't want them to think I was a sissy little girl," she explained.

"Anyway, I was pretty gullible then. They said it would be more fun if we played blindfolded. They took me out into the field, turned me around, then told me I had to wait ten minutes before I could come find them. They took off and left me there—for a lot longer than ten minutes. Eventually I figured out they had no intention of playing hide-

and-seek—that they'd tricked me. I took off the blindfold, but it was late August and the crop was good that year. The cornstalks were ten feet high, giants to a little girl like me. I started walking down the rows, calling out their names. Finally I heard one of the boys call me from far away. I changed direction and crossed more rows, then I heard another call, changed direction again, and soon I was so confused I didn't know which way I was going." She didn't mention that by then there were huge tears rolling down her cheeks.

"I remember being very hot and the locusts buzzing all around my head. I started to think that the giant stalks were walking toward me, trying to suffocate me. I tried not to panic, but I began to think I would never get out of there. Finally I reasoned that if I just kept going in one direction, I would eventually come to the end of the row. I did get out, on my own, but it really frightened me. Ever since then I can't stand tight places, and I have *no* desire to roam among the cornstalks. I know there's no logical reason to be afraid, but I can't help it. There, now you know my greatest flaw. I'm a chicken at heart."

He smiled. "I can see why you didn't want to go into the maze, then."

She nodded, smiling ruefully, and turned her head toward him. "Thanks for taking Allison. You two seemed like you had a good time."

"She's a good little girl. You've done a great job with her."

"Thanks," she said. The smile left her lips and she turned away again.

"What were you thinking a few minutes ago?" he asked, not willing to let the conversation lag for too long. He found he enjoyed listening to her voice. "You seemed deep in concentration."

"I was trying to come up with that list you wanted of Julie's friends and acquaintances. It's sad, but other than her ex-husbands, I can't think of anyone. She was my best friend, but we had no friends in common, at least not since college. She did her thing, and I did mine, and we just got together occasionally when she was in town. That's not much of a friendship, is it?"

"I don't know. It sounds like you were there for each other when you needed to be. Isn't that what friendship is all about?"

"I wasn't there Friday night."

"No, you weren't. That's probably a good thing, because if you had been there . . ."

"It might have been me," she finished for him.

He saw her shiver and reached over and brushed his fingers across her hand where it rested on the seat.

"Don't be so hard on yourself. We'll get to the bottom of this. My cousins are damn good at their jobs, and so, I might add, am I."

"I'm counting on it," she said, and though she didn't look at him again, she also did not pull her hand away from his.

They picked up Elizabeth's car without incident, although the way Drake insisted on going over it before he let her get behind the wheel gave her the creeps. Finally, after looking in, around, and underneath it, he started it up.

Elizabeth followed him back to the hotel. Safely back in their suite, she popped the extra ham and biscuits her mother had insisted she take with them into the refrigerator, then sat down at the table across from Drake. She listened as Drake checked in with Andi, trying to glean what she could from his half of the conversation. From what she could tell, there was not much new in the investigation. Drake confirmed this when he flipped off his phone.

"Andi and O'Reilly and a couple of other detectives canvassed the neighborhood again today," he said. "So far, no one's admitting seeing anyone suspicious that night—except me, of course." He shook his head irritably. "They also did a check on Julie's ex-husbands. Everyone's squeaky clean, including the current husband, Stephan Parks. Andi had crime technicians out again to see if they could lift any more fingerprints from your apartment. Nothing there yet, either, just like she said earlier, only yours, Allison's, Julie's, Mrs. Parisi's, and Donny's."

"You can't still think Donny had anything to do with this."

He scrubbed his hand across his jaw. "Not with the actual crime, perhaps, but I still think he's the key. Sometimes it's not always going from point A to B to C in an investigation. Sometimes you just have to find the key—Donny's that key, I'm sure of it. There's something there. I need to talk to him again."

"I wish you wouldn't press him, it upsets him so much. Haven't they turned up anything else?"

"No. Now, we may still be looking at a stalker, a psychopath who gets his jollies from stabbing women, although there've been no crimes similar to that in the area for some time. Is there anything you can think of that was a little off in the last week or so? Anything you noticed that set your nerves on edge or didn't seem quite right? Has anyone been following you?"

Elizabeth wanted to help him, but nothing came to mind. "I can't think of anything. My days are pretty routine. I have rounds at the center in the morning, then I'm in surgery for a couple of hours, or the catheterization lab. I have clinic in the afternoon, then when I'm through, I come home, collect Allison from Mrs. Parisi, and then I have dinner."

She stopped there. She didn't feel the need to tell him that after dinner she usually helped Allison with her little bit of homework, then watched some TV with her before tucking her into bed. He didn't need to know that after that, she usually worked on more cases, then turned in herself. No, she didn't need to tell him just how dull and sedate her life had become, that her social life had become virtually nil. Although to be honest, she had come to enjoy her routine.

"No, I don't remember anything out of the ordinary," she said. "No nutcases lurking in the shadows or hiding in the bushes," she added flippantly.

"This is serious, Elizabeth," he said, flashing her an irritated look.

She laughed, feeling the hysteria rise in her throat. "Don't you think I know that?" she said, clasping her arms across her chest. "I'm out of my apartment, my best friend's been murdered, and I can't even tuck my daughter into her own bed at night. Frankly, this bites!"

Elizabeth stood and strode to the window. Glancing out, she tried to get her emotions under control. The moon was rising over Lake Michigan, its glimmer stream reached toward shore from far out across the lake. It looked so pretty, she mused. So serene, and so completely opposite of the emotions that churned inside her. *It also bites that I'm riddled with guilt,* she told herself. She needed to tell him about Allison, and the sooner the better—whether he hated her for it or not.

She'd lied earlier when Drake asked her what was on

her mind. She hadn't been thinking about that list at all, but had been mulling over the implications of coming clean with him. Seeing him with Allison had ripped at her heart. She'd been wrong not to try harder to get in touch with him when Allison was born. But so much was going on then, and she'd wanted to keep her daughter safe.

Oh, admit it! she scolded herself. *You wanted her all to yourself and you were afraid of what Drake might do if he found out your weekend together had its own special little consequence.*

She was aware when Drake rose from the table. She closed her eyes when she felt him draw near, tried to ignore the little tremors that raced through her when he put his hands on her shoulders.

Tell him! a little voice inside her screamed. *Tell him now!*

He turned her toward him. She placed her forehead against his shoulder, unable to meet his eyes, afraid he could read her thoughts. But he wouldn't accept that. He traced his finger down her cheek, then lifted her chin.

"Look at me," he demanded.

She opened her eyes and saw the deep clouds that had built in his. Her heart raced. She held her breath.

"I think it's time we put this thing between us to rest," he said. Then, deliberately, slowly, he lowered his lips to hers.

Elizabeth closed her eyes again, fully absorbing the gentle touch of his lips against hers. Tiny sparks of kaleidoscopic sensation ripped through her as moist flesh met flesh. Her lips opened to taste him, her tongue ventured to explore him—rough and soft, sweet and masculine all at once. She heard a groan let loose from deep within him, then his tongue was circling hers, his mouth opening wide to take her further into himself.

"God, Elizabeth!" he breathed into her mouth as he wrapped his arms around her and plastered her against his chest, his waist, his loins.

Liquid silver spread through her. Her own arms reached up to pull him closer. Her breath came in sharp pants against his open mouth.

When he wrenched his lips from hers, she moaned and buried her flaming face against his shoulder. His heart hammered against her chest where he still held her fiercely. She didn't want to move—ever.

Drake lowered his face to bury it in her auburn curls, unwilling to let her go, despite his better judgment. He forced himself to concentrate on the earthy, sweet scent of her hair while he brought himself back to reality. He tried to draw on all his FBI training to slow his heart.

Hell, he hadn't expected that! He thought he would just kiss her, just one simple kiss to get it out of the way. He told himself that it would prove he'd been imagining how devastating her kisses were.

And he had been dead wrong.

He couldn't let this get out of control. Not this time. It had always goaded him that perhaps he was distracted in Atlanta when his team moved in on the raid, although since then, he had gone over everything again and again, trying to see where they could have done something different. He hadn't come up with anything other than more manpower. They'd been ambushed, outgunned. Word had leaked out that they were coming, but they had still prevailed. Still, there was that nagging sense of guilt that his time with Elizabeth had somehow distracted him, made him less keen than he should have been, and resulted in his partner's death.

He couldn't allow those distractions now, he told himself, although he knew the real truth was he was afraid to let her mess with his heart again. He didn't need anyone, he told himself. He worked better alone.

He tried to convince himself of this, even as his senses surged with her, the scent of her hair, the honey sweet taste of her lips, her moist, welcoming mouth. And the way her hips fit so snuggly against his.

The incessant ringing of his cell phone finally brought Drake to his senses. Slowly he released her and turned back to the table to answer his phone.

It was Andi calling from the lobby. She had something she wanted to show him. "Give me five minutes," he told her, then flipped the phone shut.

He turned back to Elizabeth. She stood there, once more hugging her arms in a protective stance.

"I'll go with you," she offered.

He shook his head. "No, you get some rest. I'll let you know if it turns out to be anything important. Keep the door locked and don't let anyone in."

With one last glance at her, he shoved the phone into his pocket and left the room.

ten

Drake met Andi in the hotel foyer. O'Reilly was with her.
That alone sent his already jumbled nerves flying.

"What's up?" he asked, eyeing them suspiciously.

Andi motioned him over to a table. "This won't take
long, Drake, but O'Reilly insisted we talk to you about it."
She gave O'Reilly a look that told him to keep quiet. Judging by the smug look on O'Reilly's face, Drake was sure he
wasn't going to like what they had to say. He wondered
what the hell garbage the guy had dug up now.

"Take a look at this." Andi handed him a computer
printout. "It's the call logs for the precinct the night of the
murder. The first two pages are the ones that went through
the central 911 system."

"Yeah, so what? It's got Elizabeth's 911 call," he said as
he thumbed through them.

"Take a closer look," Andi suggested.

"It might help if you tell me what I'm looking for."

O'Reilly couldn't keep quiet anymore. "Try page three," he said snidely. Drake flipped a page and scanned the document. His eyes narrowed as he spotted an item halfway down the page. Hell, O'Reilly wasn't going to make a case of that, was he?

"You want to tell us why you called the station asking for your girlfriend's address?" O'Reilly asked. "If you two were so buddy-buddy, don't you think you would have known it already?"

Drake shook his head and threw the printout on the table. Ignoring O'Reilly, he glared at Andi. "Are you going to let him pull you into his madness? I would think the two of you would have much better things to do than try to find bogus evidence on me."

"It's a legitimate question," Andi said softly. "One I assured O'Reilly you'd have an answer for."

"Yeah, like you have an answer for everything else!" O'Reilly spat. "How come the phone call happens to be around the time of the murder?"

"You don't know that! You can't give an exact time of the attack."

"I still want an answer," O'Reilly insisted.

Drake clenched his fist. He would like nothing better than to pop the blowhard in the mouth. "Get your head out of your ass, O'Reilly. I'm not the murderer. I called the station on the off chance that Sarah Perkins, or someone else I knew from when I worked the district, would be on duty. As luck would have it, she was. She did me a favor for old-time's sake."

"Why did you need her address? Did you know Julie

was there? Maybe you and Julie had something going on the side?"

Now he was really going to punch the guy. He raised his fist, but Andi quickly placed her hand against his arm. "Settle down, Drake, and answer the question.

He stared at O'Reilly for a long time, then finally shook his head and ran his hand through his hair.

"Shit!" he swore. "I had just seen Elizabeth at the alumni banquet. I didn't know where she lived, but I felt we had some unfinished business. I thought I'd drop by so we could talk. I got there before she did and waited for her, which I've already told you!" He glared pointedly at O'Reilly. "Hell, Andi, do you think if I was up to anything I'd call the local cops to get her address first? I could have done a search myself through FBI data banks, but it was just easier at the time to call the station. That's all it was!"

"That's what I figured," Andi said, gathering up the printout. "Anyway, we think we've narrowed down the time of the attack. We checked Mrs. Parks's cell phone records. She was on the phone talking to her soon-to-be-ex-husband between 7:15 and 7:44. We called him and asked him about it. He says it was not a pleasant conversation but nothing seemed out of place with Julie at the time. She most likely took her shower after that. Giving her fifteen, maybe twenty minutes for that, it puts the attack some-where around 8:15, maybe later if she didn't get into the shower right away. Seems odd, though, when she was sup-posed to meet Elizabeth downtown by 7:45."

Drake shook his head in disbelief. "If you already knew the approximate time of the attack, why did you let Bozo here question me about the phone call?"

She smiled. "I guess I just wanted to hear your answer."

"Thanks."

But O'Reilly wasn't giving up yet. "And maybe you already murdered her and made the phone call to make yourself look good."

"Right, and hightailed it downtown to catch Elizabeth's speech."

"That would be a neat alibi, but who else saw you there?"

"Hell, I can't say."

"Did you talk to anyone when you got there?"

"No, just Elizabeth."

"What time was that?"

"I don't know, but I must've left around nine, considering I made that phone call for the address at 9:09 according to your printout! Look, this is ridiculous. Andi?"

"Okay. Listen, O'Reilly, we're done here," she said. "Let's knock off for the night. Sorry, Drake, but it was just a technicality I had to get out of the way."

"Hey, you can't just let this go," O'Reilly blustered.

"Yes, I can," Andi said, staring him down. Drake smiled inwardly, despite his irritation. For a little thing, Andi could be quite intimidating. "And Drake," she added, "Mama DeLuca expects you at the house Wednesday night for the usual family dinner."

He nodded. "I'll be there if I can."

"Well, isn't this the cute family picture. You know, your husband may be a bigwig in Investigative Services, but he's not in charge in this investigation. I think I should talk to the captain about this."

"You go ahead, only I suggest you don't call him tonight with your complaints. Try tomorrow." She turned to Drake. "Call me if anything comes up." Andi put her hand firmly on O'Reilly's shoulder and steered him toward the door. Drake watched them leave, an angry taste still in his mouth.

Back in the suite, Drake was surprised to find Elizabeth asleep on the sofa. She was curled up against the armrest, her feet tucked beneath her and her head resting where it had nodded sideways against the backrest. An open file lay beside her on the floor next to her discarded shoes. It must have slipped from her hands when she nodded off. He picked it up, closed the folder, and set it on the table. Elizabeth was certainly dedicated to her work, he mused. Even after all that had happened, she couldn't ease up. Well, they had that in common. His lips twisted in to a wry smile. He wasn't sure that was a good thing.

"What am I going to do with you?" he whispered, then slipped his arms under her back and lifted her. She curled into him, moaning softly as she wrapped her arms around his neck. Her head nestled neatly beneath his chin as if it belonged there. He stood stock-still for a moment, unnerved at having her once again in his arms, and then proceeded into the bedroom.

Kicking the blanket aside, he laid her gently on the bed, then loosened her hands from around his neck. Drake could tell that even in her sleep Elizabeth hadn't give up on her worries. A line creased her brow and her lips were turned down. Her wild curls fell to rest across her cheek. Drake gently pushed them aside and tucked them behind her ear. He thought briefly of undressing her, but knew he couldn't trust himself to the task. Instead, he set her hands gently on her stomach and slowly drew the blanket up, tucking it in around her shoulders. Sighing, he gave her one last look before he left the room and closed the door snuggly between them.

Back in the living room, Drake ran his hand through his hair in frustration. There was a murderer out there, and with O'Reilly's eggheaded obsession of trying to find something on him, he was feeling less than confident in the ability of Chicago's finest to find the real murderer. He'd have to step up his own investigation.

Promptly at 7:30 the next morning, Elizabeth pulled into her reserved parking space in the side lot of the five-story concrete-and-glass building that was the Heartland Cardiac Center. Her first patient appointment wasn't until nine, but she wanted to go through the weekend discharges and see if there was anyone she needed to follow up on.

As she got out of her car, Drake pulled up a few spaces down from her. Elizabeth grabbed her briefcase and headed for the side entrance. He was at her heels within seconds. She frowned, more than a little displeased with the idea of him following her around like a puppy.

"I'm coming with you, to check it out," he said earlier when she came out of the bedroom, fully dressed and ready to return to work.

She argued that the center was perfectly safe. "Security is quite strict—our patients demand it."

"Humor me," he said with a deprecating smile that she couldn't argue with. She was embarrassed when she suddenly realized he must have been the one to put her to bed—and if she had to admit it, a little disappointed that he didn't wake her when he did and . . .

She shoved those fantasies aside now and pulled out her ID card. She slid it through the security slot, then waited while Drake opened the door for her. For security reasons, only the front reception entrance to the building was left unlocked during the day.

As they walked down the corridor, Drake whistled. "Seems O'Reilly was right for once. This place is pretty fancy. Looks like we're entering a five-star hotel, not a hospital." He nodded toward the plush carpet and the cherry wainscoting that lined the wall below the embossed wallpaper.

"It is a hotel, in a way, with all the comforts of home," Elizabeth explained, continuing down the corridor. "We try to make our patients as comfortable as possible, while at the same time offering state-of-the-art diagnostic and cardiac care."

"And charge them a small fortune for it, too, I'll bet."

She ignored his comment.

"I guess I didn't expect to find you working in a place like this," he added.

She could hear the surprise in his tone, which bordered on judgmental. It irritated her since she had good reasons to work here. "The well-to-do deserve excellent care just as much as anybody else," she said tightly. "And if they can afford to be pampered while they get it, instead of feeling like a body on a gurney waiting for their turn at the surgical room, why not?" She didn't tell him that this wasn't her first choice. She had also been offered a fellowship at the university in pediatric cardiology, but turned it down.

"Let me guess," he added, "The salary's not too shabby, either."

"I can't complain, but it's not the main reason I took the job."

"Oh?" He raised a dark eyebrow. "Then you get child support from Allison's dad? It can't be easy being a single parent."

She didn't answer him. Instead, she motioned down the hall as she guided him toward the main reception area. "The first floor houses our clinic, where we see most of our outpatients, and the CAT-scan unit and ultrasound services," she explained. "Surgery, recovery rooms, and catheterization lab are on the second floor. Physicians' offices and rehab center on the third, with patients' rooms on the fourth and fifth floors. We're basically self-contained, although if other medical issues pop up with a patient, we're close to other hospitals where they can get specialized care in those areas. Plus, specialists in other fields are associated with the clinic, and the staff can call them in for a consult at anytime."

"Impressive," he said, dogging her heels.

"It is. I'm lucky to be working here. Dr. Benson has one of the best reputations for open-heart surgery in the country. He opened the center three years ago to cater to people who feel uncomfortable in the big university hospitals. I like it here, because it's not as pressured and I get to know my patients better. I also get to concentrate on early diagnosis and treatment, which is the reason I decided to go into cardiology in the first place. As more people become aware of the importance of early diagnosis, many clients come here to have our heart scan and preliminary risk testing. You'd be amazed at how many heart attacks, and thus deaths, we can prevent with early diagnosis."

"Okay, you've sold me."

She glanced at him, to see if he was serious. At his smile, she smiled back. "Sorry, I can't help myself sometimes."

They approached the large cherrywood reception desk with its richly upholstered seating area across from it. Coffee service and rolls were laid out on a table along with freshly sliced fruit for clients to enjoy before being whisked off to an examining room; that is, for those patients who weren't scheduled for procedures. Two receptionists stood behind the desk, setting up for the day. The phone rang, but stopped before the second ring without either of the receptionists picking it up.

"We have our own after-hours call center down the hallway," Elizabeth explained. "It gives patients that personal touch. Any on-call doctor can be reached within seconds. In cardiac care, seconds can mean a life."

Elizabeth passed the elevator, opting for the stairs. "I climb the stairs whenever I can. I don't have much time for other exercise."

"Isn't that a little of the doctor not practicing what she preaches?" he teased.

"I probably put in at least three miles a day on these stairs," she assured him.

"Hey, don't explain it to me. As far as I can see, your exercise regime is working."

Her cheeks warmed as she realized he was getting an excellent view of her backside as she began to climb the steps. She smiled smugly, though, when she reached the fourth-floor landing and her breath still came easy. But then, she noted, so did his, and she hadn't set a slow pace.

Drake stepped past her and opened the door to the fourth floor. Walking past him, she headed for the nurse's station. A nurse in a blue smock looked up as they approached.

"Oh, Dr. Iverson, we really didn't expect you in today," the nurse said. Her fingers paused over her computer keyboard where she was making an entry into a chart.

"Hello, Ms. Davis." Elizabeth smiled. "This is Mr. McGuire. He's going to shadow me today. Try not to pay any attention to him."

"Oh," the nurse said again, but it was clear by her curious glance at Drake's darkly handsome features that she would be hard-pressed to ignore him. Once again he had dressed in a neatly tailored suit and tie, making him look devilishly handsome.

"Who do we have in here today?" she asked, trying to pull Ms. Davis's attention away from Drake.

"Ah, yes, well . . ." The nurse picked up a floor chart and studied it. "We kept Mrs. Thompson over from Saturday. She's in five. She didn't feel comfortable going home yet, but Dr. Benson said he's going to release her today. I guess, now that you're here, you can do that. He said all indications are that her stent is working just fine."

Elizabeth remembered she performed an angioplasty on Mrs. Thompson on Friday. It seemed a lifetime away now. During the procedure, she inserted the small, tubelike stent into Mrs. Thompson's artery to ensure it remained open and the blood flowing smoothly through it. "Yes, I'll see to Mrs. Thompson," she told the nurse. "What else have we got?"

"A couple of admits coming in later, and the patients in rooms three and four have angioplasties scheduled. We're getting ready to take them down to surgery. Dr. Young will be doing those. Oh, and Dr. Benson will be doing a bypass this afternoon on Mr. Solomon. He's in six."

"I see. Do you have the discharge list for the weekend?"

The nurse reached into a folder and pulled it out.

"Yes, here it is."

"Thank you. Is there anything out of the ordinary I should know about?"

"No," the nurse said, then hesitated. She looked embarrassed as she glanced from Elizabeth to Drake, then back again, as if trying to decide if she should say anything more. Finally she said, "Dr. Iverson, I just want to say I was sorry to hear about what happened Friday at your apartment. It must be awful for you."

"Yes, it was tragic," Elizabeth responded quickly, shoving the niggling fear that crept into her mind to the back of her psyche. She didn't want to think about any of that this morning. "I'll check on the patients, then I'll be in my office briefly before my appointments if you need me."

Ms. Davis lifted an eyebrow, but Elizabeth decided not to explain any further. She took a few minutes to review the cases from Saturday, then placed a follow-up call to one of the discharged patients from the nurse's station. Afterward, she checked on Mrs. Thompson, reassuring her that everything would be just fine now that her artery was clear. Then she stopped in with the other two patients, before heading down to the second floor and the cardiac intensive care unit. They had five cardiologists on staff and four cardiovascular surgeons, of whom Dr. Benson was the chief surgeon. The ICCU was busy this morning. Two patients had just recently undergone surgery, and three others were awaiting diagnostic tests. They didn't normally get acute heart attack cases at the center, as ambulances generally took those to other hospitals. Their business was more for ongoing care and preventive care for future heart attacks. If they did their job right, there should be less heart attack cases.

Elizabeth looked in on a couple of patients, then headed back upstairs to her office. Somewhere along the way, she lost Drake. She'd been so involved with examining her patients, she hadn't noticed when he disappeared. She sat down and checked her messages. Nothing earth-shattering awaited her, except for Mrs. Beal. The woman was feeling uncomfortable this morning and wanted to know if she could come in and see her. Elizabeth called her, as Mrs. Beal was known for her "symptoms."

She assured Mrs. Beal that the medicine she was given should be working, but if she still had concerns, she would be happy to see her this morning. Since Mrs. Beal couldn't come in until after one, Elizabeth told her that she would schedule her with Dr. Young, if that was all right. Elizabeth had done CAT scans and stress tests on the woman two months ago, and although it appeared she had partial blockage of her arteries, she didn't think Mrs. Beal was a candidate for angioplasty just yet. Medication along with a low-fat diet and exercise should be enough to help prevent future problems. She called the appointment desk and gently convinced them to squeeze Mrs. Beal in for Dr. Young that afternoon.

At nine o'clock she was downstairs, seeing patients.

Drake caught up with her at eleven.

"Can we talk?"

"I can give you five minutes, tops," she said. Then she added, "I could also use some coffee." She promptly steered Drake toward the lavishly appointed cafeteria.

"How's your morning going?" Drake asked before taking a sip of his black coffee.

"The usual," she replied, looking out the window which looked out onto a water garden.

"Good, well maybe that's not the right thing to say in a place like this."

She smiled. "It's okay."

"Yeah, anyway—your patients, that's what I want to talk to you about. Have you lost any recently whose loved ones might hold a grudge against you?"

Elizabeth stopped stirring her coffee. "You're kidding,

right? That's about as crazy as some of the other ideas you've had."

"You think so?" he asked. "You have some pretty wealthy patients here. It wouldn't be the first time someone blamed a doctor for what might seem to them an untimely death of a loved one. You have had a few deaths here in the last month, haven't you." It was a statement rather than a question.

"How did you find that out?"

He shrugged. "It's my job." When she continued to stare at him, though, he explained further. "Okay, although I found most of your nurses very discreet."

"They're paid to be discreet, to say nothing of being ethical, as their profession demands."

"Yes, well . . ." He smiled, his blue eyes lighting with mischief. "Let's just say my good looks and my ID can go a long way. Some clam up, but others don't realize what they're telling me."

"Oh, great. So now the whole place knows you're FBI and keeping an eye on me."

"Not the entire place, just a couple of nurses. I told them the investigation was top secret."

"Uh-huh. And the ones who went ahead and spoke to you, you expect them to keep quiet, do you?"

"No, but that's okay, too. It won't hurt for word to get around that we're investigating. Now, why don't you fill me in on those deaths."

Elizabeth could see that he wasn't going to let it go.

"We're a cardiac care center. We're bound to have some morbidity," she explained, angered that he would question her on it. "We know we're not God, we just do what we can. Often people wait too long for care, and by the time we get them, their bodies or their blood vessels are too weak to accommodate the procedures. It happens."

But a shadow crept across her memory. She was thinking about last week and Mr. Babcock. The man had died on the table. His wife was devastated, but Elizabeth wasn't sure she wanted to tell Drake about it.

"There is something, isn't there?" he prompted.

Damn, she swore to herself. She'd have to get better at hiding her thoughts.

"All right. There is one. Early last week. It was a patient I had seen in July. He came in again last week with chest pain, but I couldn't see him this time because I was involved in a procedure with another patient. Dr. Benson took the case. He conducted an angiogram and decided to do a bypass. I found out later that the man died on the operating table from an allergic reaction to one of the anesthetics he was given. They couldn't revive him."

The memory of how she'd found out about Mr. Babcock's death still plagued her. Mrs. Babcock had walked into her office, the shock and pain evident on her face. Elizabeth recognized the look of grief immediately. "You said he would be fine," the woman accused her. "If he just took his medication." Elizabeth had gone over the man's file at least five times since then. By all accounts, he seemed very healthy except for high cholesterol levels and high blood pressure. All the tests she'd taken showed no sign of acute arterial disease. Of course, one could never be completely sure without an angiogram.

"Does that happen often?" Drake asked her.

"What?" She'd been distracted by her thoughts.

"Patients dying in surgery from the anesthetic."

"It can, although usually we can counteract any reaction with other drugs."

"Sounds like his death might be enough to tick someone off."

Elizabeth thought about that for a moment. But no, Mrs. Babcock had seemed more distressed than angry. She shook her head. "No," she said more firmly now. "I think you're barking up the wrong tree there. Now, I've got to get back to work."

"Fine, but if you think of anything else, let me know. I've got some other things to check up on, but I'll be back by one and we'll head out to Julie's service together."

"Uh-huh," she acknowledged, but her mind was still on Mrs. Babcock.

eleven

Elizabeth walked into Dr. Benson's office and handed his secretary Mr. Babcock's file. "Sorry I didn't get this back to you Saturday." She had taken it home on Friday intending to return it the next day.

Claire Daniels looked up from her desk. "Uh, no problem," she said, taking the file and smiling warmly at Elizabeth. Claire was in her late twenties, a few years younger than Elizabeth. She could hate Claire for being so pretty and efficient, but Elizabeth wasn't that kind of woman. Absently she wondered why Claire wasn't married yet. As for Dr. Benson, he seemed to take a special interest in Claire, treating her almost like a daughter. Actually, it was not unlike the way he treated Elizabeth, herself, in some respects. The surgeon had taken her under his wing, often choosing her over the other cardiologists to assist him in his cases. Elizabeth admired and respected the man for his mentorship, which is why she felt a little guilty asking her next question.

"Do you know if Dr. Benson has Mr. Babcock's films? I'd like to take a look at them."

"Let me check." Claire opened the door to the inner office and Elizabeth followed.

"You know, Dr. Iverson," Claire said as she searched the files on Dr. Benson's desk, "Dr. Benson didn't expect you in today. We were all set to let someone else handle your patients."

"Thanks, Claire. But the work helps."

"Well, you sure seem to be taking it well. If it was my friend who was killed, I'm not sure what I would have done. It's a little spooky, isn't it? Just think what might have happened if you had been there instead."

The shiver that Elizabeth had managed to avoid most of the morning snaked up her spine. She'd heard that supposition too many times already.

"Unfortunately, Claire, I wasn't there," she said tersely. "Perhaps if I had been, the attacker might have thought twice with two of us in the apartment. As it is, I'm attending Julie's funeral this afternoon."

"Yes. Well, I'm not finding them here. Perhaps on the credenza." Claire moved over to Dr. Benson's credenza, which sat along the side wall. White viewing screens hung above it. Elizabeth noticed a series of films clipped up there. While Claire continued her search, Elizabeth flicked on the light and scanned the films. A quick examination revealed they were not Mr. Babcock's.

"I'm sorry," Claire said, "but they're not here, either. I don't remember him giving them to me to send down to records yet, but perhaps they're there. It's where they should be, of course."

Elizabeth sighed. "That's okay. I'm sure we've got the images on a CD downstairs. I'll just have to find it in the lab."

"Ah, Elizabeth, I heard you were in today."

She turned at the sound of the male voice. Dr. Noel Young stood in the doorway. Another young protégé of Dr. Benson, he was only a couple of years older than Elizabeth. If she had to use one word to describe him, it would be *suave*. He wore his dark blond hair slicked back. His face was lightly tanned, probably from his weekly tennis matches, and his lips were more often than not curved into an arrogantly charming smile. His hands rested comfortably in his pants pockets now, his arms holding back the opened front of his white physician's coat.

"Dr. Young, hello," she acknowledged. She'd never grown used to calling him Noel, especially since he tried that charm on her when she started at the center. At first she was flattered by his attention, but it soon grew annoying. She wasn't interested in a relationship with him, or anyone for that matter. Not now, not yet. Still, he kept trying, although not so often as of late.

"How are you?" he asked, with just the right touch of sincerity and understanding as he strolled farther into the room.

"Under the circumstances, I'm doing quite well, thank you," she replied. She noticed that his smile did not completely fill his light blue eyes. It didn't surprise her. She was certain he held a certain amount of animosity toward her since she refused his advances. No, his eyes were more assessing, and coldly calculating, very different from Drake's, which smoldered with emotion whenever she was with him. She quickly purged that thought form her mind, annoyed to find herself comparing Noel Young to Drake.

"That's great. And how's your little girl? It must be tough on her."

She frowned. She didn't like anyone linking Allison to what had happened. "She's well, too. She's visiting my mother until all this dies down," she said, then winced inside at her poor choice of words.

"That's probably wise."

Claire cleared her throat. Rumor had it that Dr. Noel Young was involved with Claire Daniels. He had been seen escorting the young woman out of the building on more than one occasion and once or twice returning in the morning with her in his car. It was further reason for Elizabeth to dismiss any thought of a relationship with the esteemed Dr. Young. She was pretty sure the rumors were on target as she glanced back at Claire and spotted a hot twinkle in her eye for the slickly groomed Dr. Young. Suddenly Elizabeth felt like a fifth wheel.

"Excuse me," she said quickly, "but I have to run." Far be it for her to keep the two of them from whatever lunchtime tryst they had cooked up.

In the catheterization lab Elizabeth hunted through the CDs trying to find the one that contained Mr. Babcock's images. Frustrated and clearly having no luck, she glanced at her watch. It was 1:05. Drake was probably having kittens now, looking all over the building trying to find her. They needed to stop at her apartment and pick up her gray suit before heading out to the funeral. She had forgotten to grab it last night when they picked up her car. It was further proof of how unnerved she was by the events of the last three days. Normally she planned everything out so carefully.

She gave up looking for the CD and left a note for the technician to find it for her and send it up to her office. She was just stepping toward the doorway when Dr. Young entered the room.

"So, Elizabeth, how are you *really*?" he asked, stepping up beside her and putting a hand on the wall alongside her head, virtually blocking her exit. For a brief second he seemed to scan the room, as if trying to figure out what she had been doing in there. Or did she imagine it? Were Drake's questions suddenly making her suspicious of everyone? Then he leaned in and poured on the charm, making her decidedly uncomfortable.

"You know, if you need the time off," he said, "I can cover for you. I really don't mind, and, I hate to say it, but you do look a little ragged around the edges."

"Gee, how nice of you to notice," she said sharply, giving him a cold look. "If you'll excuse me, I really do need to get going."

He blocked her way for a moment longer, then finally put up his hand, palm out, and stepped aside.

He laughed. "All right, I get it. You're not interested in me in any way, shape, or form. But I wasn't kidding. I'd be glad to help out if I can."

Elizabeth eyed him suspiciously.

"Hey, I just want you to know you've got friends here. Use them. You're not an island unto yourself, although you act like it most of the time. The only time I see you smile is when you're with your patients."

"That's not true. I—" she started to protest, but he cut her off.

"Sadly, my dear Dr. Iverson, it's true, although it pains me to say it."

"Now you're being melodramatic."

"Perhaps."

She pursed her lips, ashamed to admit, even to herself, that he was right. She lifted an eyebrow. "Actually, I could use your help."

He smiled. "Name it."

"I've scheduled a Mrs. Beal to see you this afternoon."

"There you go again, talking about work."

Elizabeth ignored his comment and continued. "She's complaining of weakness and discomfort, but she's done that in the past. All my tests indicate she should be fine. I have her on Lipitor and a low-fat diet and exercise. Still, it won't hurt to look at her. I know she suffers from anxiety. Maybe you can use some of that charm of yours to get her to relax."

His smile deepened. "I'll do my best."

And that much Elizabeth believed. Whatever his personal life was, she knew he was a good doctor. If anything were truly wrong with Mrs. Beal, he'd find it. She could feel confident leaving the woman in his hands.

"Thank you."

"Sure, now let me give you one more piece of advice before you go." A strange glint came to his eye before he added, "Watch your back."

She cocked her head sharply. She couldn't have heard him correctly. "Excuse me?"

"You heard me," he said evenly, the words bringing fresh chills to her spine, then he smiled again. "I'd hate for something to happen to our best cardiologist, after me of course."

Elizabeth tried to shake off the chill as she hurried out to her car. It was 1:15 and Drake was nowhere in sight. She decided she couldn't wait for him if she didn't want to be late for Julie's funeral. She got in her car and headed up Clark Street toward her neighborhood, then picked up her cell phone. It rang just as she was about to punch in Drake's number.

"Sorry I'm late," he said quickly. "I got caught in traffic. I'll be there in ten minutes."

"It's okay," she assured him. "I'm headed for the apartment. You can meet me there."

"Elizabeth . . ." he started, but she clicked off. She wasn't in the mood to argue. It was all very silly anyway, she thought. Even if someone was after her, they certainly wouldn't attempt anything in broad daylight—would they?

She let herself into the building, then slid under the yellow police tape and hurried up the stairs. The evidence unit had been there twice already. She reasoned that if there was anything more to find, they would have found it by now. She slowed, though, when she reached her landing. A wave of memory from the other night swept over her, and she almost backed away, wondering if maybe she had been hasty in not waiting for Drake. But this time the door was locked. She stuck her key in and slowly opened the door.

An eerie quiet greeted her as she entered. Filtered sunlight spread out across the carpet and highlighted the evidence powder, which was everywhere, coating the furniture, the doorknobs, and the windowsills. The sight of it left her feeling even more violated than before.

She crept down the hallway, telling herself to ignore the blood stains on the carpet and what she knew she would find in the bedroom. *Walk directly to the closet,* she told herself. *Get your suit, then leave quickly.* But despite her best efforts, her eyes were drawn to the tape on the carpet beside the bed, outlining Julie's body, and the dark stains that surrounded it.

She leaned against doorjamb, trying to keep her memories in check, but the horror of that night would not be stilled. It played itself out again in her mind, each moment flashing grotesquely by like scenes displayed in a quickly accelerating slide show.

A cat screamed outside her window. The crash of breaking terra-cotta sounded on the porch boards. If there really was such a thing as jumping out of your skin, she was sure she just about accomplished it. She placed a hand over her racing heart and stepped to the window, carefully walking around the tape. A quick glance told her there was no one there.

"What did you expect, you fool!" she scolded herself. Elizabeth hurried to the closet and retrieved her suit, then retraced her steps to the living room. She slipped out of her slacks, then pulled on the slim skirt and threw the jacket on over her blouse. Then she repinned her curls at the top of her head and took out her compact to attempt a quick touch up of her makeup, ignoring the ghostly look in her eyes.

Closing the door on her way out, Elizabeth made a mental note to get someone in to clean the apartment. She would talk to Andi about it. She knew there were people who did that kind of work.

Downstairs she stopped to retrieve her mail and wait for Drake. She didn't have to wait long. As she slid her mailbox shut, she spotted him bounding up the sidewalk. Clutching her mail to her chest, she opened the door to face him, ignoring the look of murder he held for her in his eyes.

"I told you to wait for me!" he shouted as he approached, rage creeping into his voice.

She shrugged and sidestepped around him to continue down the stairs. "You're overreacting," she said over her shoulder.

Drake looked at her retreating backside, at her hips neatly swaying in that suit, and he wanted to strangle her.

"Am I?" he said caustically. "You know that much about these things, do you? You've been through this before?"

Elizabeth stopped and turned back to face him. "Of course not. Now you're sounding childish. Let's go, I don't want to be late. The service starts in forty minutes." She challenged him to say more with those amber eyes of hers, but she couldn't disguise the slight trembling in her lips.

Drake realized in an instant that she wasn't nearly as cool as she sounded. He threw up his hand. "Fine, let's go, but we'll talk later."

He pulled away from the curb and headed for the expressway that would take them south toward Orland Park. His mood was so black, he couldn't even look at her. Truth was he was feeling more than a little inadequate. He hadn't turned up much of anything, and Andi and the force were drawing a blank, too. There was nothing concrete to point to either Julie or Elizabeth as the intended victim. He'd spent the last two hours tracking down and questioning Mrs. Babcock. As luck would have it, she lived relatively close by, in a stately two-story house in Evanston, the closest northern suburb to Chicago along Lake Michigan's shore. Mr. Babcock had been a trader who had made his fortune during the golden years of the 1990s and had managed to keep it during the following recession when most people lost big when the stocks tanked. Yes, the woman had money, and could hire someone to get back at Elizabeth if she wanted to, but she didn't strike him as the sort. Filled with grief, she was coping with trying to figure out her new life. Still, he told himself, it wouldn't hurt to do a little more checking in that direction.

Drake couldn't shake the feeling that the murder had something to do with Elizabeth. Hell, maybe he was overreacting. Maybe he *was* barking up the wrong tree, as she was so quick to suggest. Maybe he just wanted an excuse to stay near her. Man, that was sick!

As he turned onto the ramp to the expressway, he heard Elizabeth gasp, then sensed her go very still beside him. He glanced over at her.

"What is it?"

She was staring at the piece of paper she was holding in her hands. The shock in her features turned his blood cold.

"It seems I owe you an apology," she whispered.

twelve

You were lucky this time. I won't make the same mistake twice.

Elizabeth read the note again. The electronically printed words certainly got straight to the point. A smear of what looked to be dried blood ran across the bottom of the page.

"Give me that," Drake demanded. She held it out to him, her hand shaking. He grabbed the corner and tried to read it, keeping one eye on the traffic.

"Damn!" he swore. "I was afraid of this. I'm calling Andi. She needs to take this in for evidence. This came in your mail?"

Elizabeth nodded, unable to speak. Panic rose in her throat, threatening to squeeze off her airway. She couldn't understand why anyone would single her out for murder. Worse, if someone was after her, then Julie was an innocent bystander in this whole mess.

"That's the envelope?" Drake asked, indicating the plain white business-sized envelope that lay in her lap. "No, don't touch it. Do you have a tissue or something?"

She reached into the backseat and grabbed her shoulder bag. She rummaged through it and came up with a half-empty packet of tissues. Grabbing a corner of the envelope with one, she turned it over so the address faced up. It was printed the same as the note in what looked to be standard twelve-pitch font from an ink-jet printer. There was no return address.

"Check the postmark."

She could barely read it, but finally made out last Saturday's date and Irving Park Road.

"That's the main sorting plant for anything mailed in this area. We probably won't get anything on that. It could have been mailed from any one of a hundred drop boxes. Damn!"

Elizabeth felt numb. Drake quickly dialed Andi on his cell phone. His voice became a blur in the background as an overwhelming sense of guilt washed over her.

The feeling only grew stronger an hour later as Elizabeth sat through Julie's service and stared at the beautifully carved ivory coffin. They'd arrived late after all. Drake had pulled off the expressway onto a side street and waited for Andi to meet them to get the letter before they continued on. They made it to the funeral home mere seconds before the funeral director closed the casket to prepare it for the journey to the church. Elizabeth requested a few moments with Julie. Looking at her friend's beautiful blond hair and serene smile brought a terrible ache to the pit of her stomach. When the lid was finally closed, Elizabeth had the intense urge to run from the room. She couldn't shake the thought that it should be her lying in that locked casket, not Julie.

Elizabeth glanced briefly now at the other mourners, recognizing among them Julie's parents, her brother, his wife and children, two of Julie's ex-husbands, and her current husband, Stephan Parks. He actually looked somewhat grieved. She realized that whatever their relationship was like, Stephan must have loved Julie at some point. Maybe he still did. Julie was easy to love, even if she was a little flighty. As Elizabeth watched Stephan rub at his reddened eyes, a fresh guilt washed over her. How could they have considered him, even briefly, a possible murderer?

"I just want to tell you how sorry I am," Elizabeth said later at the luncheon, forcing her tears back. "And how terrible I feel about all this." Somehow, though, words just didn't seem enough. She had trouble meeting Julie's parents' eyes.

"It wasn't your fault, dear," Julie's mother told her, hugging her fiercely, then dabbing tears from her own eyes. "God knows why these things happen. I just hope they find the murderer and put him away so he can't do this to anyone else," she said, clinging to her husband's arm.

Julie's dad echoed his wife's sentiments. "We just thank the Lord that no one else was taken with her, and that you are safe."

Elizabeth nodded, unable to say anything more for fear that she would break down in front of them. She wanted to scream at them: *You don't understand! Julie should be here, ALIVE. I'm the one who's supposed to be dead!* But she knew that would do neither of them any good. She was humbled by their faith and wished she had as much.

Glancing around the room, Elizabeth spotted Drake talking with Stephan Parks. As she approached them, she

noticed that Julie's estranged husband seemed to have re-
covered from his grief; he didn't look all that choked up
now. She wondered why Drake was talking to him, if it had
anything to do with the investigation. Surely that angle was
a dead end now, since, like Drake had thought all along,
she was the intended victim, not Julie.

Elizabeth wanted to pull Drake away. They needed to
get back to the city. She needed to get this thing solved for
Julie. Then another sobering thought hit her. She needed to
solve it for herself—for Allison. That letter made it clear
that the murderer was still out there, waiting for his chance
to strike again.

Drake looked up at her, then nodded at Stephan. "Thank
you for your time," he said, shaking Stephan's hand.

"Anything I can do to help," Stephan replied. He turned
toward Elizabeth. "Hi, Elizabeth."

She bit her lip, reminding herself to keep her tone civil
even though Stephan Parks was not her favorite person.

"I'm sorry for your loss," she said, extending her hand.

"Thanks." He took her hand, then surprised her as he
held it for an extra moment longer than necessary. "You
know, even though Julie and I were not on the best of terms
lately, I did love her." There was a slight tremor in his
voice. Elizabeth realized his grief was still there, just below the surface. It reminded her of how desperately she,
too, missed Julie. On impulse, she reached up and hugged
him. He returned the hug, holding on while they shared
their grief for a few moments.

"Excuse me, I see some other people I need to talk to,"
he said, releasing Elizabeth and turning from them. Elizabeth could see his eyes were red again.

"You okay?" Drake asked as he touched her arm.

She nodded, despite the fresh tears that wet the corners

of her own eyes. He reached over and grabbed a clean napkin from a nearby table and handed it to her. He gave her a
few seconds to pull herself together, then said, "If you're
ready to go, I think we should get back and see if they've
found any fingerprints on that letter, although I'm guessing
not."

"I'll just get my bag," she said. She made her way to
Julie's parents to say goodbye before meeting him at the
restaurant entrance.

"You wait here, I'll bring the car around," Drake said.

Elizabeth glanced at her watch. It was five-thirty. She was
afraid it would take quite some time for them to get back
through the city to district headquarters.

When they finally approached the entrance to the
Stevenson Expressway nearly a half hour later, Elizabeth's
nerves were clearly on edge. She willed herself to calm
down as Drake headed up the ramp and onto the expressway, joining the ribbon of traffic heading into the city,
which, although still heavy, was moving at a decent speed.

"I think I'll drop you off at your car and let you drive to
the hotel, if you promise to go directly there," he said as he
sped along in the lane, a little too close to the car ahead of
them for her taste.

"Do you have to drive so fast?" she asked, making a
conscious effort to unclench her fists.

"I want to see if the crime techs have come up with anything on that letter. Make sure you lock yourself into the
suite when you get there. I'm going to have Andi send up a
cop to guard the place. There's a couple of other things I
want to check out, too."

"What things? And why were you questioning Stephan

Parks? I figured he was off the list now that it's obvious Julie wasn't the intended victim."

"Just crossing my *t*'s and dotting my *i*'s, as my old supervisor used to say. It's possible that Stephan was ticked off at you for your influence on Julie, but again, the one he sent to take care of you mistook Julie for you."

"Gee, that's a creepy thought, especially since I was just beginning to give the guy the benefit of the doubt. How do you come up with these scenarios? It must be terrible to think like that all the time, always looking for diabolical plots and hidden agendas. The scary thing is I'm afraid I'm beginning to think like that, too."

He glanced over at her. "That's not such a bad thing right now."

"Do you really think it's possible that Stephan is the murderer?"

"Right now, anything's possible. I just—"

Suddenly, an explosion rocked the car, accompanied by a chaotic release of sparks and multicolored flames that shot out in every direction from the backseat. Elizabeth's heart raced as clouds of caustic smoke billowed around them.

She couldn't breathe; she couldn't see. The smoke blocked her vision. She knew Drake couldn't see, either. She screamed, but she couldn't hear herself. Sparks landed in her hair and on her clothes. She put her arm over her face, grabbed for the dashboard, and braced for the inevitable crash. Her mind flashed to Allison. She wondered what her daughter would do without her as another wave of sparks let loose upon them.

Miraculously Drake kept the car under control. The smoke began to clear.

Elizabeth felt a rush of air *whoosh* through her window. It carried the smoke up and out the now open sunroof, even as a fresh onslaught of sparks filled the car. She gasped in the clear air and tried to look ahead. Through stinging eyes she was able to make out the car in front of them moving quickly away. More cars zoomed around them, their drivers seemingly unconcerned for a car speeding down the highway filled with smoke and flames.

Elizabeth looked at Drake. She saw his lips move, saw new alarm burn brighter in his face, but she could not make out what he was saying. Quicker than she thought possible, though, he swerved across two lanes of traffic, flew onto the shoulder, and braked the car hard. Seconds later he was yanking her from the car, smothering her with his suit coat and throwing her to the pavement.

"Hey, what the—" she started to protest when he landed on top of her and took her with him as he started to roll. Fresh panic flashed through her like lightning—*she was on fire!*

Drake finally stopped rolling. His heart hammered violently in his chest as he sat up and pulled his coat from her head. He was afraid of what he would find. Elizabeth's haunting eyes questioned him as he examined her. The ends of her auburn curls were badly charred, but there was no evidence of burns to her scalp. *Thank God!* He shook his head in answer to her unspoken question, then she collapsed against him. He held her tightly as her body began to tremble with the shock of what had just happened.

Rubbing his hand up and down her back, he tried to sooth her, tried to sooth himself, to reassure himself that she was really all right. Then she began to sob—huge wrenching sobs that tore at his heart. He whispered against her ear, but he was sure she couldn't hear him. It didn't surprise him as his own ears were ringing like a fire alarm at close range.

"Call the police!" Drake shouted at a truck driver who stopped to help them.

"Already done!" the man shouted back as he sprayed the smoldering interior of Drake's car with a fire extinguisher.

Another car stopped in front of them. A woman came over and asked them if they were all right. Other cars were finally slowing, almost coming to a dead stop as drivers realized something interesting was happening.

Where the hell did that come from? Drake wondered about the firestorm as he held Elizabeth and rocked her.

"I'm sorry," she murmured into his shirt.

Drake just shook his head and held her tighter. He didn't blame Elizabeth for being scared out of her wits. Hell, his hands were shaking. He still didn't know how he managed to slow the car without crashing. Thank God he hadn't panicked. His years in the FBI had obviously done their job.

He tipped Elizabeth's chin up with his thumb and brushed at her tears with his fingertips. Then he tugged at the hem of his shirt and gently wiped the worst of the soot from her face. She smiled meekly at him, and rubbed the back of her hand across her runny nose. Drake smiled. She was going to be all right. Elizabeth was a tough cookie, that's for sure.

"Can I use that pen for a second?" he asked the officer who stood next to him, filling out a report.

The paramedics had finally come, along with the cops and a fire engine, although by then the fire was completely out. Drake left Elizabeth briefly in the paramedics' hands while he examined the car. The backseat was burned through the leather and the whole interior of the car was pretty much blackened. Shreds of Elizabeth's shoulder bag lay strewn about the back. The initial explosion must have torn right through it.

"I don't think you should touch anything," the cop told him.

"It's okay," he said. "I'm FBI."

The cop shrugged, then gave him his pen. Drake sifted through the mess of molten metal and burnt cardboard on the seat. He lifted the charred tube with the tip of the pen. If he wasn't mistaken, it was what remained of a common Fourth of July–variety Roman candle. He realized someone must have slipped it into Elizabeth's bag during the funeral.

"Damn! How the hell did I let that one get by me?" he exclaimed.

"Excuse me?" the officer asked.

"Never mind. Do you have an evidence bag?"

While the officer went to his car to retrieve one, Drake asked his second question to himself: *How the hell did someone detonate it while we were speeding down the expressway?*

The police towed Drake's car so they could scour it for evidence. Drake wanted Elizabeth to go with the paramedics to the emergency room since her hearing still hadn't returned, but she refused. At his continued look of concern, though, she promised him that if it didn't improve during the night, she'd have one of the doctors at the clinic take a look at her in the morning. Right now, though, she felt it was more important to accompany Drake while the officer drove him to headquarters to meet Andi. She was sure her hearing loss was only temporary, brought on by the sudden percussion of the explosion in the enclosed car.

By the time they reached the station, she was pleased to notice that her hearing was, in fact, returning, although it was accompanied by a distinct ringing that made it difficult to make out what Andi was telling them.

"We've got a release going out on the nine and ten o'clock news," Andi said as they walked into a conference room. "Hopefully someone saw something. There were certainly enough vehicles on the expressway at the time. However, there might not have been anything to see. I'm afraid your hunch was right, Drake. Preliminary investigation seems to uphold your theory that the Roman candle was indeed in Elizabeth's shoulder bag. Any idea how it got there?" she directed the question toward both of them.

Elizabeth shook her head. "It wasn't there earlier, when I was at the apartment. I'm sure I would have noticed it when I took my makeup out of my bag, or a few minutes later in the car when I searched for my tissues so Drake could examine the letter we gave you earlier."

"Are you sure? You could have been distracted by finding the letter," Andi offered.

"I suppose it's possible." She realized the mention of the letter no longer sent shivers snaking up her spine, nor did the mention of the Roman candle and their miraculous escape on the expressway. She had finally gone numb.

"Do you remember at any time feeling added weight in your shoulder bag? It wouldn't be much, only a couple of pounds or so."

"No. I guess I wasn't thinking much about it at all. It often weighs more, depending on how many things I've crammed into it for the day, between Allison's things and my work files, which I occasionally carry home with me. With everything that's on my mind, it probably wouldn't have registered that it was a pound or two heavier than when I started the day with it."

Andi sighed. "I can certainly understand that." She turned toward Drake. "You didn't see anything suspicious while you were driving in?"

"No."

"Well, we've got speed cameras stationed along that stretch. Maybe one of them caught something on tape, although at this point, it's probably going to be like looking for a needle in a haystack." She took another look at her notes.

"The forensic team is trying to come up with an origin for the firework," she went on. "Looks like it was electronically detonated from what they've found so far. Could have been anyone in any of those cars who set it off, or even someone on a street below, or in a nearby building, just waiting for you to pass by. Obviously, it was someone who knew you were at Julie's funeral and that you'd be taking that route home."

Drake ran his hand through his hair. "That could have been anyone in the city. Julie's murder had plenty of news coverage, and it was no secret as to when and where the funeral was. There were even a couple of TV cameras there."

Elizabeth could tell that he was frustrated, blaming himself for the attack. She knew he was beating himself up, thinking he'd failed at protecting her.

"Maybe we can use their video," Andi said, tapping a pencil against her chin. "I'll check with the television stations and take a look at their tape. Someone might have got something on camera. Someone had to put that firework in your bag at some point, Elizabeth."

"The only time I didn't have it with me was when I came over to talk to you, Drake, when you were talking to Stephan Parks, just before we left."

His eyebrows came together as he focused on past events. She could tell he was trying to remember everything that went on in the room at the time.

"It could have been then," Andi said, "or it could have

been someone just brushing past you during the service. Did you notice anything during the service, Drake?"

"No one and nothing I could put my finger on. Believe me, I scanned the mourners." He looked toward Elizabeth and explained. "A murderer often shows up at the victim's funeral and mixes in with the crowd. It satisfies some sick need to secretly flaunt his or her deed in front of the family and the authorities."

"Yes, I've heard of that."

"But for the life of me, I didn't see anything suspicious. Damn!"

It pained Elizabeth to see him so upset about it. She reached out and touched his shoulder. "It's okay," she said. But the fire in his eyes told her it was far from okay. She felt an intense need to hold him, console him.

He cleared his throat. "Andi, I think I'd better get Elizabeth back to the hotel. We both need a shower and some clean clothes. And I think I'll make her call in a doctor, despite her protests. When you get hold of that tape, swing by and let me take a look at it. And get that cop on duty. He can keep watch outside our door. I'm not afraid to admit we could use a little more help at this point. Right now I don't think any place is safe."

Elizabeth pulled her hand back. Her control over her life ebbed more with every word he spoke. She realized that her hope for getting back to a normal existence was further away than ever.

"Sure," Andi said. "I'll have Hank drive you, and he can stick around. But before you go, I need that list of acquaintances and coworkers from you Elizabeth. It's time we started checking out every one of them."

Elizabeth felt the tremors return to her fingers. Someone was out to get her—there was no denying it now. And it was probably someone she knew. Someone she had worked with, or helped or . . .

She clasped her hands tightly in her lap, refusing to let the tremors take over. The ringing in her ears made her head pound.

thirteen

"I think you should pack up and come home right now!" Sharon Iverson insisted. "It's too dangerous to stay in the city with someone after you."

Elizabeth tried to keep the strain from the day's events out of her voice as she spoke with her mother from the hotel suite phone. But Sharon caught on right way. Elizabeth had explained what happened, trying not to make it sound as terrifying as it was.

"I can't," Elizabeth said. "I need to work. I have patients who are counting on me, and frankly, I don't want to give whoever is doing this the satisfaction of knowing he is affecting my daily routine. I also have to think of Allison. I can't bring any danger to her."

There was silence on the line as her mother digested the argument.

"Mother, trust me," Elizabeth said, trying to ease the woman's worry. "I'll be careful. Drake is with me and they've got another guard on duty outside the room. This last attack only provided the police with more evidence to help them find the person who's doing this. Please, let me talk to Allison."

Elizabeth heard a long sigh. Then her mother said, "I'll be glad when this is all over."

The understatement of the year, Elizabeth thought.

"Do you want me to wake her?" Sharon asked next. "She had a long day playing with her friend. The poor thing fell asleep on the couch watching a movie. She tried so hard to wait for your call."

Elizabeth closed her eyes. She really needed to speak to Allison, but it wouldn't be fair to wake her.

"No, it's okay. Tell her that I called, though, and that I'll call her in the morning. And that I love her, and—give her an extra kiss and a hug for me. I love you, Mom."

She heard a soft sob from her mother. "I love you, too, Elizabeth. For God's sake, be careful!"

Elizabeth hung up the phone, then sat still for a minute. A tear stung her eye, and an aching emptiness filled her. She'd give anything to hold Allison in her arms right now.

The sound of the shower streaming in the bathroom penetrated her stillness. Elizabeth set the phone down and stood, letting her feet carry her to the door. She wouldn't think about tomorrow, or the next day, or the day after that. All she knew right now was that she needed heat to burn away the ice that had settled into her bones. She needed to feel life flowing, ebbing, surging through her. She needed to block out Julie's funeral, and the awful drive back, and the vision of all her acquaintances' and colleagues' names written in her handwriting in black and white on a police pad. She needed to be wrapped in someone's arms. No, she needed Drake's arms.

Slowly she turned the door handle and entered the steamy room, then closed the door softly behind her.

Drake was aware of her the instant she stepped into the room. Hell, he'd been achingly aware of her all day. He was standing now with his hands flat against the wall tile, letting the scalding water splash down over his head and shoulders, trying to ease the tension in his body, trying to get the ache for her out of his system. He needed to drive away the memory of the way his heart had slammed against his chest when that firework had exploded in the car, when they had been a split second from disaster, and when he saw her hair in flames. Drake's heart filled again with pain as he remembered her sitting beside him, not knowing the full danger she was in, all because he missed someone slipping that firework into her bag.

He had admonished himself a hundred times already for missing that. He also vowed to never let his guard down again, not even for a second. Which is why he groaned inwardly now as he sensed her shedding her clothes. He closed his eyes, willing his body not to react to her. There were a million reasons why she shouldn't be doing this. She was vulnerable right now. Hell, he was vulnerable. They shouldn't let the terrible events of the past three days push them into this.

But his body pulsed with his need for her. Heat seared him, and it wasn't just from the scalding water. His arms ached to crush her to himself. His legs went slightly weak from the knowledge that he needed this woman against him, beneath him, inside him. His breath came hard and he thought his chest was going to explode.

Elizabeth pulled the shower curtain aside. "Drake?" she whispered.

Slowly he let his hands fall to his sides. He turned to face her. Another groan froze deep in his chest as he looked upon her. In the billowing steam from the shower, she stood like a gift out of the mist. Damn, he but she was beautiful—even with her auburn curls singed from the fire—thank God there wasn't more damage. The singed curls hung down out of the knot atop her head and lay along her throat.

This time unimpeded by the flimsy nightgown, Drake took in her perfect breasts, the nipples taut and hard, rosy dark against her fair skin. His gaze roamed down along her ribs, outlined against her smooth skin, and down to her slender waist, then on to her hips, sculptured round like one of Michelangelo's nymph's. He sucked in his breath. Slowly he let his eyes wander back up to her face. The heat spread deeper within him as he recognized his own need mirrored in her amber eyes. But there was something else there, too, a touch of fear and helplessness.

Damn him, but he felt helpless, too. Drake's gaze held hers as she stepped into the shower. He watched as she raised her hand to brush it gently against his chest where the water spilled over him. Then she twisted her hand in the coarse hairs and sent a firestorm of sparks raging through him. He grabbed her hand with the sense that he was holding on for dear life, then slowly, drew her to him. If he thought he could hold out against her, he was out of his mind.

Drake could no more deny her than he could deny his own need. He reached up and loosened the knot in her hair, letting the rest of her curls fall down around her neck. With the water splashing all around them he captured her mouth, taking in the taste of water and sweetness and hunger. The groan escaped his lips at last as he crushed her to him.

Elizabeth clung to him, need exploding within her, turning to hunger so desperate it took her breath away. Suddenly she felt as if she could never get close enough to him. She reveled in the coarse touch of his chest hairs rubbing against her breasts. She ground her waist, then her hips against his. He pulled her tighter, nestling his arousal against her belly. Liquid fire rose within her. She tore her lips from his and pressed them against his chest, licking, tasting; exploring the sensations that ripped through her at every bite. He nipped at her neck, her shoulder. Her loins filled with hot pressure. His hand traced her hip and slid between her thighs. He stroked, feeding the flames. She pressed against his hand, demanding, needing, wanting more. She moved with his stroke while the water sluiced around them, creating their own cocoon of passion.

The pressure built. She was nearing the peak and she wanted him with her. He seemed to sense this because he pressed her against the tile. Elizabeth looked up and their eyes met as he grabbed her buttocks and lifted her. She opened for him, welcoming him as he guided her over his sex. She wrapped her legs around his waist, cradling him as he slid deep within her.

"Drake . . ." she breathed as the connection rocked her, completing what she had missed for all these years. In answer, he kissed her again and she closed her eyes, taking in each liquid thrust as he began to move within her. Her need built. She clung to him fiercely, unaware of her nails digging into his back.

He groaned against her mouth. Through the pulse of the cascading water she heard her own voice whimpering, purring. The crescendo built, but she needed more, deeper, harder. He picked up the pace, and she went with it, pulling at his shoulders, demanding more. There came a moment where she thought she might die with sensation as he plunged deeper and she felt a splintering within herself. The lava burst through and she clung to him, holding on as he took her over the abyss into a netherworld where only the two of them moved in a primal release as old as time itself.

Drake held her, not knowing how he'd managed to stay on his feet. Slowly he became aware of the shower turning cooler. Her legs were still wrapped around his waist, his hands still held her buttocks, keeping her firm against him. He nestled his head in her wet curls, drinking in the odd scent of smoke mingling with her own special perfume. His breathing began to slow. He could feel her breath against his neck where her chin lay against him. He didn't want to let her go. He didn't want the moment to end. He nudged her curls aside and kissed the tip of her ear.

"Elizabeth?" he whispered.

"Hmmm . . ." she said, her voice dreamy. "Don't talk." She lifted her face, her amber eyes molten in the afterglow, and brushed her lips against his, sending another shower of sparks spiking into him. He could have sworn right now that that wouldn't be possible. He smiled and grabbed her tight with one arm then reached back with his other hand and flipped off the shower.

"Let's take this into the bedroom."

"Hmmm," she said again, and nibbled along his neck.

He was actually surprised he kept hard inside her as he stepped out of the shower and grabbed a towel, then threw open the door to the bedroom. He considered it a major feat as he walked with her, then turned and sat upon the bed with her on top of him. He swabbed at the water dripping from her shoulders, ran the towel through her curls, then took her with him as he rolled onto the bed.

"I need you again," he whispered as he began to move inside her once more.

"Hmmm . . ." she murmured. Her smile deepened the amber color in her eyes. She moved with him. This time it was slower, and smoother and softer with blankets around them and Elizabeth beneath him, and it tugged at his heart even more. Yeah, she was really getting underneath his skin now. She was sleek and tight around him, her velvet folds cushioning him. He grabbed her hands and pulled them over her head, then let his lips slide down her neck, on down to a taut nipple that beckoned him. He grasped it between his teeth and teased and suckled, then took as much of the soft mound of her breast into his mouth as he could, milking her desire. When he had his fill of one breast, he let his lips drift over to the other, not wanting to play favorites, and teased and sucked and milked again.

But as the rhythm of their joining took hold and grew stronger, he raised his lips to her face and captured her mouth once more. He drew the essence of her into himself as the storm of their passion built again toward its towering crescendo.

"Drake, are you in there?"

An annoying rapping assaulted Elizabeth's ears. She moaned, willing it away, then pulled the blanket up tighter around her shoulders. Then she started to smile. She felt delicious, languid and rich like warm maple syrup poured over pancakes. Mmmm, she was hungry. Sex, good and hard. God, she'd missed it. She snuggled her butt up against Drake and felt him curl against her, his thigh muscles tight and firm against her legs, his hips caressing hers. Elizabeth refused to think about anything else right now. Life was too short—it was the one thing that had been drilled into her over the last couple of days. Of course, in her profession, that thought was always in the back of her mind. Too many people were gone before their time.

Julie.

Damn, that's what she got for letting her mind ramble. *Go away! Leave me alone!* she wanted to scream. *At least until tomorrow. Let me have this one night.*

The rapping came harder.

"Drake, open up!"

They'd left the door to the bedroom open and Andi was now pounding on the outside door of the suite.

"Shit!" Drake swore at her side. "I can tell her to get lost."

Life drenched her, crashing in like a Mack truck against a case of marshmallows. She groaned and stuck her head under the pillow.

Drake slid his lips against her shoulder. "You okay?" he asked.

"Yeah," she grumbled beneath the pillow. "You better let her in."

"That's not necessary. She's probably got the tapes. We can look at them tomorrow."

The thought that there might be something on those tapes to help them find the killer sobered her. She shoved the pillow aside and turned to face him. "No, it's all right. The sooner we get this solved, the better." She had been a fool to think she could have this one night. Julie didn't have any more nights, and if they didn't catch the killer, she wouldn't have any more, either. Death didn't really frighten her so much as the thought of not being able to hold her daughter in her arms and watch her grow up or to lay with Drake like this again.

Drake's eyes narrowed. "Elizabeth, I . . ." he began, but Andi's persistent pounding on the door interrupted him.

"I swear I'll break this door down!" Andi called. "You're scaring me, Drake."

Elizabeth put her fingers over his lips.

"Shhh, let her in. We can talk later."

Not willing to leave her just yet, he rolled her onto her back and kissed her soundly, sending her toes curling. "This isn't over yet," he said, his voice husky with meaning. He slid out of bed, took a step, then paused and looked around as if confused. Elizabeth's heart leaped at the sight of him standing naked in the moonlight. He was the picture of masculine virility with his broad chest, trim hips, and strong, long legs. Her eyes were drawn to his sex, somewhat hard again from their kiss.

"Shit, I don't have any clothes in here!" he said.

She laughed. "She's not in the suite yet. Go grab some pants out of your suitcase and open the door before the poor woman shoots the lock off!"

But as Elizabeth watched him walk out of the bedroom, a chill slithered up her spine, a ghost of déjà vu. She was in this situation before, and he walked out. He'd almost gotten killed. And she hadn't seen him again for over six years. She shook her head, willing the thought aside as she got out of bed and grabbed her robe. She headed back to the shower, deciding she needed the warm water to help wake her.

fourteen

Elizabeth glanced at her reflection in the bathroom mirror. She was horrified, realizing once more how close she had come to disaster. She rummaged through Drake's shaving kit and found a small pair of scissors. Snipping at her curls, she diligently cut out the burnt tendrils. With most of the burnt curls in the sink, she pulled what was left of her hair into a barrette at the nape of her neck.

Andi and Drake were huddled in front of the TV in the living room. As Elizabeth entered the room, Drake reached for the remote to turn off the VCR, but she waved her hand to tell him to forget that idea.

"It's okay," she assured him. "I'm not that fragile." She came to sit beside him on the sofa.

The picture showed the steps of the funeral where people were entering before Julie's service. A female news correspondent stood in the foreground explaining the situation. The sound was turned down, enabling Andi and Drake to concentrate on the images.

Drake gave her a slow smile, his deep blue eyes filled with a mixture of admiration and intimacy that sent her heart astir again. Grabbing her hand, he rubbed his fingers caressingly over hers then turned his attention back to the screen.

Across from them Andi cleared her throat. "Well, then . . ." she started to say. Elizabeth caught her knowing look as Andi glanced from Drake to her. A slight blush warmed her cheeks, making her feel down right ridiculous. She and Drake were consenting adults—there was nothing to be embarrassed about. Still, it was clear that Andi was aware that their relationship had moved up a notch—or rather, had taken a major leap. Were they really that transparent? Thinking that it wasn't such a good idea at this point for everyone to know she and Drake had slept together, Elizabeth slowly drew her hand from his while Andi continued to talk.

"As I told Drake," Andi explained, "I managed to convince the local networks to give me copies of their footage. Three networks thought it newsworthy enough for video. This is Channel Five's. They took the most tape, but I'm afraid that it isn't much. This is the unedited version. If you could just look closely, Elizabeth, and see if there's anyone you recognize that shouldn't be there—or anyone who seems even just a bit suspicious."

Elizabeth studied the screen. She recognized some of Julie's relatives and a couple of their friends from school, but other than that, no one. Then she watched herself hurry up the steps with Drake at her side. The camera zoomed in on her. She didn't think the picture especially flattering. Her face was pinched, and pale. She remembered they had just finished talking with Andi and handing over the threatening letter for evidence. Another video frame popped up in the corner of the screen, overlaid over the first. It showed the scene outside her apartment the night of the murder.

The tape went blank for a second. Then a talking head came on with a video frame over his shoulder that showed the view from a helicopter looking down on the expressway. "In another bizarre twist to this story," the newscaster said, "an incident on the Stevenson Expressway this evening appears to be another attack on Dr. Iverson's life. A bomb exploded in the car she and FBI agent Drake McGuire were driving home from the funeral. . . ."

"This hit the six and ten o'clock news," Andi explained. "It was taken a few minutes after the incident. We don't need to watch this."

"No, leave it." Elizabeth leaned forward as the picture zoomed in. Traffic had slowed drastically around them as two cop cars and a fire engine blocked one of the lanes beside them. She watched as a tow truck arrived and she and Drake got into a police car. The camera again moved in close on her.

"Our sources tell us that the FBI have been called into the case to help solve the attempted murder of Dr. Iverson. Police are asking anyone who was in the area and saw anything suspicious to call the eyewitness hotline." The screen went blank.

"I'm afraid this coverage isn't going to help us much," Andi said, reaching for another tape. "Whoever did this wanted you dead, and he's not going to be happy to see that he failed to get his mark again."

"If he wanted me dead, why didn't he use a bomb that would blow up the whole car? Why did he choose that crazy firework?"

Drake took the new tape from Andi, flipped out the old one, and slid the new one into the VCR. "This person is not happy just to kill you, Elizabeth," he explained hotly. "He wants you well aware of the fact that you are dying. He wants blood and gore and fear. He's really sick."

"That's right," Andi agreed. "And he doesn't seem to care now if he takes out others along with you. You're both going to have to be on your toes from now on."

Elizabeth shuddered. She glanced at Drake, not happy with the thought that having him around her put him in just as much danger as she was.

"This one pans the parking lot of the funeral home for a couple of seconds before settling on the front steps," Andi continued. "Drake and I thought we could check out the cars there, maybe match them to ones going back on the expressway. I have IDOT developing the film from some of the surveillance cameras along the route. If we can match it up with someone going through around the same time as you did we might have a lead we can work on."

"I'd like to run these by the FBI," Drake offered. "Check their databases. I can get computer wizards to blow up the license plates."

Andi shrugged. "It's fine by me. But first, we need to know if you see anything out of place, Elizabeth. Again, is there anyone here who strikes you as odd, someone that perhaps shouldn't be there?"

She studied the screen again. After a few minutes she shook her head. Nothing looked odd to her, except of course if you considered the whole macabre notion of watching these tapes at all. Once more, the camera zoomed in on her. It seemed she'd become a celebrity overnight. The thought made her queasy.

"I'm sorry," Elizabeth said, "but this just doesn't seem

to be helping." After forty-five minutes of viewing the tapes, all she got for it was a raging headache. She rubbed at her temples.

Andi sighed. She gathered up her coat and notepad. "That's okay; it was a long shot anyway. I'll leave the tapes with you, Drake. I think we should all get some rest. It's been a long day—Joe will think I fell off the face of the earth."

"Thanks for everything, Andi." Drake stood and hugged her.

She shrugged. "It's my job. Just be careful. Mama DeLuca would have a fit if anything happened to you."

Elizabeth frowned. The only reason Drake was in danger was because he was helping her. But Drake didn't seem a bit upset by it. He winked at Andi. "You tell Aunt Jennie I can take care of myself."

"That's what we all try to tell her, but she still worries, you know," Andi said with a laugh. "She wouldn't be a good Italian mama if she didn't. Oh, and I'm sure I'll talk to you again before then, but I'm supposed to remind you not to forget dinner Wednesday night." She glanced at her watch. "I guess that would actually be tomorrow night now, wouldn't it?"

Elizabeth stood and walked Andi to the door. "Thanks, Andi."

"Like I said, it's my job. And don't be too disheartened. Sometimes memory can trigger later. You might wake up in the morning and realize something struck you in those tapes, after all."

"One can hope."

Once Andi left, Elizabeth turned back to Drake. He came toward her and drew her into his arms. "Let's get some rest," he whispered into her ear.

In the bedroom she stepped out of her sweatsuit and into a nightgown. He slipped off his pants, and once more naked, pulled her down onto the bed. She lay cuddled against him, her head resting on his chest while he pulled the blankets up around them. She kissed his skin where his ribs poked out along his side, then ran her hand slowly down over his belly, enjoying the feel of him.

He let out a deep, tight breath. "As much as I'd like nothing better to make love to you again," he said, his voice husky, "I suggest you still your hand so we can both can get some sleep. Morning is just a few hours away."

Her lips curled slowly with the knowledge that holding her was enough for him for now. Then another thought struck her. He'd said "making love." Well, he hadn't exactly said he loved her, but it was close, and it opened up a whole new realm of possibilities for her to consider. What future did they have once they caught the killer?

It felt odd to watch herself on TV. The last time they were together, it had been Drake on the TV screen. It was his body being wheeled into an ambulance—and she had run from that, not wanting to deal with the potential violence and danger that would be a part of a life with him. Now they had come full circle. Violence and danger had sought her out despite the fact that she had tried so hard to run from it.

Elizabeth's hand traveled to the spot just below the joining of his hip and thigh where she had discovered his new scar earlier. An inch or so higher and it could have done severe damage. She lightly traced the scar with her fingertip, realizing wryly that fate seemed to have its own designs for them.

As if aware of her thoughts, he grabbed her hand, brought it to his lips, and kissed it, then pulled her tighter.

Her heart thudded with a fear deeper and stronger than she had ever felt before. She could feel his matching beat against her ear. She raised her head and slowly rolled above him. Bending, she kissed his lips, then his eyes, his cheeks, his chin. Slowly she worked down along his neck to his chest, laying tender kisses along the old scar just below his shoulder, feeling the need to connect with him there, then slowly she worked her kisses down along his belly, to the new scar. She lingered there briefly, then grazed over to the tip of his arousal. He buried his hands in her hair and groaned deeply. She responded by teasing him with her tongue. Holding her might be enough for him, but it wasn't nearly enough for her. She needed as much of this man as she could get—for now.

While Drake headed downtown to the FBI field office, another officer drove Elizabeth to work. Drake didn't want to lose any time getting the videotapes to his agent friends, who would analyze them and glean from them what they could. Before he let them loose on the tapes, though, he planned to make copies. He also wanted to question Julie's parents again.

That morning Drake had been full of energy. He had already talked to Andi by the time Elizabeth managed to pull herself out of bed after calling Allison. He was obviously one of those men that sex fortified, making them feel like they could tackle anything. She looked him over, envious of his energy, as she padded into the room. He smiled at her while she brushed her tousled curls aside and handed her a cup of coffee. His stamina could be a good thing for their future, if they had a future, Elizabeth thought with a smile.

Drake kissed her before explaining that the police hadn't obtained much helpful information from the threatening letter she received. It was printed on standard, twenty-pound paper with an ink-jet printer that was compatible with any number of business systems or home PCs. If they found the particular printer they might be able to match it up, but again, like Andi had said last night about finding something on the expressway cameras, that would be like looking for a needle in a haystack. There were no fingerprints or other identifying marks on the letter, either. The blood, however, did appear to be Julie's—probably wiped from the murder weapon. As for the Roman candle that had gone off in the car, it was one of a variety that could be picked up at any of the roadside fireworks stands that popped up in the summer just on the other side of Illinois' borders with Indiana and Wisconsin where it was legal to sell them. Illinois didn't keep records of people who bought pyrotechnics in neighboring states, unless, of course, they got caught. As for the detonator, it was a common hobby shop variety. It wouldn't take a genius to figure out how to hook one up and detonate it. They were, in a word, nowhere.

Still, as Elizabeth did her rounds that morning, she was thankful that Drake wasn't with her. At least when he wasn't near her he wasn't in danger.

"Mrs. Beal is in surgery?" Elizabeth asked pointedly as she glanced at the room assignment chart, shocked to discover the woman's name there. The nurse turned from putting fresh sheets on the bed.

"Oh, Dr. Iverson. Yes, Dr. Benson's performing a double bypass on her this morning."

"A double bypass?"

"Ah, yes," the nurse returned.

Elizabeth shook her head. It didn't make sense. Mrs. Beal was the patient she had sent to Dr. Young yesterday afternoon. There was nothing in the woman's tests that indicated surgery was necessary at this point, as far as Elizabeth was concerned. Furthermore, Mrs. Beal was a severe diabetic—surgery could be more complicated and recovery more difficult for her than for most patients. That was the main reason Elizabeth had opted for treating her moderate arterial blockage with drugs and diet.

"When did she go down?" she asked.

"Over two hours ago."

They were well into the surgery by now. Elizabeth frowned and left the room, heading for the stairs. She wanted to know what had changed so drastically that Dr. Young had decided to consult Dr. Benson and make the two of them decide a bypass was necessary.

Her shoes clicked rapidly on the tile floor as she headed down the second-floor hallway toward the surgery department. She scrubbed, then slipped on a gown and gloves.

"Dr. Iverson?" the scrub nurse asked as she turned toward the operating room. Elizabeth ignored her as she pushed into the room. Mrs. Beal was her patient and she felt she had an obligation to her.

Elizabeth walked around to the head of the table. "How's she doing?" she asked the anesthesiologist.

The hiss of the respirator and click and beeps of the monitors filled the room. Glancing at the team of surgeons and nurses surrounding the operating table, she immediately recognized Dr. Benson by the glasses which peeked out from beneath his green surgical cap. A quick glance at the heart pump told her they were sending Mrs. Beal's blood around her heart now, which meant they were well into the work on her arteries.

"So far, so good," the anesthesiologist told her.

"Elizabeth," Dr. Benson said, without looking up from his work. "Nice to see you here. Looks like you missed this diagnosis, heh?"

There was a slight cough from one of the other doctors. The surgical nurses avoided looking at her while the team continued to work on Mrs. Beal.

Elizabeth's irritation rose as she stepped to the other side of the table to observe the procedure. She watched as Dr. Benson sutured the end of a small segment of vein he had taken from Mrs. Beal's leg to her aorta. She could see the graft of the other artery already in place. "With all due respect, Carl," she said, "I didn't think surgery was indicated just yet. I would have consulted with you had I thought she'd reached that point."

"And your patient might have been dead by then. More suction, please."

Elizabeth winced at his words. Dr. Benson had never been quite so curt with her before. A nurse reached over his hands to suction blood from Mrs. Beal's open chest cavity.

"You did an angiogram?" Elizabeth asked, still trying to figure out how her patient's disease had progressed so rapidly.

"Yes, something you should have done months ago, the first time she came in complaining of chest pains. It's a good thing she came in when she did yesterday."

Elizabeth's gaze focused on Mrs. Beal's heart where Dr. Benson's fingers were expertly maneuvering his instruments to tie off the delicate suture. "But all my tests indicated no heart attack, and the stress tests and scans indicated no major blockage. Mrs. Beal is prone to nervousness. Dr. Young was going to look at her and assure her she was okay."

"Dr. Young was busy. Okay, that's the last one. Let's take her off the machine and see what we've got here."

Dr. Benson carefully removed the aortic clamp to allow blood to flow once more through Mrs. Beal's heart into her main arteries. Elizabeth held her breath, as did the rest of the surgical team, waiting for the heart to begin beating again. She knew this was a crucial time. They would know within seconds whether or not the sutures would hold.

A red squirt pulsed across Dr. Benson's blue scrub front and against his glasses.

"Damn!" he shouted. "We've got a leak here!"

Elizabeth clenched her fists in frustration. This was what she'd been afraid of. Mrs. Beal's arterial walls were weakened by the diabetes. Wisely though, she realized it was not the time to bring this to Dr. Benson's attention.

"More suction!" Dr. Benson screamed. She watched as his fingers flew, attempting to stop the flow of blood and repair the leak. If anyone could save Mrs. Beal at this point, it was he. The man was a master at his craft.

"Pressure's dropping," the anesthesiologist warned. The pulse monitor beeped faster as Mrs. Beal's heart tried to compensate for the lower pressure.

"Son of a bitch! Hold this!" Dr. Benson ordered the doctor across from him.

It had been a tough day. Elizabeth sat at her desk, rubbing her hand across the back of her neck, trying to ease the tension. She stayed with the surgical team until Dr. Benson stopped the leak and Mrs. Beal had stabilized. Then she was called to the catheterization lab, as her patient was ready for angioplasty. She performed two angioplasties that morning and then grabbed a quick bite to eat in the cafeteria before checking on Mrs. Beal in recovery.

Elizabeth glanced at her watch. It was after five, and she still had unfinished business to attend to. She did not appreciate the dressing-down Dr. Benson had given her in surgery in front of the other doctors and nurses. She wanted to see that angiogram he had performed.

Her cell phone rang, a new cell phone, which was delivered that afternoon, since her old one was toast. It had melted in her shoulder bag during the firework episode. She lifted the phone out of the pocket of her physician's coat. The caller ID told her it was Drake.

"Hello."

"Tough day?" he asked. He must have heard it in her voice.

"Yes, and you?"

There was a brief silence, then, "Tough day here, too." Elizabeth sensed that he meant they hadn't gotten any further in the investigation. She sighed. Amazingly, she'd been able to push Julie's murder and the fact that someone was after her out of her mind for most of the day. Now it all washed over her again, making her feel oddly depleted.

"How about I pick you up in a half hour and we grab some dinner," Drake offered.

"That would be great, but what I really need is a nap."

"I'll see what I can do," he said, his low voice filled with sexual promise. "Make it twenty minutes," he added before hanging up. She smiled, despite her fatigue, realizing with a slight twinge of guilt that she was looking forward to the evening. She tapped her fingers on the desk, allowing her mind to wander briefly back to the euphoria of the night before, then she reached for her desk phone and dialed Dr. Benson's office number.

"Is he in?" she asked when Claire answered the phone.

"I expect him in about five minutes. He's just finishing up with a patient."

"Tell him I'm coming to see him."

Dr. Benson was seated in the chair behind his desk when Elizabeth walked into his office. She had taken a few minutes to go down to radiology and take another look at the films of Mrs. Beal's heart scans, which she had taken two months ago. She'd brought them with her.

"Ah, Elizabeth, I understand you had quite a scare yesterday," Dr. Benson said, looking up as she walked into the room. "Please, sit down."

"Thanks, and yes, it was, but I'd like to discuss something with you if I may?" she said, ignoring his invitation to sit.

He eyed her over the rim of his black Armani glasses. "Difficult case this morning. That's what you want to discuss, isn't it. Yes, I wanted to discuss that with you, also." He stood and came around the desk. "Are those Mrs. Beal's?" He nodded toward the large envelope she had in her hand.

Elizabeth hesitated. Her hands felt a bit clammy. Dr. Carl Benson was the picture of the distinguished surgeon, dressed in crisp black slacks, blue shirt and tie, and suitcoat. His eyes were a deep brown beneath bushy salt and pepper eyebrows and graying hair that was receding at the temples. In his late forties, he was at the zenith of his career. Although of medium height, he had a commanding yet knowing demeanor, which put patients at their ease.

And he'd been very good to Elizabeth. She felt a bit guilty questioning him, as she owed her current position to him. He had taken her under his wing these past few months, showing great faith in her skills by hiring her when he could have hired any number of competent cardiologists in the Chicago area, then guiding her further to improve her skills. Still, having faith in her meant he should also have faith in her judgment.

She took a deep breath and plunged forward. "Yes," she said, slipping her hand into the envelope and walking toward the viewing screen above the credenza. "May I?"

"By all means." He smiled and flipped on the backlight while she took out a series of six films and slipped them up onto the screen. "You can clearly see by the scans that Mrs. Beal's arteries, both the right main artery and left anterior artery, do show some signs of mild stenosis, judging by the slight calcification in them." She pointed to various points on the screen. "Further thallium scans during her stress test indicated that there was indeed, some stenosis, but at most, thirty to forty percent." She indicated points on another film of a scan. "As you can see, there is nothing so severe as to indicate surgery, or even an angiogram for that matter."

"Ah, yes," Dr. Benson said, rubbing his chin. "I concur with your diagnosis. Her condition would not appear to be life-threatening at that time."

"Exactly," Elizabeth agreed. "Based on this, and her severe diabetes, I decided it would be wise to try and control her atherosclerosis with medication and diet."

Dr. Benson nodded. "A very conservative approach, and perhaps appropriate in most cases. But as I told you this morning, your patient came in complaining of severe chest pain. Sometimes, it is necessary to go further in order to ease the patient. And the diabetes might only damage her arterial walls further with time, making surgery virtually impossible. Therefore, I felt it necessary to conduct an angiogram to be sure there were no severe blockages. As you know, stenosis can progress rapidly in certain patients and the only way to be one-hundred percent sure of the condition is with angiography. I did the procedure, and judging by the significant amount of occlusion I found, decided that bypass was clearly indicated. It was best to do it now to give her a better opportunity for a successful outcome."

"I'd like to see that angiogram. Mrs. Beal—"

Dr. Benson raised his hand. "No, Elizabeth, enough," he said softly, but firmly. "You are, in essence, questioning my judgment. In fact, this is the second time in as many weeks that you have done so. You are very young and very bright, or I would not have hired you, but you have a lot to learn. Consider this a learning experience. And next time I think you should think twice before questioning the call of those who have so much more experience than you." He smiled sweetly, but for the first time since she'd started at the center, Elizabeth felt uncomfortable with that smile. It was as if he was trying to placate her, basically patting her on the head like he would a recalcitrant child.

"With all due respect, I think a good physician should question all those involved with her patient's case," she said, her cheeks flushed with frustration.

Dr. Benson smiled, flipped off the viewing screen, and started taking down the films. "You're right, in most cases. But next time, don't do it while the patient is on the operating table."

Elizabeth grew incensed at his stark dismissal of her

concerns. "Unfortunately, I didn't have a chance to confer with you before the surgery. Frankly, I don't understand why bypass had to be performed so swiftly."

His smile faded. "Yes, you were unable to perform your duties here as required and someone else had to step up to the plate."

She opened her mouth to protest, but he waved it aside.

"No, it's okay, I understand. You are under extreme pressure right now, anyone would be. May I?" He held out his hand for the envelope. She stared at it for a moment before handing it over to him. "I'll see that these get back into her records. And in the future, if you'd like the records to a case, come to me first. Don't go through Claire. That way we can have this conversation ahead of time and not take up the precious time of my secretary." He slipped the films into the envelope and set them on his desk.

Elizabeth knew he was speaking of Mr. Babcock's records. It had taken Claire over a week to get the file to her, and she still didn't have the films yet.

"Now, let's talk about you," Dr. Benson continued. "I think it would be a good idea if you took a couple of days off, until this thing settles down."

"My work is not being affected."

"Perhaps you don't see it, but I still think it would be wise to take some time off. Which reminds me, there were two detectives in here questioning me earlier today, a woman and some gruff chubby guy. I can't say as I appreciated his attitude."

"I'm sorry about that." Elizabeth swallowed hard, trying to adjust to the change of subject. "It must have been detectives DeLuca and O'Reilly." She'd been so busy she hadn't realized they were in the building. "O'Reilly is a bit of a boar. I'm afraid I had to give them the names of my coworkers. They have to check everyone out."

"You can't think someone here has it in for you?" Dr. Benson raised an eyebrow.

"No, I . . ." she began, but realized she truly didn't know what to say. "Listen, I'm sorry, but they insisted. They're just being thorough."

"Well, under the circumstances, I suppose I can understand that. But please, Elizabeth, think about that time off. Perhaps you should go spend it with your daughter. But first, you will be at the cocktail party tonight, won't you?"

"Cocktail party?"

"Don't tell me you've forgotten. Well, I suppose that's understandable, too, under the circumstances. We're celebrating the center's third anniversary. The board of directors and many of the investors will be there. I expect all of my staff physicians to attend."

"Oh, yes, of course."

"Great. Now if you'll excuse me, I have a report to dictate before I leave, and my wife won't like it if I'm late to our own party." He smiled at her as he sat down at his desk and picked up a patient file.

Elizabeth wanted to say more, but realized he had already closed the subject on Mrs. Beal. Still frustrated, she turned on her heel and walked out, nodding to Claire who sat at her desk smiling sweetly as she stepped past her and out into the hallway. She wondered just how much of their conversation Claire had heard. Probably all of it, she reasoned, and it just served to irritate her more.

What the hell just happened in there? she wondered as she leaned against a wall in the hallway. Dr. Benson completely dismissed her concerns about Mrs. Beal, and then he turned the conversation around to put her on the defensive regarding the investigation. The encounter didn't sit well with her, although she knew she had to consider the possibility that she might have been wrong about Mrs. Beal's diagnosis and care. That possibility made her feel even worse. Lowering her head, she rubbed at her temples. The headache from last night had returned with a vengeance. Footsteps approached, causing her to look up. Drake was walking toward her. He paused to exchange a few words with the policeman standing just ten feet from her, whom she had managed to ignore for most of the day.

"It's a good thing you have this guy watching out for you," Drake said, a welcoming light in his eye as he came up to her, "or I'd never be able to track you down." She smiled weakly, realizing she was going to have to disappoint him as their plans for the evening had now changed.

fifteen

Drake's hand rested protectively against Elizabeth's back as he rapped his knuckles against Bensons' door. A doorman hired for the occasion swiftly answered.

"Nice digs," Drake said under his breath.

Dr. Carl Benson and his wife, Eve, lived in a luxury condo on the forty-first floor of a high-rise building along Chicago's Gold Coast, only a mile south of the Heartland Cardiac Center. Judging by the sound of laughter and clinking glasses that mingled with the dulcet tones of a string quartet, the party was already in full swing. Within seconds, Elizabeth and Drake were whisked down the hallway into a brightly lit, spacious living room. Two walls of floor-to-ceiling windows dominated the high-ceilinged room. A third wall held a modern white-tile fireplace topped with a black granite mantel. Above it, a vivid oil painting of large lilies done in tones of whites and grays against a deep green and red background graced the wall. Elizabeth recognized the painting as the work of an up-and-coming Chicago artist whose original work now came at a hefty price. A series of gray and red sofas and chairs were artfully arranged around the room, along with a few glass-topped tables. The back wall sported a sleek granite bar to match the mantel and glass shelves where Eve's crystal collection was displayed.

"Dr. Benson knows how to live," she replied.

Elizabeth walked farther into the room and was awed again by the panoramic view the full-length windows offered of the city. Lake Michigan stretched out before them, its waters glimmering now in the light beams from the rising moon. To the right, Chicago's famous skyline twinkled back at them in breathtaking splendor.

Elizabeth had been to Dr. Benson's condo only a couple of times before, for staff parties thrown by his wife. She spotted Eve now, offering a tray of hors d'oeuvres to two men she recognized as members of the board of directors. Elizabeth liked Eve, for no matter how glamorous the "digs," she still made the place feel warm and inviting by taking an active role in serving her guests, even as a butler, also hired for the evening, approached Elizabeth and Drake with a tray filled with glasses of champagne. Drake waved him off, but Elizabeth grabbed for one.

"Thank you," she told the butler, then lifted her chin to Drake when he raised an eyebrow at her. "For medicinal purposes," she explained.

He nodded. "Just stay close."

Elizabeth polished off half of her champagne, then put on her best face and made the rounds. She greeted colleagues and directors alike, sharing snippets of conversation with each one before moving on. Drake followed at her side. She introduced him merely as Drake McGuire—a friend. Although most there must have known the circumstances of the previous few days and some surely knew Drake was a special agent for the FBI, they were kind enough not to mention any of it. As she and Drake neared the far side of the room where Dr. Benson was holding court with some investors, one of the directors on the Heartland Center's board clinked his glass, commanding attention.

"Ladies and gentlemen, if you please . . ." he said, his voice raised. The room gradually quieted and the music stopped. "I just want to say how proud we are of Dr. Benson and the Heartland Cardiac Center," the director declared. "On this, our third anniversary, I am happy to report, the venture has been a great success; both in the number of people we've managed to save and return to normal lives, and in the financial growth of the center. I don't think I'm overstating it when I say we owe the bulk of our success to Dr. Benson—for the great surgeon that he is and for his forsight in convincing us that this is the way to go for cardiac care of the future. So please, all of you, lift your glasses in a toast. To Dr. Carl Benson, may we all continue to reap the benefits of his expertise and wisdom."

"Hear! Hear!" A general cheer went up from the party-goers.

Elizabeth raised her glass along with the rest. As she took a sip, she studied Dr. Benson. He was clearly enjoying the praises of his guests; he virtually beamed with pride beneath those Armani glasses. His next words, though, held just the right touch of humility as he turned the accolades from himself to those in the room.

"Thank you, all of you, but I could not do it without my

excellent staff, or the faith that you all have in me. Now, please—eat, drink, and be merry. This is a celebration for all of us. Here's to our continued success!" He raised his glass to salute his guests and the music started up again.

As the guests began milling about again, Dr. Benson spotted Elizabeth and Drake.

"Ah, Elizabeth," he said, motioning them over. "I'm so glad you could make it."

She slid away from Drake as Dr. Benson grabbed her hand and pulled her forward, then placed an arm around her back, welcoming her into the fold.

"Gentleman, let me introduce you to our latest acquisition," he said proudly. "This is the brilliant and oh-so-talented Dr. Elizabeth Iverson, come to us fresh from a fellowship at the University of Illinois Hospital. I can tell you, gentlemen, that watching her perform a procedure is like watching an artist at work. Oh, and she's also great with the patients."

He winked and a small chorus of laughter echoed around the group. It was well rumored that surgeons and cardiologists didn't always have the best bedside manners.

"Thank you, Carl," she said, appreciating his praise but feeling a bit surprised by it considering the conversation they had only a little over an hour ago in his office. She tried to put it out of her mind as she shook hands with each investor.

"Yes, if I had a daughter," Dr. Benson said after he made all the introductions, "I couldn't ask for a better one than Elizabeth. She's a tribute—to the medical field." She glanced at him. By the warmth in his eyes it was obvious that he meant what he said. It would seem that their disagreement had not damaged their relationship. She supposed that was a good thing, although she couldn't help but feel a bit uncomfortable by his remarks. She caught Drake's eye. He'd been observing the encounter and gave her a proud wink now. Crazily, that made her feel better.

"That's not to say we always agree," Dr. Benson went on.

Uh-oh, Elizabeth thought, *here it comes*. But Dr. Benson's smile only widened. "But that's to be expected. I wouldn't want anything less. The young doctors keep us on our toes, agreed?" He looked up at the small group that had now grown, a few of her colleagues walking over to witness the accolades Dr. Benson was bestowing on her. She spotted Dr. Young among them. Claire, not surprisingly, was at his side. A couple of the physicians laughed their agreement to Dr. Benson's remark, but Noel Young did not laugh with them. Instead, he lifted his glass to her. Beside him, Claire's smile looked brittle, or did she imagine it?

"Carl, that's enough." Eve Benson stepped through the throng and grabbed Elizabeth's hand. "You can't monopolize your protégée all evening; I need her for some girl talk!"

"Thanks," Elizabeth whispered as Eve pulled her toward the other side of the room.

"No problem. I could tell Carl was making you squeamish, although I don't know why. You do deserve all the praise, from what he's told me, but enough shop talk. Tell me how that little girl of yours is doing."

With that, Elizabeth launched into her favorite subject, bringing Eve up to speed on Allison's latest antics, and thankfully, for a few minutes, letting go of all the turmoil in her life.

Later in the evening Elizabeth stood at the windows gazing out at the brightly lit city when Dr. Young cornered her.

"You look like you're holding up well. Another glass of champagne?" he asked as the butler approached them.

"I think I've had enough, thank you," she said shaking her head. The one she drank earlier had definitely gone to her head, its effect no doubt intensified by her state of fatigue. She glanced around, looking for Drake, wondering where he'd gone. She was surprised he was no longer glued to her side.

"That was quite a speech Benson gave on your behalf, given the dressing down he gave you in surgery this morning," Dr. Young said.

"Yes, nice of him, wasn't it." She wasn't surprised that Dr. Young had heard about the incident—nothing stayed quiet within the walls of the center. "He wants me to take a few days off, although you'd never know it by what he said tonight."

"Not a bad idea, under the circumstances."

She slanted her eyes at him. Was it her imagination, or was everyone suddenly trying to get rid of her? "Yes, well, maybe I'll consider it. So, where's your girlfriend?"

"Claire?"

"The one and only."

"Trust me, she's not my girlfriend, although she doesn't always choose to believe that. She's gone to powder her nose. I see your boyfriend's deserted you, too."

"He's not my boyfriend."

"Right," he said, but it was clear by his tone he didn't believe her.

"Carl said you didn't get a chance to see Mrs. Beal yesterday—that he stepped in for you."

"That's right. I was called in on another emergency."

"Do me a favor, take a look at her cardiac scans if you get a chance. I left the films in his office, but he said he would get them back down to records. I'd like your opinion on them. Maybe I did miss something."

Suddenly he looked uncomfortable. This time she knew she didn't imagine it as his gaze shifted to glance out across the skyline. Well, she wasn't completely surprised. Dr. Benson was his bread and butter, too, and doctors didn't like to second-guess their colleagues, at least not on record. "I suppose I could have a look at them," he said, finally, "but surgery is always a tough call in these kinds of cases."

Her gaze narrowed. "Not always."

"Right, well . . ."

Drake appeared beside her again. "Ready to leave?" he asked. It seemed he was reading her thoughts again.

"Yes, but first I'd like to introduce you to Dr. Noel Young. I don't believe you two have met yet."

"Yes, we've met," Drake said. His eyes turned a bit steely. "We had a nice chat the other day."

Dr. Young nodded, a smile touching his smooth lips. "Agent McGuire questioned me regarding my alibi for Friday night. I assume it checked out, since he hasn't bothered me since."

"The fact that you were on call checks out," Drake said. "Although there is the matter of your claim that you were in your office going over paperwork for over an hour. No one seems to have seen you there."

Dr. Young's smile grew cockier. "Ah, that's a tough one, isn't it? Sorry, I can't help you there, but I'm sure Elizabeth will vouch for the fact that we're always up to our ears in paperwork. Tell you what, Agent McGuire, why don't you let me know when you have some real evidence against me."

"You can count on it," Drake said, his voice dead level, full of threatening promise. "Now if you'll excuse us, it's been a long day."

"Of course," Dr. Young replied, then as they turned to leave, added, "Have a good night."

Elizabeth could swear she heard a smirk in his voice, but she was unable to turn around as Drake had taken her arm and was already leading her toward the door.

"Let's get out of here before anyone else commandeers you," Drake said under his breath.

"You've been awfully quiet," Elizabeth said back in their hotel suite, a police guard standing vigil outside the door. "Where did you disappear to? You were gone a good ten minutes."

"I was having a look around the place," he said as he made a quick search of the suite, making sure no one was there and no surprise packages were lying about. "Dr. Benson lives rather high on the hog, wouldn't you say? He must command one hell of a salary—Eve Benson has a rather nice assortment of fine jewelry. And I had a hard time keeping count of their original oil paintings and crystal."

"You spied on them?" She followed him into the bedroom while he searched it.

"I can't help myself, it's my job. Looks like we're all clear here."

She turned to the bureau and began slipping pins out of her hair. "I think maybe you've been at your job too long," she said. "You're starting to see villains everywhere you turn. Of course Dr. Benson commands a high salary. He's head of the cardiac center. He put the whole operation together. It's his baby. He works hard, so why shouldn't he live well?"

"Hey, don't bite my head off, I was just making an observation." Drake stood still, staring at her as she removed the last few pins from her hair, then shook her head to let her curls lay across her shoulders.

"And Noel Young?" she continued grilling him. "I know he's a bit glib at times, but you're suspicious of him, also?" she asked, although, to be fair, she had her own doubts about Dr. Young. That creeped her out even more. Perhaps she should tell him about her encounter with Dr. Young in the lab yesterday.

"Until we find the murderer, everyone's under suspicion."

"I'm beginning to think you have a problem with doctors, Agent McGuire."

His eyes darkened. "No, not *all* doctors. Just the ones who can't keep their eyes off my woman."

She moved her hands through her hair and shook her head again, loosening the curls even more, not completely oblivious to the effect it was having on him. "I'm not your woman," she stated matter-of-factly.

He ignored that, adding, "And he has the hots for you. You must know that—his girlfriend certainly does."

She glanced sideways at him, her gaze turning mischievous. "Why, Agent McGuire, you're jealous."

Her pulse picked up a beat as he came toward her and brushed a curl off her forehead, then trailed a hand down her neck. She decided she'd tell him about Dr. Young later.

"Damn straight," he said. He reached behind her and pulled her up against himself, causing her breath to catch in her throat. "Now, how about that nap?"

She tilted her head and eyed him knowingly. "Nap, huh?"

His smile deepened. "Yep."

But as he lowered his lips to capture hers, it was obvious that sleep was the farthest thing from his mind. Her insides curled with hot anticipation as she slid her fingers around the nape of his neck. She was thankful she had the foresight to make her nightly call to Allison on their way back from the party.

"Allison!"

Elizabeth bolted upright in the bed, clutching the sheet and trying to blink back the darkness of the room. Gasping for air, she tried to catch her breath. She had awakend in a pool of sweat. Her curls lay damp against her neck. She realized she must have been dreaming for quite some time. *She couldn't find Allison. Someone had taken her.* Her heart still raced with the terror.

"What is it?" Drake asked, sitting up beside her.

She swallowed hard.

"Nothing," she managed to croak. "A nightmare, that's all."

He reached for her, trying to comfort her. The guilt she'd managed to push aside earlier washed over her with the force of a tidal wave. She knew she had to tell him the truth about Allison. But the dream left an icy dread within her. She never liked to analyze her dreams, but this one seemed obvious. She was sure the nightmare was the direct result of her fear that when she told Drake about Allison, he would be so angry with her that he would try and take Allison away from her. But he couldn't be that cold or unfeeling, could he?

"Just hold me," she whispered.

He drew her into his embrace, and like a coward, she let him. He gentled them down between the sheets and rubbed his hand across her arm, trying to soothe her. He nestled his chin against her hair.

"It's okay now," he murmured. "Get some sleep."

But sleep was a long time coming. She vowed to herself that before night fell again, Drake would know the truth, no matter what the consequences. She had to steel herself for the repercussions first. Yes, she chided herself, she was a coward, and selfish, too—but only for a few more hours.

Work was hectic the next day. So much so that by mid-afternoon, Elizabeth was beginning to consider taking Dr. Benson up on his offer for that time off. The cumulative effect of the events of the last few days, her worry over Allison and Drake, and her extracurricular activities at night were taking their toll on her. And now she had a new worry. In the light of day another thought occurred to her. What if the nightmare hadn't been about her and Drake at all, but a premonition? What if it was really about Allison's safety, or lack thereof, given recent events?

Elizabeth stood at the nurse's station staring at a lab report that she must have read at least three times already without comprehending it. The stress was clearly starting to have an adverse effect on her work, too, something she definitely could not allow.

She read the report one more time, forcing herself to concentrate, then handed it back to the nurse, made some notes on a patient's chart, and headed for the stairs to go back down to the clinic. She had more patients to see. Sliding her hand into her pocket, she reached for her cell phone, then stopped herself. She couldn't call Allison again, she'd already phoned her twice today—once, first thing in the morning, then again just before noon. Allison would become alarmed if she called her too often. Sighing, Elizabeth flung the door open and headed down the stairs, patently aware of the police bodyguard who followed her.

No more attempts had been made on her life, yet that unnerved her, too. She was sure the killer was just waiting for an opportunity to make another move. Drake had called her a few minutes earlier, sounding tense and frustrated. He told her they had no new leads and the ones they did have were going nowhere. Nothing from the expressway tapes matched the funeral tapes, but then the funeral tapes had limited views. Still, they were running every license plate they could get a read on from the expressway cameras around the time they would have been passing them. So far, though, nothing looked promising.

"I went out and interviewed Donny again," he added.

"Drake, no."

"I didn't get anywhere, he's still not talking."

"Maybe that's because he doesn't know anything. He's probably just upset about the murder and all the activity at the apartment. He doesn't like anything messing up his daily routine."

"Yes, I suppose that's possible."

She decided to approach him with what had been bothering her since the morning. She took a deep breath, almost afraid to put her fears to voice.

"Drake . . . I'm worried about Allison. The killer's been quiet since the attack Monday night and that worries me. I can't believe he's given up—that letter sounded so vindictive. What if he decides to go after Allison as a way to get to me?"

There was a pause, then, "I was wondering when you'd figure that one out. It's already taken care of, I just didn't want to worry you."

"What's taken care of?"

"I put a man on it yesterday. He's watching over your mother's place."

For a moment she couldn't speak. Emotion welled in her throat, and a tear formed in her eye. In that moment she knew she loved him.

"My mother didn't mention it," she whispered.

"He's trained to be inconspicuous, but it's difficult in the middle of farm country, so I called her and told her. I didn't want her to be alarmed by a strange man lurking about," he explained. "So I'll pick you up at six? Mama DeLuca's Italian feast is definitely the prescription for tonight. Our family gathering should be fairly entertaining. It might take your mind off all this for a while," he went on, quickly changing the subject.

Elizabeth smiled weakly. "Six sounds fine."

Now as she trod down the stairs, she felt emboldened by her decision to come clean with him after the dinner tonight. No matter how he felt about her, she was sure he would not abandon them until the investigation was over.

Before heading out to the parking lot to meet Drake, Elizabeth looked in on Mrs. Beal. Just one day out of surgery and the woman was propped up in bed, smiling weakly, when Elizabeth entered the room. By all accounts, she was doing fabulously. A glance at her chart told Elizabeth that all her vitals were stable.

"You're looking well, Mrs. Beal," Elizabeth said. "How are you feeling?"

"A little sore," Mrs. Beal said hoarsely. "My throat, too. Would you be a dear and give me a few ice chips? I can't quite handle it."

"Sure." Elizabeth picked up the cup and spooned some chips between the woman's parched lips. When Mrs. Beal indicated she had enough, she set the cup back on the side table. "Now, let me take a quick peek at your staples," she said, then began a quick examination.

She noted that the incision looked okay. There was some oozing, but that was to be expected. She listened to Mrs. Beal's heart, then, satisfied that all was going well, said, "You're doing just great."

Mrs. Beal nodded. "You doctors are all so wonderful here. You saved my life, especially Dr. Benson. He is just the greatest, isn't he? I'm so lucky to be here."

Elizabeth's smile twisted slightly. She still wasn't entirely sure that Mrs. Beal's surgery had been necessary, but she couldn't deny that her patient seemed to think so.

"I may have to give a huge donation to this hospital," Mrs. Beal went on. "You are all treating me so well." As if to emphasize the point, a nurse came in and offered her a rubdown. "That would be wonderful," Mrs. Beal murmured. "And then you can give me some of that wonderful pain medication again and I'll take a nice nap." She smiled contentedly, despite the pain she must be in, obviously very happy to have all the attention. Elizabeth shook her head as she left the room. She had a feeling they might have a hard time getting Mrs. Beal to leave the hospital when the time came. She knew the woman was a widow and lived alone in a big house in Evanston with a maid who came every other day to take care of the household duties. She had two sons who had moved away and only visited a couple of times a year. Elizabeth was surprised that they weren't here now, but she heard one was flying in tonight, the other tomorrow. "They're very busy professionals, you know," Mrs. Beal told her once, pride shining in her eyes. Well, if Mrs. Beal wanted a little TLC, Elizabeth couldn't begrudge her that, as long as she didn't act too helpless and hinder her recovery.

sixteen

Drake steered the black LeSabre Joey had lent him into the parking lot just as Elizabeth exited the center, the cop/bodyguard beside her. He could have used Elizabeth's car while his was in the impound lot for testing, but he figured the black LeSabre was more low profile than her red Grand Am and he'd just as soon draw as little attention to himself as possible right now. Drake parked the car at the sidewalk, then ran up to her and grabbed her briefcase, placing a hand on her arm.

"You searched this?" he asked the officer.

"Yep, it's clean."

"Good. Tell you what, why don't you follow us. You can stake out the DeLucas' and maybe get a meal out of it if you're lucky."

"Sounds good."

The officer headed for his cruiser while Drake guided

Elizabeth toward the LeSabre. A quick survey of her features revealed her fatigue. Dark circles shadowed her eyes and small lines he hadn't seen there before etched the corners of her mouth.

"Something on your mind?" he asked a few moments later as he pulled out of the parking lot.

"You're kidding, right?"

"Yeah, I guess that was pretty lame—of course you've got a lot on your mind, but you seem more preoccupied than usual. Something going on at the center? Something I should know about?"

She shook her head. "No, it's just one of my patients. Well, *was* one of my patients, I'm not so sure, now. I just checked on her. I think she's actually pleased to have had open-heart surgery just to get the attention."

"That sounds a bit extreme."

"Yes, it does, but mostly, it's sad." She leaned back against the headrest and sighed. "Do you ever wonder if everything you've learned, every assumption you've based your life on, was false, making your whole life just one big false statement?"

"Wow. Where did that come from? You really did have a rough day, didn't you?"

She didn't respond, which alarmed him even more. He'd never seen this side of her before.

"Are you sure nothing else happened? If it has anything to do with the investigation, you'd better spill it. You didn't get another threatening letter did you?"

"No, it's nothing like that."

"Then what's this all about? Where are these negative vibes coming from?"

"Dr. Benson and I disagreed on the treatment for this patient."

"Oh, I see," he said, relieved that the killer hadn't approached her again. "And now he's making you doubt your skills?"

"Something like that. Unfortunately, I'm afraid he might be right, this time."

"And that makes you wrong? What, you've never missed a diagnosis before?"

"Well, no. I mean, yes, of course I have, but . . ."

"Gee, you're not perfect. Welcome to the real world, Doc. Although from where I sit, you look pretty damned perfect to me." He grasped her hand, raised it to his lips, then turned it over and kissed her open palm.

He had meant it to soothe her, but it only seemed to make her more upset. Her smile turned shaky. "No, you were right the first time, I'm far from perfect." She turned her head away, but not before he caught the shimmer of tears in her eyes. It puzzled him—there was something else here she wasn't telling him. He didn't let go of her hand.

"I hope you brought your appetite tonight," he said a short time later as he turned onto Diversey, heading west to Milwaukee Avenue. "Mama DeLuca always prepares a feast for these Wednesday night get-togethers."

"I'll try to eat enough to be respectable. Why Wednesdays?"

"You mean as opposed to Saturdays or Sundays or some other day?"

"Yes."

"According to Mama DeLuca, Sunday is her day off. She cooks every other day of the week, but she refuses to cook on Sundays. Since cops are usually busy on Friday and Saturday nights, she picked Wednesdays. Whoever can make it, comes. It's nice, because as the family has grown, it's given my cousins the weekends to spend with their own

growing families. Did you know Andi and Joey have a toddler of their own?"

"Really? I can't believe I didn't realize Andi has a child.
Moms usually have a certain connection, you know. I wonder how they manage with their busy schedules."

"They hired a nanny."

"Mmmm. That sounds like heaven to me."

He glanced at her again. "It must have been difficult
with Allison, these past few years." He could imagine how
impossible it must have been raising her daughter while
putting in grueling hours as a resident with multiple nights
on call.

She smiled wistfully. "You don't know the half of it, but
I'd give anything to have her with me right now."

His jaw tensed. He was reminded, once more, that they
were virtually nowhere in the investigation. He could see
that mother and daughter needed to be reunited, and soon.
He changed the subject.

"My aunt and uncle own a brownstone near the Six Corners area. They moved out there around the same time I
came to live with them. It's bigger than the apartment they
lived in before, but it still seemed crowded with the seven
of us kids running through it every day. I often think my
aunt and uncle are saints! We weren't an easy bunch. I
shared a room with Joey and Tony."

"How many of your cousins do you expect tonight?"

"Let's see, Joey and Andi; Tony and his wife Debbie
and their three kids; Frank, if he's not on duty; Kate and
her husband and their two kids; and maybe Louis if he's in
town. He travels a lot. He's an engineer."

"Oh, I see, the black sheep of the family," Elizabeth
teased.

He smiled. "Something like that. And my cousin An-
gela. She's not a cop, either, she's a paramedic."

"That must have been rather daunting, coming to live
with them when you were so young. You were an only
child, weren't you?"

"Yes. It was hard to get used to, but my aunt and Uncle
Joseph—Joey Senior—were very welcoming. They treated
me like one of their own from the start. "When it got nuts,
I would hide out in the attic. Although my cousins liked to
play cops and robbers, I played my own little games of investigation, interrogating the bad guys and coming up with
the missing clue. I had my own chalkboard and maps and
even a fake lie detector test."

"You were an odd kid, Drake McGuire."

He laughed, glad that he'd finally gotten her mind off
her troubles for a while. "I guess I was. Even then I wanted
to get the thugs that caused my parents' deaths, and I don't
mean the ones that drove the car that smashed into them—
I mean the big guys. Drugs were rampant back then, as
now, and even at that age I knew we weren't going to stop
it by cracking down on the users and small-fry dealers. I
wanted to go after the heads of the drug cartels and the
money-launderers, although at the time, I didn't know
that's what they were called."

"So you set your sights on the FBI?"

"Weird, huh?" They reached the intersection with Milwaukee Avenue and he turned right.

"Not really," Elizabeth said. "It makes sense, I guess.
Was your dad a cop?"

He shook his head. "No, Dad was an elevator mechanic.
He met my mom at the Drake Hotel, where she was a waitress. He hadn't been in the country long. He got the job

through a distant cousin. The rest of his family was still in Ireland—*is* still in Ireland," he emphasized. "I've never been back there, although I think I'd like to go someday. Anyway, Dad used to stop in and have lunch at the restaurant, and you might say he courted her. They spent their honeymoon at the Drake—thus my name."

"How romantic."

Drake glanced over to see if she was kidding, but there was a tender light in her eyes. It brought a catch to his throat. He grimaced slightly, knowing that the thought of his parents could still affect him like this. He wondered, briefly, but not for the first time, what his life might have been like if his parents had lived. Perhaps he would have ended up as an elevator mechanic instead of an FBI agent. Now, that was a switch for you.

He signaled and turned into the parking lot of a deli. "Rule is everybody brings something," he explained. "I'm dessert tonight." He looked in the rearview mirror to make sure the police car pulled in behind them. "I'll just be a minute. Sit tight," he said, stepping out of the car.

The thought of meeting all of the DeLucas at once sent Elizabeth's nerves even more on edge. She couldn't imagine what it must have been like growing up with so many children in one household. She only had her sister when she was growing up in their large farmhouse. As Drake pulled up in front of the comparatively small, two-story brick home, its windows filled with light now in the gathering dusk, she wondered how the DeLucas had survived it. And how they'd been able to afford raising so many children on a policeman's salary.

"Ready to face the inquisition?" Drake asked.

"Give me a minute." She pulled down the visor and studied her reflection in the mirror. She smoothed her errant curls back up into their barrette, then slicked on some lipstick. "As ready as I'll ever be," she said, and stuffed the lipstick back into the side compartment of her briefcase.

Drake leaned across, took her chin in his hand, and turned her head until their eyes met. She swallowed deeply, a keen awareness rushing through her. "You look beautiful, as always, Dr. Iverson," he said, then he leaned in and kissed her. The kiss lingered, turned more heated, until he finally pulled away. "I guess we better get in there before I change my mind."

But she didn't want to let him go just yet. She touched his face, leaned forward, and kissed him back. "Before we both change our minds," she said against his lips.

"Hey, Irish! Glad you could make it!" A man Elizabeth guessed was Drake's Uncle Joey shouted at them from the opposite side of the room as they entered the living room of the DeLuca household. He had a fairly full head of dark hair, just beginning to gray at the temples, and dark, deep-set eyes. As he came forward to greet them, Elizabeth could see that he was only a few inches taller than her own five-feet-five, and he sported a well-fed pouch that protruded somewhat over his buckled waistband—most likely due to his wife's excellent cooking, Elizabeth mused. The tantalizing aroma of simmering red sauce and warm garlic bread filled the room, sending Elizabeth's mouth watering.

The man came forward and grabbed Drake in a bear hug, not an easy task given Drake's height and the man's pouch.

"Hey, Uncle Joey," Drake said, hugging him back while

juggling the box of cannolis he'd picked up at the deli. "How's retirement treating you? I can see you've been eating well. Time to buy that treadmill, hey?"

Uncle Joey laughed. "Don't get smart with me, boy, I'll box your ears back!" He looked toward Elizabeth. "Who's the pretty lady here?"

Andi came forward, carrying her two-year-old in her arms. "Now, Papa Joey," she said, "you know this is Elizabeth, Dr. Iverson. Remember? Joey and I told you about her."

"Yes, yes, I remember, but you didn't tell me how beautiful she was. Hey, good for you, Irish, I didn't think you had it in you!"

Elizabeth held out her hand. "It's nice to meet you, Mr. DeLuca," she said. He smiled, took her hand, then before she knew it, he wrapped his arms around her and engulfed her in a bear hug, too.

"I'm just helping her out until we catch the person who murdered her friend," Drake said at her side.

Uncle Joey took a step back, still holding her shoulders in his hands, and raised an eyebrow at Drake. "Yeah, and that must be beet relish you've got on your lips. How many times have I told you, 'Don't kid a kidder!' "

He winked at Elizabeth. Drake smiled ruefully and rubbed at his mouth with the back of his hand.

"So, Dr. Iverson, what do you think of my youngest grandson?" Uncle Joey said, releasing her to pluck Andi's child out of her arms and bounce him on his shoulder. The boy laughed and grabbed his grandfather's cheeks.

"A handsome boy, I think," Elizabeth said. "Is this one going to carry on the DeLuca tradition and be a police officer, also?" She laughed as the toddler let lose of one of Uncle Joey's cheeks and held his hand out to her.

"Nope. We've got enough of those for now. I think this one's going to be an astronaut."

"An astronaut. Wow!" She grasped the child's tiny hand between her thumb and forefinger and shook it. "How do you do . . ." She looked to Drake for help.

"Michael," he provided.

"Michael?" she finished. The little boy simply laughed in reply. She reached up and ruffled his dark curls, remembering Allison at this age.

"So, you're a doctor," Uncle Joey went on, studying her again, this time with a much steadier gaze. Elizabeth could feel him sizing her up, the cop's instinct obviously still strong in him. She forced herself not to squirm under those keen eyes. "We could use a doctor in this family," he said, "considering how it's been growing by leaps and bounds."

As if on cue, four kids of various ages came tearing down the stairs and into the living room.

"Uncle Drake, Uncle Drake!" they screamed in unison as they ran for him. Drake laughed, shoved the cannoli box into Elizabeth's hands, then knelt, bracing himself as all four children plowed into him at the same time. A ritual of giggling and tickling and kisses ensued. A smaller child, a girl who was around three, Elizabeth guessed, walked slowly into the room, then stopped. She waited for the ruckus to subside, then took a step closer.

"And how are you, Miss Margaret?" Drake asked, holding the other kids at his sides. Freeing a hand, he tapped his cheek. "How about a kiss right here for your uncle Drake." The girl smiled shyly, then laughed and ran into his arms. He swooped her up and gave her a big hug.

Elizabeth's heart did a thousand flip-flops. Drake was so good with these kids. It was obvious how much he loved his cousins' children. Her traitorous mind imagined Allison running into his arms, calling him Daddy, him catching her up like this, showering her pretty face with kisses. She imagined the light of love in his eyes and Allison's pretty blue eyes reflecting it right back. Guilt shot through her again, this time like a sharpshooter's bullet, almost felling her. She knew how desperately wrong she'd been to keep Drake's daughter a secret from him.

The guilt weighed on her as Andi shooed the kids away and Drake led her into the kitchen where the real party was taking place. She pasted a smile on her face as he introduced her to his cousins and his aunt Jennie, Mama DeLuca as he called her. But Elizabeth found it difficult to concentrate amid all the familial ribbing and laughter. She felt as though she couldn't breathe, as if she were drowning in the icy, lonely, dark depths of Lake Michigan.

They all sat down to dinner at the huge dining room table. The conversation never ceased as homemade ravioli, meatballs, and red sauce were passed around. Elizabeth watched, dazed, while the family chatted on. Her ears buzzed and although she took a sizable helping of food, she knew she wouldn't be able to eat the respectable amount she'd promised Drake. Then another thought knifed through her, bringing a new ache to her chest. What if something did happen to her? What if the murderer was successful in his goal of killing her? The only one who knew Drake was Allison's father was Julie, and Julie was gone. What if Drake *never* knew the truth?

She couldn't let that happen. Drake would know tonight—she'd already decided that. Sipping her wine, Elizabeth felt fortified with new determination. He might hate her for it. He might even threaten to sue for custody, and she couldn't blame him if he did, but he'd finally know the truth. Buoyed by that thought, she tried to relax and enjoy the rest of the evening.

Drake kept an eye on Elizabeth throughout dinner. He'd been afraid she would be overwhelmed by the DeLucas. In fact, at first she did seem a bit overcome, but then she managed to somehow take his boisterous family in stride. She had an easy, natural way with her, and he liked that. But he could tell she was preoccupied. He caught her looking at him with sadness in her eyes, more than a few times— missing her daughter, no doubt. He felt like a jerk, bringing her here. Of course she was missing Allison with all these kids running around. Louis was out of town, but the rest of his cousins were here; it was a kind of homecoming party for him. His eyes narrowed as he watched Elizabeth help gather the dessert dishes and carry them into the kitchen. He wished the circumstances weren't so pressing.

He was half listening to Joey and Joey Senior discuss the problems in the hierarchy of the Chicago Police Department when Andi touched his arm.

"Drake, can I talk to you outside?" The look in her eye did not bode well.

"Sure," he said, setting down his coffee cup.

They walked out onto the porch. Once more the night was warm, but the humidity had moved in, making the air sticky and uncomfortable. A cold front was promised for the end of the week, reminding him of just how fickle Mother Nature could be in the Windy City.

"What's up?" he asked, loosening his tie. Andi shifted away, as if reluctant to talk now that they were alone. In the few years he'd known her, he never knew her to be particu larly reticent. It brought an odd chill of foreboding to his heart.

"Nice night, huh?" she asked, looking out toward the street where the trees waved in the warm breeze.

"Yeah, great, now cut the crap. You didn't ask me out here to talk about the weather."

She turned and cocked her head at him. "Just how well do you know Elizabeth?"

He folded his arms across his chest and leaned against the cement railing, trying to ignore the alarm bells that went off in his head. "What does that mean? Well enough, I guess."

"You're lovers," she said matter-of-factly.

"A recent development."

"How recent?"

His eyes zeroed in on her. "I'm not sure that's any of your business."

"Were you lovers six years ago?" she went on relentlessly. "Actually, a little more than six years ago I would guess. Joey said something went on between the two of you back then, when you were assigned to the Atlanta field office."

"Joey should keep his damn mouth shut." He had confided in his cousin one night on a trip home not long after the raid in Atlanta. The two of them had tried to see how many bars they could hit along Rush Street before they couldn't walk. "What does that have to do with anything?"

"Nothing, maybe everything." She shook her head and leaned back against the rail to study him. "It never ceases to amaze me how the smartest men can be so blind."

"What the hell's that supposed to mean?" He didn't like the cat-and-mouse game she was playing with him. "Come on, DeLuca, if you know something I don't, spit it out."

"Fine. Here it is. When we asked Elizabeth for that list of her friends and acquaintances, she left off Allison's father."

"Man, that's what you're worried about?" He let his shoulders relax a little. "Jeez, Andi, she explained that to me. She said the father's been out of her life since before Allison was born. She said he didn't want anything to do with the baby. It didn't fit into his lifestyle. He was going to be some hotshot lawyer or something."

"And you believed her?"

"Why wouldn't I?" he asked, but a knot began to form in his gut. He remembered how neatly Elizabeth had answered his questions. He unfolded his arms, turned and grasped the railing.

Andi stepped over and placed a hand on his shoulder. When she spoke again, her voice was softer, sympathetic. It didn't make him feel any better. "Listen, I didn't want to bring this up," she said, "but O'Reilly insisted we discuss it with you, and I have to say he's right on this one. We have to consider all angles. We were looking into the possibility of the killer being an ex-boyfriend, or a pissed-off father. You can't say you didn't think about that, too?"

"I did, but I took her word for it."

"And you didn't follow up? Bad form, Irish."

"Hey, only Uncle Joey can call me that," he protested, but he was beginning to fear that his closeness to Elizabeth had clouded his judgment. That thought made his gut coil tighter.

"We talked to Mary Parisi," Andi went on. "She told us Elizabeth hasn't had more than two dates that she knew of the whole time she's lived there. That's over a period of four years. It doesn't sound like Elizabeth is a woman who sleeps around. A call to her mother, along with interviews with a couple of her medical school classmates, seemed to confirm it. Elizabeth had a fiancé in med school. They broke up shortly before the end of her fourth year. It seems he wasn't replaced. We decided to go through some of her records at the apartment."

"Andi . . ." He slid her a look of disdain, but realized it was something he would have, *should* have done, even if it was unethical.

"Anyway, we came up with Allison's date-of-birth— January, a little over five-and-a half years ago. The date struck a chord with me, given what Joey told me about your relationship with Elizabeth. That was in April, wasn't it? The spring of the previous year? When you were shot? It doesn't take a rocket scientist to do the math."

Drake grabbed the rail tighter, this time for support. When he'd first seen Allison, he guessed her to be much younger than that. She was definitely small for her age, although still quite precocious. A cold sweat worked its way up between his shoulder blades. He never thought to ask Elizabeth how old she was, and Elizabeth hadn't offered the information. Damn! Why the hell would Elizabeth lie about something like this?

"Well, O'Reilly wouldn't leave it at that," Andi continued. "He found a copy of the kid's birth certificate."

"And?" he asked between clenched teeth.

"The father is listed as 'unknown.' "

He turned and let out a deep breath. "See, there you have it. She didn't know who the father was."

"Or she didn't want to list it. If it was the fiancé, why wouldn't she? She'd have nothing to lose and everything to gain. I would think she would have at least tried to sue for child support. My guess is, she knows exactly who the father is, but doesn't want anyone else to know—especially the father."

"And why would that be?" he asked, playing devil's advocate. "What would she gain by that?"

"A child, with no claims on her from anyone. Elizabeth is noted for being a control freak. She likes things ordered. I don't think I need to spell it out any further for you."

Drake's pulse buzzed in his ears. He remembered how Allison had tugged at his heart, her big blue eyes connecting with something deep inside him . . . and how Elizabeth had watched. Damn her! Fury boiled up within him. Why was she doing this?

"Like I said, I didn't want to be the one to tell you this, but if I didn't, I'm afraid O'Reilly would have. He doesn't know as much as I do, but he's pushing. To him, this would be just one more reason to suspect you in Julie's murder. *Enraged father returns home to discover child he never knew he had. Botches attempt to murder mother, kills mom's college roommate instead.* The news agencies would have a field day with that one."

"Shit!" he swore. "O'Reilly's such an ass."

"True, but that's not the point right now. I suppose I could have talked to Elizabeth about this first, but my loyalty is to you."

He blew out a breath, trying to rein in his emotions. "Thanks Andi," he said, but right now it was more than he could deal with. He knew he couldn't go back into that house and face Elizabeth. The fury that was building within him threatened to explode into a raging storm. "Make sure she gets back safely to the hotel," he said. Then he stalked off the porch.

"Where are you going?" she shouted after him.

"Not now!"

He escaped into his car and slammed the door. Scrubbing his hands across his face, he tried to absorb all Andi had told him. It was just supposition, he told himself. It didn't *prove* Allison was his. *Yeah, but where there's a smoking gun . . .*

"Damn!" he swore again, then smashed the heel of his hands against the steering wheel. He started the engine and peeled out into the street.

seventeen

Elizabeth glanced at her watch while she rocked little Michael in her arms. The evening was growing late and she still needed to call Allison. She was torn between the idea of finding a quiet corner in order to call Allison, or hanging around to find out just what Andi and Drake were discussing out on the front porch. When they had stepped out earlier, Elizabeth started to follow, but Joey ran a blocking pattern, thrusting Michael into her hands. It didn't take a brain surgeon to realize Joey didn't want her in on the conversation. But Elizabeth was anxious to know if there was some new development in the investigation.

"I think you're little one is ready for bed," Elizabeth said to Andi when she finally came through the front door. Still cuddling Michael in her arms, Elizabeth had rocked and cooed him to the point where his eyes were now closed. She noted that Drake wasn't with her, and an alarm bell went off in her head.

"Yes, I see that," Andi said. Her eyes lit with motherly love as she gazed upon her child. She took Michael in her arms and gave him a kiss on the forehead. "Thanks, Elizabeth."

"No problem." She'd found it comforting having a little one in her arms again, to the point that she felt a little sad giving him up. There was something soothing about holding a baby in your arms. She was fully aware, though, that Andi was avoiding her eyes, and her unasked question of where Drake was.

"Where's Joey?" Andi asked, glancing around the room.

"Upstairs, with the kids."

"Then I guess I'd better corral him so we can head on home." She started to walk toward the staircase.

"Andi," Elizabeth said, her eyes narrowing. "Where's Drake?"

Andi paused in mid-step, then turned slightly. "He had something he needed to take care of. He asked me to make sure you got safely back to the hotel. I'll grab Joey, and then we'll walk you out to the squad car after we say our goodbyes. The officer can drive you back, if that's all right?"

Elizabeth tensed. Something definitely didn't feel right. She sensed an odd coldness in Andi's demeanor. In fact, now that she thought about it, Andi had been somewhat distant to her all evening. But she had just been too preoccupied with her own thoughts to give it much notice. The alarm bell pealed louder.

She didn't understand why Drake would leave her here

with his family. It seemed uncharacteristically rude of him. Maybe she was just being paranoid, she chided herself. Andi and Drake could have discussed any number of things related to the investigation that they didn't want her to know about.

But her woman's instincts told her it was more than that—much more. Elizabeth stepped forward and placed a hand on Andi's arm, forcing her to meet her gaze.

"What did you tell him?" she asked. "I need to know." She held her voice low, even, despite the panic that was building inside her.

Andi's features twisted as she studied Elizabeth, as if she was trying to make up her mind about something, then suddenly they softened and she sighed. "Later," she said. "After we've said our goodbyes."

It was fifteen minutes before they were able to leave the house. Elizabeth expressed her thanks to the DeLucas for dinner and their hospitality and accepted their hugs along with a plate of leftovers. "You can't possibly be eating anything worthwhile staying in a hotel like that," Mrs. DeLuca insisted. After what seemed like eons, they finally walked to the curb. Andi handed Michael to Joey and continued on with Elizabeth toward the squad car.

Halfway there she stopped. Elizabeth turned to face her. Under the dim light of the streetlamp, she tried to read the other woman's guarded eyes.

"Man, I wish I hadn't given up cigarettes," Andi said as she shoved her hands into the pockets of the short, stylish jacket she wore. "I sure could use one now."

"It's a good thing you did," Elizabeth said, trying to be patient as she realized Andi was just stalling for time. "I could show you some disgusting pictures of diseased lungs and a few clogged arteries and dead heart muscle if you need further encouragement."

Andi smiled at that. "Thanks, but I don't think that's necessary. It's just that after these big dinners all I want is to kick back, put my feet up, and have a good smoke. Anyway, It's probably best if I just come right out and say this. Elizabeth, my instincts are pretty good, and right now, those instincts are telling me to like you. They're telling me that deep down you're genuinely a good person. God knows it's not up to me to judge why people do what they do. But I have to say, I also feel like you're playing some kind of game with Drake. I don't know why, but I'm definitely sure I don't like it."

"Hey, Andi, I . . ." she started to say, but Andi waved aside her protest.

"No, give me a minute. I'm speaking to you now woman to woman, one mother to another. You probably know by now that Drake doesn't forgive easily. None of the DeLucas do, and they'd hate it if they found out one of their own was duped. Believe me, I know from experience. But for Drake it's even worse, judging by what Joey's told me about him—it's that Italian and Irish all wrapped up in one. Elizabeth, if you truly love him, which I think you just might, you have to come clean with him. And the sooner the better."

Elizabeth's gaze leveled on Andi. "I'm not sure I know what you're talking about," she said, nor was she sure any of this was Andi's business.

"Oh, I think you do," Andi said, meeting her gaze now with steely conviction.

Elizabeth clenched her fists at her sides. Her heart beat faster as the panic she felt earlier threatened to take hold of her again. Andi's look told her much more than she wanted to know. And, woman to woman, Andi was warning her to be careful. She was also warning her not to hurt Drake any more than he already would be when he heard the news that Allison was his daughter.

"How did you find out?" Elizabeth asked tightly.

A slight twist of Andi's features told her that Andi hadn't really known for sure, until now. A sick feeling dropped like lead into the pit of her stomach. She looked away. "I had planned to tell him tonight," she said, "when we got back to the hotel."

Andi nodded.

Elizabeth bit her lip, trying to block the pain. She was fully aware of how angry Drake would be with her. "Where did he go?"

Andi shook her head. "I have no idea."

Elizabeth convinced the officer to drive her to her apartment. Although he clearly wasn't happy about it, she insisted she needed to pick up some more clothes, which was true, but not her most pressing need. On the way she phoned Allison. Her daughter was all excited about her visit to the mall and the Rain Forest Café with her grandmother.

"There were parrots in there, Mom. For real! Cool ones, with orange and yellow feathers. And fish. Can we get some fish? Then we went across the mall and saw snakes." Her words reminded Elizabeth of how thrilled Allison had been the few times she'd taken her to the zoo, and how long it had been since their last trip. She'd have to schedule another visit again soon.

She smiled while Allison rattled on, knowing just how

her daughter's eyes would be shining with her excitement and the wonders of the world. She closed her own eyes, wishing Allison could stay that way forever.

When she hung up, she was more determined than ever that Drake should know his daughter. He deserved to witness her exuberance and innocence while it lasted. She wondered briefly how Allison would take the news that Drake was her daddy. Then Elizabeth smiled. Her daughter would take it in stride, just as she did everything else. There seemed to be a bond between the two already. Allison would be thrilled to have a daddy—*for real!*

Elizabeth stepped out of the car and was halfway up the outside steps before she realized she didn't have her keys. They were in her shoulder bag, along with her wallet when the Roman candle went off in Drake's car. Everything was kept for evidence testing, although Andi said there wasn't much left anyway, except for some charred pieces of credit cards.

The officer was at her heels as she buzzed Mary Parisi's apartment. There was no answer. She pushed the button again. She knew Mary was home because Donny's form was silhouetted against the shade that was drawn at his window. Elizabeth frowned, wondering if the precaution of pulling the shade down was enough to protect him from whoever was out there.

"Yes?" Finally, Mrs. Parisi's voice sounded over the intercom.

"Mary, it's Elizabeth. Can you let me in?"

"Elizabeth? Oh, yes, of course!"

Moments later Mrs. Parisi approached the door, dishtowel in hand. "Hello, dear," she said somewhat breathless as she opened the door wide to let them into the foyer. "I was in the kitchen, finishing up some baking. I didn't hear you at first. How are you, dear?"

"Fine, thank you, but I need to get into the apartment."

"You don't have your key?"

"No, I'm afraid not. It was in my shoulder bag Monday when—"

"Oh—yes, of course it was. You don't have to explain further. How stupid of me to ask." She reached into her pocket and pulled out a full set of keys, then took one off and handed it to Elizabeth. "Here, take this one. I'd go with you, but my cake is almost done. Chocolate—Donny's favorite, you know. Allison's, too, for that matter. You know, I was thinking of changing the locks anyway, now that that nice police lady was here and said it was okay to get into the apartment. I thought I would have the carpet in the bedroom changed, too, so that you won't have to look at those nasty stains. And maybe have the walls painted. Are you sure you want to go up on your own? If you give me a few minutes, I can go up with you."

"Thank you, but I'll be fine," Elizabeth assured her. "You said a policewoman was here?"

"Yes, with that nasty partner of hers. I don't like him."

Elizabeth nodded. "That would be Detective O'Reilly, no doubt. Were they here long?"

Mrs. Parisi creased her brow, trying to remember. "About thirty minutes or so, I'd guess."

"I see." She glanced anxiously up the stairs. She realized her apartment was a crime scene, but that didn't give Andi the right to go through her private things without a warrant.

"I'll come down when I'm through and have a quick cup of coffee with you," she said, turning back to Mrs. Parisi. It was her way of getting rid of her landlady quickly. She didn't need an audience right now.

"You do that," Mrs. Parisi said, patting her arm, "and I'll cut you a nice piece of cake to go with it. You, too, Officer," she added.

The officer insisted on preceding Elizabeth up the stairs. He took the key from her and unlocked the door, then told her to remain at the door while he entered first and checked it out, making sure the apartment was clear. The whole procedure brought home again how fragile her situation was. A killer was still out there—waiting for her. Finally the officer came back and told her she was free to enter.

"I'll just be a minute," she told him, and headed for her bedroom. Thankfully, he waited in the living room.

She ignored the bloodstains this time, heading directly for the closet. She flipped on the lightswitch and made a quick inspection of the shelves, searching for any sign that they had been disturbed. Seeing nothing changed since the last time she'd been there, Elizabeth allowed her tension to ease for a moment. Whatever evidence Andi and O'Reilly had found, they didn't find it in her closet. Standing on her tiptoes, she reached up along the top shelf and ran her hand between a stack of books and some old purses she meant to throw out long ago. But when her hand came up empty, her heart picked up a beat. Not allowing herself to panic, she reached in further, behind the books, and was rewarded as the smooth surface of a small leather pouch met her fingertips. She shoved the books aside and pulled the pouch out, then held it to her chest.

Quickly Elizabeth worked the tiny combination lock. When it gave way, she tore open the pouch and thumbed through the contents. It was all there—the picture of her and Drake in Atlanta taken by the restaurant photographer;

the envelope with the results of the paternity test showing her fiancé was not Allison's father, not that she had really thought he could be, but she had needed to be 100 percent sure; and the second envelope, addressed to Drake, telling him about his daughter.

She had never sent it. She didn't have the nerve. She convinced herself that she was protecting Allison, that Drake's profession was far too dangerous to expose a young child to. She needed to keep Allison safe. She realized now that she had only been kidding herself. Keeping Allison safe was only part of it. She was the one who didn't want to deal with Drake's violent lifestyle, and the possibility that he could be snuffed out of her life in a split second. But that wasn't the only thing she'd run from. The depth of passion he awakened in her terrified her, too. She ran in fear, fear of new possibilities. By her fourth year in medical school, Elizabeth's life was well on track. She didn't need Drake throwing a wrench under the wheels to derail her. She wanted more for herself than being a farmer's wife, or a teacher, or an office receptionist, or even a small-town store owner—not that there was anything wrong with any of those. It was just that Elizabeth had always known she needed to do more. She couldn't remember a time when she didn't want to be a doctor.

She had run from Atlanta and Drake and buried herself in her work. Then, when Allison came, she poured all of whatever remaining energy she had left into her new baby daughter. Yes, she gained control of her life the best way she knew how.

"Everything okay in there?" the officer called.

"Yes, thank you." Elizabeth jammed the picture and envelopes back into the pouch and closed the clasp, spinning the combination to lock it again. Then she shoved the pouch beneath her belt and pulled the hem of her blouse out, letting it lay loose against her hips. She reached for a garment bag, grabbed a couple of pairs of slacks, a blouse, a blazer, and a sweater, and tossed them in. As an afterthought, she grabbed a pair of jeans, too. She thought she might spend tomorrow afternoon at the farm. It was just as good a time as any to start that vacation Dr. Benson was pushing on her. Elizabeth slung the bag over her shoulder and stepped out into the hallway, heading toward Allison's room. Allison had been asking for one of her dolls.

Entering the brightly decorated pink-and-green room, she immediately sensed someone else had been in the room very recently. Andi and O'Reilly hadn't been subtle in their search. One of Allison's brightly colored shirts protruded from a dresser drawer, a photo album lay open on the bed, and Allison's baby book rested beside it. Elizabeth cringed, knowing the snooping detectives could easily have gleaned plenty of information from that—incriminating information, like the date of Allison's birth, her illnesses, and the fact she had been hospitalized at eighteen months for pneumonia. Armed with that information, they could very possibly get into other records, including Allison's hospital records.

"Damn!" she swore under her breath. Elizabeth looked toward the dresser again. One of the photos normally displayed there was missing from its frame. Anger fused within her. They had no right to take that without asking. She decided she would have to have words with Ms. Andi DeLuca—the sooner the better. Grabbing the doll, two pairs of jeans, and a couple of sweatshirts, she stuffed them into one of Allison's knapsacks, then left the room.

"Could I trouble you to hold these for a minute?" she asked the officer.

"Sure."

"Thanks." She handed him the knapsack and her garment bag, then stepped over to the small computer desk in the corner of the living room. She'd need some pieces of identification—her Social Security card, a copy of her license certificate, credit card numbers, her extra set of keys. She took out her metal file of important papers, then pursed her lips. Someone had jimmied the lock, not even bothering to disguise it. The lid flipped open in her hands. Allison's birth certificate lay on top of the rest of the papers. "Damn again!" she swore.

"Something wrong?" the officer asked.

"No. Sorry, it's all right."

There was a knock at the door.

"I'll get that," the officer said.

Moments later she heard Mary's voice. "Sorry to disturb you, Officer."

"Mrs. Parisi," he said. "What can we do for you?"

"I just wanted to see if Elizabeth was all right."

"Yes, I'm fine," Elizabeth called out. "I'll be right there." But Mrs. Parisi didn't wait. She pushed past the officer and into the living room.

"You know, I was thinking," she said as Elizabeth slammed the file box shut and turned to face her. "You could bring Allison back to my apartment if you like. It seems okay here now, and I could watch her. That way, she would be close enough for you to drop in and see her, or I could bring her by the center. Besides, Donny misses her, and so do I."

Elizabeth frowned. "I don't think that's such a good idea, but I appreciate the offer, Mary, I really do. You've been a lifesaver more than once."

The woman's eye turned critical. A flash of disapproval,

and possibly anger, sparked briefly in her brown eyes. An odd fear touched Elizabeth's heart, passing over it like a shadow. *This is ridiculous,* she told herself. *Mary would never hurt her, or Allison.* But despite her mental protests, her analytical brain clicked on rapidly. But she *did* have opportunity—she had the keys to the apartment and she could have let herself in at any time while Julie was taking her shower. *And* Mary wasn't home the day of the funeral when Elizabeth stopped by to pick up her suit. Was she already out on the expressway, waiting to push the button to detonate the firework, or was she waiting at the funeral home, or the restaurant, to slip it into her bag first? But surely she would have seen her at the restaurant. And would Mary know enough to rig the Roman candle to go off in the car? *But,* Elizabeth thought, her ex-husband had ties to some unsavory characters. She could have picked up a few skills from him along the way.

Elizabeth tried to force the doubts from her mind. The idea that Mary Parisi could be a killer was insane, a result of paranoia from lack of sleep and stress. The woman surely would have known it was Julie in the shower and not Elizabeth. *Or maybe not,* the persistent little voice inside her head murmured. She hadn't told Mary that Julie was visiting *and* Julie was attacked in a darkened bedroom while wearing Elizabeth's robe.

"Maybe after this is all over," Mrs. Parisi said, her voice practically dripping syrup, "you'll finally be able to spend more time with that pretty little daughter of yours."

Ridiculous or not, the shadow returned. Mary had grown increasingly more proprietary over Allison in the past few months, criticizing Elizabeth more often about how she raised her. The incidents had left her with the unsettling impression that her landlady resented her for having such a healthy child while Donny was disabled. Elizabeth tried to ignore those feelings, but realized now, it was time to move on. She'd have to start looking for a new apartment—soon.

"Mary, it's getting late," Elizabeth said, forcing her lips into a smile. "I'm sorry, but I'm going to have to take a rain check on that cup of coffee. You understand." The onslaught of thoughts had made her stomach queasy.

Mrs. Parisi nodded. Her look turned to one of concern, and all hint of criticism vanished from her eyes. Elizabeth felt a sense of guilt wash over her. She wondered if she had, indeed, imagined the undercurrent of anger and disapproval in the woman's demeanor.

"Yes, poor thing, you must be exhausted," Mrs. Parisi said, patting Elizabeth's hand where she still held the file box. "We'll wait until you're back here, and then we'll have a nice long talk, just the two of us, like old times. In the meantime, I'll get this place cleaned up."

"Thanks, you're a sweetheart, Mary."

"It's the least I can do. Can I help you take your things to the car?"

"No, that won't be necessary. The officer and I can handle it."

"Well, okay then," she said, but she hesitated briefly before giving Elizabeth a hug. "Be safe, dear," she whispered, then turned and headed back for the stairs. Watching her leave, Elizabeth still felt a shiver of uneasiness.

Drake rose slowly from his crouched position outside Elizabeth's bedroom window. When he heard them coming up the front stairs, he'd barely had time to escape out the kitchen door before the officer came in to check out the apartment. Although relieved he wasn't discovered, he didn't like the fact that the officer didn't search the back porch, too, before giving Elizabeth the okay to enter. The cop was damn lucky it was just him crouching outside and not the deranged killer.

Drake rubbed his hand against his back pocket, making sure Allison's picture was still there. Seeing the photo again tonight, he realized instantly why it had touched him so much when he first saw it the night of the murder. The image brought to mind a photo of his grandma McGuire as a young girl. That particular photo was tucked away in a shoebox along with some other family memorabilia in his apartment in New Orleans. It'd been a long time since he'd gone through that box, but if he wasn't mistaken, Allison was the spitting image of his grandmother at the same age. He felt like a fool for not recognizing the resemblance immediately.

After snatching Allison's photo, he'd picked up her baby book and started thumbing through it. Gazing at the images of the cute little infant wrapped in pink, he couldn't help but wonder what it would have been like to hold her as a tiny baby. Then he'd flipped through her photo album, stunned that a third of the girl's childhood was already gone—and, thanks to Elizabeth, he hadn't had a chance to see it firsthand.

But he absorbed more than images from those albums. He had her date of birth, and the dates of her hospitalization. There was more sleuthing he could and *would* do, but it wasn't really necessary. In his heart he already knew the truth.

*   *   *

Elizabeth rubbed her fingers absently along the edges of the leather pouch where it lay beneath her pillow. She would show its contents to Drake. It wasn't much, but maybe it would help explain her reasons, as flawed as they were. Maybe he would understand—even a little. She could only hope.

Elizabeth's anxiety had grown when Drake didn't return to the suite. When another officer came to relieve the one outside her door, she decided she should at least get ready for bed. She had undressed and slipped beneath the covers, but left the light on, willing herself to stay awake despite the exhaustion that weighed heavily in her limbs.

Reaching out now, Elizabeth ran a hand across his pillow, then down along the sheet, wondering if it was possible she had dreamed his presence there the previous two nights, wondering if, after what she told him, he would ever lay beside her again. Maybe, given time, he could forgive her. It was a big maybe. Like Andi said, he didn't forgive easily. That's why he was still chasing down the drug lords he thought were responsible for killing his parents. She pulled the pillow to her. The scent of Drake's aftershave lingered on the case. Closing her eyes, she breathed in the spicy scent, not allowing herself the luxury of the tears that threatened at the corners of her eyes. She didn't deserve them.

eighteen

When Elizabeth awoke the next morning, Drake still hadn't returned. Full of anxiety, a million thoughts swam through her head. While she dressed, her anxiety gave way to anger.

If Andi had told him about her suspicions about Allison, after what they'd been through the last few days, why didn't he at least come to her and confront her with it—give her a chance to explain? But that annoying little voice in her head wouldn't let it go at that. What if he couldn't come to her? What if something had happened to him? No one seemed to know where he'd gone last night. What if he followed up on a lead, found the killer, and the killer "offed" him?

God, Elizabeth, now you're being melodramatic! She grabbed her briefcase and took the elevator down to the lobby, the officer beside her.

Elizabeth walked into the Heartland Cardiac Center a bundle of nerves. She started to punch in Drake's number a dozen times on her cell phone, but clicked off each time before the call could go through, telling herself that if he wanted to contact her, he would. She wouldn't call him after he'd left her last night without any explanation or even a goodbye.

She tried to hold on to her anger, letting it fortify her while she did her rounds, then headed downstairs for her morning appointments. Stopping briefly at the main desk, Elizabeth told the clerks to free up her P.M. schedule since she was taking the afternoon off. Her decision involved a good deal of rescheduling for them, but for once, she didn't care. She was putting herself and her needs first. And the truth was there were plenty of competent doctors here who could fill in for her. That thought gave her an odd sense of freedom. Elizabeth realized she was finally acknowledging the fact that everything wasn't always on her shoulders.

"So, Mr. Meyer," she said as she scanned the chart of the patient who sat on the edge of the examining table in front of her. "You're taking your medication as we discussed?"

"Yes, ma'am! I've lost ten pounds, too." He pulled the front of his shirt out from his body to show the extra couple inches available there now.

Elizabeth smiled. "I see that."

At age fifty-three, Mr. Meyer, the owner of a retail hardware chain, had come in earlier this summer complaining of moderate shortness of breath. Preliminary testing followed by a CAT scan and ultrasound revealed he was one of the lucky ones who caught the warning signs early. He could turn his life around with some lifestyle changes. He reminded her of one of the reasons she chose this field of medicine in the first place. Although Mr. Meyer had some vascular disease, Elizabeth elected to treat him conservatively and followed his condition closely.

"You've obviously been watching your diet and exercising," she said. "Your tests results show significant improvements in your cholesterol, and I see your blood pressure is down, too."

Mr. Meyer complained good-naturedly. "Your diet is killing me, Doc, but I do feel better. I've even taken up riding my bicycle to the office. My wife thinks it's pretty funny since I never walked farther than the end of the driveway to get the paper before. It's affecting other parts of my life, too, if you know what I mean. Giving me a lot more energy. My wife doesn't seem to mind that part, either." He winked at her.

Elizabeth laughed. "I'll bet she doesn't. Now, if you'll just unbutton your shirt, I'll listen to your heart."

She set the chart down and pulled her stethoscope from around her neck. She was positioning the ends in her ears when the wall phone buzzed.

"If you'll forgive me for a second, Mr. Meyer?"

He nodded. "You've got to do your job. I'm not going anywhere."

"Thanks."

She stepped over to the wall and picked up the receiver. "Dr. Iverson."

At first no one responded, then a raspy voice graveled out, *"Three's the charm."*

Her blood froze. She gripped the receiver tighter.

"Excuse me?" she asked, trying to still the tremor in her voice. She must have heard wrong.

"Three's the charm," the voice repeated, then the line went dead.

She stood there a moment longer, half in shock, still wondering if she had heard correctly.

"Something wrong?" Mr. Meyer asked from the examining table.

She glanced back at him. The sight of her patient waiting for her, needing her, stirred her. Anger replaced the shock, bringing a hot fire to her veins to replace the chill.

She slammed the phone back onto the receiver. "I'll be back in a minute," she told him, then stormed out of the room.

"Allison is very sick," Drake said, lying to the clerk. "Her doctor needs the records right away."

It made sense that Elizabeth would bring Allison to this hospital where she was doing her residency and where the doctors knew her. At first he was given the runaround when he tried to get Allison's records, even when he had pulled out his FBI shield. The clerk at the University of Illinois Hospital guarded the records as if her life depended on their secrecy. He knew he could get around her with other means, if he needed to—all UIH records were retrieved electronically now; it would just be a matter of finding an empty terminal and getting in past the passwords. But on a whim, and to speed things up, he finally told her he was the child's father.

"Well, that's going to take time. They'll have to be printed if you expect to take them with you. If it's really that urgent, I could e-mail the file to her doctor." She eyed him doubtfully. "Which hospital did you say your daughter was in?"

"Northwestern. And I'd prefer to take the records with me."

"Uh-huh." She punched a few keys on the keyboard, then, after a few moments, studied the screen briefly, then looked up again, this time with a hint of incredulity in her eye.

"What did you say your name was?"

"Drake, Drake McGuire."

"Can you show me that ID again?"

He brought it out. She examined it, then studied him as if she were looking at a frog under a microscope. Still suspicious, she asked, "Why didn't you tell me you were the child's father in the first place?"

"Sorry, I wasn't thinking. It's been a stressful time. Do you have the records?"

"You need x-rays and all? You'll have to go to radiology for that. Or just the charted info and lab reports?"

"The charted info and lab reports will do."

"Hmmm. That'll cost you."

"It's not a problem," he said coolly, but his head buzzed. Could Elizabeth really have listed him as Allison's father on the admittance papers? And if so, why? Maybe there was something genetically wrong with his daughter and Elizabeth wanted a record somewhere that he was the father. She's a doctor, so she would think of something like that. But Allison looked perfect to him. . . .

"You'll have to sign a form," the clerk said, handing him a piece of paper. "And wait over there." She pointed to a bank of chairs across the room. "It'll take me a few minutes."

When the clerk left the room, Drake slipped around the desk and scanned the computer screen. She'd left the admission record open. His name, bright and bold, blazed at him under the heading of "Father," right beside the mother's name, "Elizabeth Marie Iverson." His address was listed as unknown.

He hit Print, then drummed his fingers impatiently on the desk. He just finished tucking the printed sheet into his shirt pocket when the woman came back into the room. She eyed him suspiciously as he stood over her desk, signing the release document.

"It will be a few minutes. I'll give you a voucher and you can pay at the cashier on your way out. Being an FBI guy, I can assume you won't stiff us?"

He smiled. "Right."

He put the pen down, slid the paper toward her. The woman leaned over and studied his signature. "Have I seen you before?" She eyed him suspiciously again.

"No, I don't think so." Although, he reasoned, if she watched any amount of television in the last few days, she'd probably caught a glimpse of him on the newscasts. He hoped she didn't put the two together.

"Like I said, you can wait over there," she said.

"Thanks."

But Drake couldn't sit still. He paced the floor, wishing he had gone with his first instinct and just found a vacant computer terminal where he could have worked his magic. He hated waiting for anything, though it was an integral part of his job. From behind her desk, the clerk glanced up occasionally at him, her look now turning to one of sympathy. Well, whatever works, he thought.

Finally the clerk produced a large envelope. "Here you are, Mr. McGuire. I hope it helps."

Drake allowed himself a few steps outside the door before he flipped open the file and scanned the pages. The baby girl had trouble breathing and a fever of 105 when she was admitted. They put her on a ventilator briefly. His heart thudded against his chest as he imagined how terrified Elizabeth must have been. *Damn, why had she insisted on doing this on her own!* he wondered again for the umpteenth time. Then another piece of information caught his eye, a lab sheet, identifying Allison's blood type as "B+." It was a rare type—his own.

Allison spent five days in the hospital, her fever finally breaking on the fourth day, but it looked like they kept her another day to make sure there were no complications.

Nothing he'd discovered during the night he'd just spent at the FBI bureau office, going through databases and following the short trail of Allison Iverson's existence, held a candle to what he had discovered this morning in those hospital records. Drake zipped out from the hospital parking lot and into traffic now, cursing the late morning congestion as he listened to Andi on his cell phone. His discovery would have to wait. It seemed the killer was ready to make another attack.

"Where's Elizabeth?" he asked.

"She insisted on keeping her schedule and seeing her patients."

"What!"

"Calm down, my officer's on guard. I wanted him in the room, but she said that wasn't ethical."

"She picked a fine time to be ethical," he said, eyeing the file that sat on the seat beside him. "Make sure someone stays with her. Did you trace the call?"

"We're working on it, but I don't hold out much hope. The call came in through the distribution center to the main desk console. The receptionist passed it on to the examining room from there."

"Did you talk to the receptionist?"

A pause. Drake guessed Andi wasn't pleased with his second-guessing her. "I know my job, Drake," she said, her tone a bit caustic, then she seemed to get over it as she went on. "The receptionist couldn't tell if it was a man or a woman who made the call, the voice was too quiet. The person just said they needed to talk to Dr. Iverson— immediately. The receptionist figured it was one of her elderly patients, and she knows that Elizabeth likes to talk directly to her patients when she can. So she put the caller through."

"Did the caller give the receptionist a name?"

"No, she didn't."

"Great. Listen, I'll be there as soon as I can. You've locked the place up tight?"

"Again, we're on it." Drake could hear the tension in Andi's voice. He didn't blame her. She was putting in long hours on this. They were all getting a little punchy.

"Okay, Andi. Thanks." He clicked off.

"Oh hell," he swore as another red light threatened to impede his progress. He grabbed the light bubble from the passenger seat, slipped it onto the roof, and flicked on the siren.

As unaffected as she tried to convince herself she was by the threatening phone call, Elizabeth now found her shield of anger weakening. An arrow of fear pierced the armor, allowing the chilling words of the caller to repeat in her mind: *"Three's the charm."* It didn't take a genius to figure out what he meant by that.

Elizabeth sighed and rubbed her fingertips across her forehead. The officer on duty shadowed her as she made her way to the stairs. She needed some time alone in her office before Drake arrived to sort out her feelings and get a grip on what she was going to tell him. She could use Drake's comforting arms around her right now, but she knew she couldn't give in to that desire. First, he had to hear her out.

Safely locked in her office, Elizabeth opened her briefcase, reassuring herself that the leather pouch was still inside before snapping it shut again.

Trying to clear her mind, she flipped through the patient files she had gathered over the last couple of days. The center had experienced eight fatalities in the last two months, a significant number since they weren't necessarily an emergency center. What Drake said a couple of days ago had made her think. Perhaps the attacks *were* from a patient's relative. Perhaps she had done something, missed something, that caused someone to go off the deep end.

At first glance Elizabeth found nothing particularly remarkable in the files, other than the fact that the patients had died. Their deaths were caused by a variety of reasons—secondary infections, surgical complications, heart failure. There was no guarantee that a patient's heart wouldn't give out while undergoing surgery, even for the healthiest person. And these patients were far from healthy.

Then a report in one of the files caught her eye. Elizabeth remembered dictating it after a patient's CAT scan and subsequent stress test, only the words typed on the page were not hers. The report indicated the CAT scan showed a significant calcium buildup in three arteries and major abnormalities in heart rhythm during the stress test. A consultation with Dr. Benson was suggested. But Elizabeth remembered this patient, and remembered performing the tests. These were not her results. Delving further in the file, she discovered another report, this one Dr. Benson's. This report ended with the words: "Patient scheduled for surgery, triple bypass indicated."

Elizabeth's fingers shook as she flipped the page. The transcription of the surgery performed by Dr. Benson followed. Elizabeth studied it intently. The surgery appeared to have progressed routinely, until the final entry: "The heart was brought back on line. It regained normal sinus rhythm briefly, then the patient's blood pressure dropped to sixty/twenty, then fell to undetectable levels. Seconds later the heart went into ventricular fibrillation, then stopped. Efforts to defibrillate were unsuccessful. Patient expired at 1:15 P.M."

Elizabeth swallowed hard. First Mr. Babcock, then Mrs. Beal, and now this patient. True, Mrs. Beal hadn't died, but she'd come close, and she still wasn't completely out of the woods.

There was a knock at her door. The officer stuck his head in. "Somebody from records just dropped this by for you. I checked it, it's clean." He set a large manila envelope on her desk.

"Thank you."

"I'll be right outside if you need me," he said.

When the door closed again, Elizabeth opened the envelope. Pulling out its contents, she discovered it contained the films from Mr. Babcock's angiogram—the one performed by Dr. Benson just before surgery—the films she'd been looking for last Monday in the catheterization lab. She stood and flipped on her viewing screen, then slid the films into the clips. After a minute she reached for her briefcase and pulled out Mr. Babcock's file, her pulse pounding in her ears. Pulling out the pictures of his CAT scan and lab reports, she studied both for a long time, then examined the films on the viewer once more. She was almost dead sure that the films clipped up on her viewing screen were not of Mr. Babcock's heart even though they were clearly labeled so. Indeed, they did show blockage in two major arteries, indicating a need for bypass surgery, but the placement of the arteries didn't exactly match those on the CAT scans. Her trained eye picked up the slight nuances of difference. Each person's heart has its own individual signature of arteries—a slight difference in size and length, a tiny bend here, an enlargement there. These two were definitely not the same. She'd bet her career on it.

More than ever, Elizabeth wanted to get her hands on the films Dr. Benson took of Mrs. Beal's heart before surgery, or should she say, Mrs. Beal's *real* films, for there was definitely a pattern here. Although she didn't want to admit it, the icy realization was staring her right in the face. Dr. Benson was switching reports, falsifying records, doctoring up films in an attempt to justify bypass surgery for patients at the center. In doing so, he was exposing those patients to great risk. And all for what? Money? Prestige? She'd heard about such things before, but she never dreamed Dr. Benson capable of it.

She wondered how many more unneeded surgeries he had performed since the center opened, how many more patients died unnecessarily, and just who else knew what was going on. Dr. Young? Perhaps that was why he warned her to watch her back.

Elizabeth sat down and closed the file as she tried to still the panic that sent her heart thudding violently against her rib cage. Her gaze darted to the door. She half expected someone to come barging in to accuse her of being a traitor to the center, but the fact remained, Dr. Benson was, in effect, killing people. The question was, what was she going to do about it?

Elizabeth's pager vibrated at her side. She glanced at

the message. "ICCU-4." Mrs. Beal was in ICCU, Room 4. She snatched the films off the viewing screen, then gathered up the files and shoved everything into her briefcase before leaving the room.

The policeman wasn't at his post outside her door. This discovery unsettled her further, but she decided she couldn't wait for him as she raced for the stairwell.

An odd muffled sound coming from behind her had her glancing over her shoulder as she started down the stairs. Elizabeth's feet froze in midstep.

"What the . . . !"

Shock registered briefly as the end of a baseball bat came flying toward her face. Elizabeth's reflexes caused her to raise her hand and duck, but not soon enough. As the bat met her skull, pain flashed in her head like an electric firestorm. The force of the blow sent her tumbling down the stairs.

nineteen

"Where's Dr. Iverson?" Drake said to no one in particular. He flashed his ID at the cop posted out front and headed straight for the reception desk.

The receptionist glanced up as Drake stalked toward her. She recognized him from his prior visits.

"Where's Dr. Iverson?" Drake asked again.

"She left a few minutes ago to go upstairs to her office. She said she'd be there if anyone needed her."

"Thanks."

He strode down the hallway to the elevator.

"Hey, Drake, wait up," Andi called after him. She'd been nursing a cup of coffee at the refreshment station while she waited for him.

Catching the look in Andi's eyes, he realized she had a million questions about where he'd gone last night. He wasn't in the mood to tell her just yet.

He hit the call button on the elevator. "Not now," he said. "I'm going up to interview Elizabeth again. She has to have some kind of idea of who's after her. She's holding back, in more ways than one. You want in on this?"

"Sure. But I already had this discussion with her not more than twenty minutes ago. What makes you think you can get more out of her?"

He didn't answer her directly. "You couldn't tell if the call came from inside or outside the center?"

"Outside, through the main line, but it could've been made from a cell phone from inside. The caller ID was blocked— we're working on it. Why? You know something I don't?"

"Just a hunch. Elizabeth was bugged by something yesterday when I came to pick her up. She said it had to do with Dr. Benson, but in my gut I feel there's more to it than that. Although she insisted it had nothing to do with the attempts on her life, I'm not so sure now. Something just doesn't feel right here."

"Joey warned me about that instinct of yours. Why didn't you tell me about this sooner?"

"I guess I didn't get around to it yet," he said.

Stepping off the elevator on the third floor, Drake instantly sensed that something was wrong. This floor was always much quieter than the other floors, with very little traffic in the hallways. This was where the doctors came to get away and make their phone calls, go over the work of the day, occasionally consult with patients. But today the third floor seemed quieter than normal. Something palpable was in the air. It was as if fear had worked its way into the corridor, slithering in like a snake through the ventilation ducts. Andi and Drake walked down the corridor and turned the corner. The cop wasn't at his post outside Elizabeth's office. The hair on the back of Drake's neck prickled.

"I thought she was supposed to be here?" he asked Andi. He opened the office door. The room was empty. "Where the hell is she?"

Andi pressed the Talk button on her radio. She put a call out to her officer. After a couple of tries with no response, she turned back toward Drake, but he was already three-quarters of the way down the hall, heading for the stair-well. He drew his gun, an uneasy feeling eating at his gut. He remembered Elizabeth liked taking the stairs. He was sure others in the hospital knew that, too.

Drake opened the heavy door. His heart leaped into his throat when he saw the spatters of blood that dotted the wall. His gaze followed the trail downward, although he'd already guessed what he would find there.

Elizabeth lay still on the tile floor of the lower landing, her body turned at an odd angle, blood pooling around her head. A baseball bat lay across her hips, placed there, he could only guess, by her psycho attacker.

"Elizabeth!" he shouted. "Andi, get a doctor in here quick!" He raced down the stairs.

"Damn!" he swore as he knelt beside her. He was afraid to touch her, afraid if he did, he might cause her more harm. "Elizabeth, can you hear me!" he shouted. She didn't move. He slid his hand to the side of her neck. A thready pulse met his fingertips, or did he imagine it?

"Elizabeth!" he shouted again, fear and anger coalesc-ing into panic. He needed to move her head so he could get pressure on the gash at her temple.

"You can't go, Doc, not like this!" he screamed at her. "Not like this! We still have unfinished business, you and I."

Her eyes fluttered open. Her brow pinched as she tried to focus on him.

"Drake?" she asked, her voice weak, barely a whisper.

"Yes, I'm here! Hold on, sweetheart, help's on its way. Who did this to you?"

But she couldn't answer him. Her eyes closed again as she slipped back into unconsciousness.

In the somber twilight of her hospital room, Drake leaned forward in his chair and scrubbed his hands across his face. Across from him Elizabeth slept what seemed to be peacefully under the glow from the night-light in the console above her bed. Part of him envied her. He hadn't had a good night's sleep in days.

It was 2:00 A.M., over fourteen hours since the attack, and still they weren't any closer to finding her attacker. He could kick himself. If he hadn't spent Wednesday night and half the day yesterday trying to prove what in his gut he already knew, he would have been here with her when the threatening call came in. He would have been at her side, protecting her, and the psychopath wouldn't have been able to get to her so easily. Instead, he let anger and his jumbled emotions rule his head while the killer prepared to strike again, right under their noses.

Andi's men had found the bodyguard across the hall, locked in Dr. Young's office, unconscious and barely breathing. He was transferred to Northwestern, where he was now on life support. Someone, presumably the killer, had shot him up with a lethal dose of morphine to the back of the neck. The police managed to piece together the events. With the morphine in his system, the officer had fallen, knocking his head on the desk, the phone still in his hand. They figured he was lured there to take a bogus phone call. There was no record of a call coming in for Dr. Young at that time. The killer locked the officer in the room, retrieved the bat, which he most likely had stored in the supply closet, then paged Elizabeth to ICU. Paging records showed the call came through the hospital's central system, but that meant it could have originated from any phone within the hospital. There was a wall phone by the elevators, very near the stairwell.

They put the hospital on lockdown, interviewing anyone who may have been on the third floor or seen anyone suspicious in the building at the time of the attack, but eventually they had to let people go home. Drake took particular pleasure in interviewing Dr. Young, still convinced that he must know something by his glib attitude, but Dr. Young had a perfect alibi again. He'd been in surgery, inserting a stent into a patient's artery between the time Elizabeth left the clinic and when she was found in the stairwell. As for Dr. Benson, he was in the clinic seeing patients. His secretary, Claire Daniels, said she hadn't seen anyone on the floor who didn't belong there, although she, herself, had gone down to the clinic to give assistance as she did every day during the lunch hours to allow the nurses and assistants to take their breaks.

Drake stood and rubbed at the small of his back, trying to massage away the kinks, remembering how frightened he'd been as he watched the doctors work on Elizabeth. He stayed with her as long as he could, until he was told to leave the room, assured that she would survive. A neurologist, Dr. Raschard, was called in on the case. He said Elizabeth was lucky that she'd sustained only a mild concussion—the bat had glanced off her skull, causing the angry cut, which bled profusely, but her hand had taken most of the force, leaving her with a broken wrist and a couple of broken fingers which would heal in time. Of course, her left side was badly bruised, too, from the tumble down the stairs, but all in all, she was lucky.

Drake sighed. Yeah, she was lucky all right. But she didn't look so lucky lying in the hospital bed, her head swathed in bandages and her wrist in a cast. She'd been in and out of consciousness since the attack, only able to verify stimulus and moan, but Dr. Raschard took that as a good sign. She just needed to be watched for a couple of days to make sure there were no further complications.

"She's a tough lady," he told Drake.

Drake walked to the window and stared out at the lights along Lake Shore Drive that lit up the night. An immense wave of loneliness swept over him, urged on by his frustration. None of it added up. Someone was mad as hell at Elizabeth, mad enough to risk taking out a cop in his efforts to get to her. But the violence hadn't been directed at the cop. The psychopath had been okay with using a needle and morphine on him. No, the violence was reserved for Elizabeth.

He told Andi he wanted every bin in the place checked, that they had to find that syringe. But he knew it was futile trying to find a particular needle in a hospital where hundreds were used every day, and where there were dozens of hazardous waste bins in which the killer could have tossed it. It didn't make sense to conduct DNA tests on every needle because even if they did find the right one, they probably still wouldn't find evidence on it pointing to who had wielded it. Preliminary tests on the bat indicated it had been wiped clean before the assault, not even leaving a skin fragment or fiber for analysis, other than Elizabeth's. He'd bet the syringe would prove just as clean.

Damn, there was something here, something that played

at the edges of his mind. He just couldn't reel it in. Drake glanced again at Elizabeth. He had a feeling she knew more than she let on. He had searched her office briefly, looking for some clue, anything that might shed light on the case. When he discovered that her briefcase was missing, alarm bells went off in his head again. He asked Andi to send an officer to their hotel suite to look for the pouch he'd seen her retrieve from her bedroom, only to find that was missing, too. If only he hadn't let his anger rule him, he might have been able to get to the bottom of all this then.

Yeah, he was still pissed as hell that Elizabeth kept Allison a secret from him, but he'd been unprepared for the jolt that ripped through him when he saw her lying at the bottom of the stairs. When he thought he had lost her for good this time, he'd felt his world suddenly tilt.

A slight movement in the bed caught his attention. Drake walked over and leaned above her.

"Elizabeth?" he asked softly, praying she was coming out of the deep sleep she'd been in. Maybe now she could give him some information. She had to have seen her assailant.

She stilled, then slowly opened her eyes.

"Ah, you're finally awake I see," he said. "Welcome back, Sleeping Beauty."

A slow smile curved her lips. She gazed up playfully at him, a soft, sensual light in her eyes. "Mmmm," she murmured, "I must still be sleeping. I don't think I'll wake from this dream."

Her eyes closed again.

He laughed gently. "Hey, sweetheart, I think you should wake up long enough to talk to me for a minute. We really need to find out who did this to you."

At the sound of his voice, her amber eyes flew open,

sharply this time. A quizzical glance replaced the sensual one.

"Drake?" she asked suspiciously. "Drake McGuire?"

"Who else calls you sweetheart?" he asked lightly. "And for the record, you gave me one hell of a scare," he added, but he didn't like that odd, almost panicked look in her eye. She was scaring him again. She moved as if to sit up, then moaned against the pain and brought her right hand to her head, causing the cast to rub against the bandage.

"What happened?" she asked, somewhat breathless. "And what in the world are you doing here?"

"You don't remember?"

She made a face, trying to concentrate. "The last thing I remember is buying a dress for the banquet."

Drake felt as if the wind had been knocked out of him. They were back to square one.

Then her eyes narrowed accusingly at him. "Where's Allison!" she demanded, her voice rising. "Where's my daughter! Is she all right?"

Elizabeth tried to concentrate on Drake's words, but her head throbbed violently. All she could think of was Allison. She needed to know she was safe, and she didn't trust Drake. The last time she remembered seeing him he was on TV, being wheeled into an ambulance.

She couldn't meet his gaze directly, for the look in those deep blue eyes was way too intimate and unsettling. He said they met each other again at the banquet, but she couldn't remember.

When she awakened, the nurse had called the neurologist in, Dr. Raschard. Although it was the wee hours of the morning, he came. Elizabeth knew him. He ran her through a series of questions, examined her, checked her reflexes, her sensitivity to touch, her eyes. She knew the drill. Then he patted her good hand.

"I think it's best if you just relax," he told her. "Your brain has suffered significant trauma. You have a concussion, which has caused selective amnesia. Sometimes that happens, you know that. It's very likely your memory will return given time, a day or two, maybe a week."

"Can I ask her a few questions?" Drake asked.

The doctor studied him closely, then nodded. "I understand the need, but don't give her too much too soon. Rest is best right now. I'll be back in a few hours."

Dr. Raschard had advised her to relax, but how could she? Drake had just told her Julie was dead, and that someone was trying to kill her. None of it made any sense.

"I need to see Allison," Elizabeth said desperately. She didn't care about anything else right now. She had to touch her daughter, hold her, make sure she was all right.

"I don't think that's a good idea," Drake said, holding tightly to the rail beside her bed.

She glanced up at him. He looked crumpled, tired. There were tiny lines around his eyes. A muscle twitched in his jaw, which showed a good day's growth of beard. It didn't detract from his good looks, though, just made him more ruggedly handsome. From what she could see, the years since they'd seen each other had served him well. But his blue eyes looked a bit desperate and lost now. She felt the oddest longing to reach out to him. It surprised her, and confused her even more. If only he would just stop talking.

"Are you sure you don't remember anything from the stairwell, or before that?" he went on ruthlessly.

She shook her head, then winced at the pain. Why

wouldn't he stop badgering her? She needed to be alone, to get her tumbling emotions in order.

"I think you should go," the nurse said.

"I'm not leaving this room," he insisted. The intensity of his tone stunned Elizabeth.

"Then no more questions for now, I mean it." The nurse turned out the light above her bed, leaving only the soft glow of the night-light to illuminate the room once again. Elizabeth closed her eyes, exhaustion spilling through her, but she couldn't sleep yet.

"I need to see Allison," she said again.

At her side Drake sighed. "I'll have her here in the morning."

twenty

It was mid-morning when Elizabeth opened her eyes again. She felt even worse than before. Every bone in her body ached, yet she refused the painkillers the nurses offered. She wanted to be fully coherent when Allison arrived.

"Feeling any better?" Drake asked as she attempted to eat a bowl of oatmeal topped with fresh strawberries. She noticed he didn't call her sweetheart this time, but seemed more businesslike as he kept his distance from her. She was surprised at the brief twinge of regret it caused her.

"Not exactly," Elizabeth said with a frown, "and before you ask, I don't remember anything yet." She had tried racking her brain, but it only made her headache worse. She dropped the spoon into the bowl and shoved the bed table aside. Glancing sideways at him, she asked, "I don't suppose I was imagining what you told me last night?"

"What was that?"

"About Julie."

His eyes narrowed as if he hated confirming it for her. Slowly he shook his head.

Sorrow welled within her. "How?" she asked, choking down the tears.

"You really want to hear this?"

She shook her head. "No, but it seems I must."

He stood at the foot of the bed. "In your apartment, the night of the banquet. She was stabbed in the back, and in the neck, multiple times. It was meant to be you."

"Oh . . ." She tried to digest this information. Why in the world would someone want to kill her? "And this person is still out to get me?"

"It would seem so."

She refused to believe it. "Maybe I just tripped on the stairs. I know I take them more quickly than I should. Maybe I wasn't paying attention?"

He leveled that deep blue gaze at her. Its intensity sent fear icing through her. "You were conked in the head with a baseball bat," he said evenly.

She raised her good hand to the bandage on the side of her head. "Yes, I see how that couldn't be an accident."

"Before that, a firework exploded in our car. You received threats prior to both incidents." He pulled up a chair and sat beside her. "I just finished talking with Andi . . ."

"Andi?"

"I guess you wouldn't remember her, either. She's one of the detectives on the case. She also happens to be married to my cousin Joey. Anyway, according to her, no one saw a damn thing. The policeman who was guarding you is still in a coma. The assailant shot him with a massive dose of morphine, which stopped his breathing. They're not sure if he'll ever come out of it—oxygen deprivation."

"Yes, that would do it." Elizabeth wished she could remember something, anything.

"Elizabeth, the other day, you seemed upset about a patient. You said you had a disagreement with Dr. Benson, but I had a feeling it was more than that. Do you remember any of it?"

"No, which patient?" she said, shaking her head.

"Mrs. Beal. She had open heart surgery."

"Really." She remembered seeing the woman in the summer, but wouldn't have thought she would need surgery, especially not this soon. "Who performed the surgery?"

"Dr. Benson."

"I see," she said, but she really didn't. She would be interested in looking at the woman's chart.

"Anyway, I was surprised when I couldn't find your briefcase in your office. I have Andi searching for it. Can you at least remember what you did with it? You've been bringing files home. My guess is they may be linked in some way to the attempts on your life. Maybe if we find the briefcase, we can get a handle on this."

She tried, she really did, but nothing came to mind. The last few days were a blank page. "I'm sorry, Drake, but I really can't remember anything." Gazing up at him, she could see the disappointment in his eyes. It saddened her, for she wanted so much to help him.

"So, you're assigned to the case, too?" she asked, wondering again why it mattered so much to him. "That's why you've been helping me?"

His gaze closed off, shuttering his emotions. "Yeah, something like that."

The phone on the bedside table rang. He picked it up.

"Yes?" he said, then after a short pause, "Meet me at the

nurse's station." Standing, he strode to the door, then turned to face her again. She couldn't read the look in his eyes. "You have a visitor," he said. He stood there a moment longer, as if he wanted to say something else, then changed his mind. "I'll be right back."

She watched him leave, wondering why the panic had suddenly returned to her chest. Pulling the bed table back to her, she slid the tray aside and raised the center mirror to examine her reflection. Perhaps seeing Allison *wasn't* such a good idea right now, she thought, for her face was uncharacteristically pale. The bandage went across her forehead, down the side of her face, then wrapped around the back of her head. That, along with the bruises along her other cheek, looked scary even to her. She ran her hand quickly through her curls where they pushed out behind the bandage, trying to bring some order to them. All was forgotten, however, moments later when her pride and joy burst into the room.

"Mommy!"

"Allison, wait!" Sharon Iverson called after her granddaughter, but Allison paid no attention. She ran toward the bed where Elizabeth caught her up, wrapping her good arm around her.

"Allison, my sweet!" she said, planting a kiss against her daughter's forehead.

But Allison quickly pulled back, alarmed by the bandages. "Oh, Mommy . . ." she said. Elizabeth watched the fear cloud her eyes, along with a look of consideration that was far too old for her age.

"What did they do to you!" Allison exclaimed. "I was so scared when Grandma said you were hurt. Does it hurt real bad?"

Elizabeth tried to put on her brightest smile. "Not real bad, now that you're here. You're the best medicine in the world for me. Now, climb up here and give me a big hug."

But Allison still hesitated, bringing a catch to Elizabeth's throat. "Can I, Grandma?" she asked, looking back to her grandmother for permission. Elizabeth looked up, too, and witnessed the horror that flashed briefly in her mother's eyes at her battered condition. Then the look was gone as she assured Allison it was okay.

But the mature little imp that she was, Allison still didn't quite buy it. She frowned as she climbed gingerly onto the bed. "I love you, Mommy," she said, wrapping her small arms around Elizabeth's shoulders.

Elizabeth pulled her close, despite the pain that shot through her body. "I love you more," she said, and showered her with kisses.

"Oh, Mommy!" Allison laughed. Then she leaned back and made a serious face. "Everything is going to be all right now," she said. "Drake is here. He said he was going to keep a close eye on you and he sent this really nice man to get us. His name is Mr. Frank. Do you know he likes farms? He said he grew up on a ranch, with some horses. He used to ride them all the time."

Elizabeth smiled deep within herself as her daughter rambled on. She pulled her close again, letting the fresh herbal scent of her curls renew her strength. She'd have to send her away soon, to somewhere safe, until the killer was caught, but for now, she needed to hold her.

Her throat worked convulsively as she tried not to cry. She looked across the bed, over Allison's head, to where Drake stood in the doorway. A look of such wonder and amazement flicked across his features as he gazed upon Allison that it stunned her. Then he raised his gaze and a connection flowed between them, reaching so deeply into her soul that it almost took her breath away, and caused another fear to wiggle its way into her heart.

In the last few days, had she told him Allison was his? She held his gaze while Allison rattled on.

But Allison would not sit still. The exuberant child twisted in the bed, then eyed the food on her tray. "What did they give you?" she asked. Then, when she noticed the food hadn't been touched, she scolded her in her most grown-up voice. "You really need to eat, Mommy. You have to get better so you can come and play with the cows. Grandma said you'll have to take a vacation now."

"I suppose I will," Elizabeth said. She tore her eyes from Drake's to smile down on her daughter. When she looked back up, he was gone.

"Now, don't tire your mother," Sharon Iverson warned, approaching the bed. "How are you, dear?" she asked as she leaned over and placed a kiss lightly against Elizabeth's bruised cheek. "We'll have to see about someone coming in here and getting that hair shampooed. Allison, sit aside and let me brush your mother's hair."

A short time later Claire Daniels stuck her head in the doorway. "Up for more company?"

Elizabeth frowned. One thing she did remember was that Claire was not her favorite person.

But Claire didn't wait for her consent. She slid into the room carrying a pot of mums in one hand and a plastic hospital bag in the other. "I brought your things from downstairs," she explained as she breezed toward the bed. "And this is from the staff." She set the bag and the plant on the bedside table. "Your pager and shoes," she explained, tapping the bag. "I'm afraid there wasn't much left of your clothes."

Elizabeth wasn't surprised. She was sure the doctors and nurses had cut her clothes off of her when they attended her, being careful not to jostle her any more than necessary until they were sure there were no other broken bones in her body.

"Boy, those are pretty!" Allison said, bounding from the bed. "Can I smell them?" Her sudden movement caused Elizabeth to wince.

"You sure can," Claire said, smiling sweetly at Allison. "And how are you today, Miss Iverson?"

Allison laughed. "Very well, thank you, Miss Daniels."

Elizabeth knew it was a game the two played whenever Allison came to visit the office and ran into Claire. Occasionally, Claire would even let Allison type on her keyboard, something that never ceased to surprise her since Claire normally didn't like anyone messing with her desk. But Allison seemed to bring out the best in Claire.

"You know, getting into this room is like trying to get into Fort Knox," Claire said, turning toward Elizabeth. "There are no less than four men guarding your door, two policemen and two plainclothesmen, very handsome ones, too, I might add."

"They're FBI," Allison whispered, as if it was a secret.

"Oh, I see," Claire whispered back.

"But they're real nice. Drake even came out with Mommy last week and went through the corn maze with me. Do you know what that is?"

"I think I do."

"Well, it's scarier than ever this year, but Drake didn't mind. Mommy wouldn't go, though. She got scared."

Elizabeth winced again, not completely thrilled with Claire being privy to her weakness.

Claire smiled. "Don't be too hard on her for that. I have claustrophobia myself sometimes."

"Clostra-what?" Allison asked.

"Claustrophobia—it's when you're scared of being trapped in places. Listen, I'd better get back to work. You're going to take good care of your mom, now, aren't you?"

"I sure will."

"Goodbye, Dr. Iverson. Dr. Benson said he would check in on you later."

"Thanks, Claire."

Too soon, the nurse came in to usher Sharon and Allison out of the room. Drake followed close on the nurse's heels. "I think we need to leave your mom alone now and let her get some rest," the nurse said.

"Mr. Frank is going to take you for a ride, Allison," Drake said, glancing up at Elizabeth. She nodded, understanding the need to get Allison out of the hospital to some place safe.

"Say goodbye now," Sharon told Allison.

"Goodbye, Mommy," she said, hugging Elizabeth again. "Now, you make sure you eat all your breakfast before you take your nap."

Elizabeth smiled. "I promise." She kissed her, holding her for an extra long moment before releasing her to her mother's care.

"I hate leaving you like this," her mother whispered into her ear when she kissed her goodbye.

Elizabeth sighed. "Just look out for Allison."

When they left, Drake followed them, but not before giving her one last piece of advice. "Make sure you get that rest, because I'm springing you this afternoon." His tone made her shiver. His meaning was clear. Even with the guards, Elizabeth wasn't safe here.

Elizabeth found it virtually impossible to relax. She thought she would go mad lying in bed, doing nothing, despite her pain. Being idle just wasn't her style, and it didn't help that Drake kept going in and out of the room to check on Andi's progress with the investigation. It seemed he was just as tightly wound as she was.

When Dr. Raschard returned just before noon, he examined her and found no changes in her condition. Her vital signs were good. Drake explained his plans to take her back to the hotel suite that afternoon.

"That's not wise," Dr. Raschard said. "I'd feel more comfortable keeping her in the hospital under observation for another day or so."

"And I'd feel more comfortable with her out of here."

"Yes, well, I see your point. Why don't we wait a few more hours, then if everything still looks good, I guess I can release her, if you promise to keep her resting for another couple of days at least."

"Understood," Drake said, not looking at Elizabeth. She glanced from one to the other, wondering if she had a say in the matter.

Elizabeth tried to eat the soup on the tray in front her, remembering her daughter's orders with a smile. Her brief moment of peace was shattered when she heard Drake's voice raised in anger just outside the door. Curious to see what the ruckus was about, she eased her legs over the side of the bed and stood. A wave of dizziness had her clutching at the rail. She waited for it to pass, then stepped over to the door and very carefully pulled it open a crack.

"You're not running this investigation!" a man yelled at Drake. "Move away so I can question Dr. Iverson!"

Drake stood not two feet from her, blocking the entrance. The man yelling at him stood across from him. From what she could see, the other man's face was turning a good shade or two darker red as he argued with Drake. She noted how his stomach bulged over his buckled pants. She couldn't help wondering if he'd had a checkup lately—he looked like a good candidate for a heart attack. Perhaps she should give him a few tips on how to avoid one, although she had a feeling this guy wasn't one to follow doctor's orders.

"Fat chance, O'Reilly. If you had spent more time going after the real killer instead of harassing me, maybe Elizabeth wouldn't be lying in that bed right now."

"Step aside, McGuire!"

But Drake wasn't budging. "You take one step inside this door and I'll make sure it's the last step you ever take."

"Hey, threatening a police officer. I could arrest you for that!"

"You and what army?"

A uniformed officer standing beside Drake put his hand on Drake's shoulder. "Maybe you better settle down, Agent McGuire."

"Just don't let him past this door. If I have to go higher up, I will."

"Yeah, you're proud of your friends on the force aren't you," O'Reilly taunted him. "Nice of them to protect you, Loverboy."

Drake had enough. He stepped forward and cocked his arm. Elizabeth was sure he would have punched the man if the officer hadn't grabbed his arm and held him back.

Then a rather petite woman dressed in a slim skirt and waistcoat approached from down the hall. "What in the world are you two up to now? Don't we have enough to worry about without you going head-to-head again? Drake?" she asked accusingly.

"Andi, he's not to go in there," he said. "Elizabeth has nothing to tell you. She still can't remember anything from the past week."

The woman's eyes narrowed. "Nothing, huh?"

Drake ripped his arm from the officer's grasp and ran his hand through his hair. "Yeah, nothing."

"I see," Andi said. She turned back to O'Reilly. "Okay, O'Reilly, why don't we take this up again later. Maybe we'll be able to get something out of her then."

"Still protecting Loverboy here, huh?"

"Jeez, give it up! There are plenty of other things we can do here besides harass Dr. Iverson."

Elizabeth let the door close and went back to bed. Weary now, she closed her eyes and wondered just what Detective O'Reilly had meant by calling Drake "Loverboy."

Elizabeth didn't know how long she had been sleeping before she was awakened by the sound of a cell phone ringing. Opening her eyes, she discovered Drake sitting in the chair across from her.

"Sorry," Drake said sheepishly, reaching into his pocket to retrieve his phone. "I forgot to switch it off."

"You're not supposed to have that on in here."

"I know. Sorry." He looked at the caller ID. "I'm afraid I have to take this anyway."

She shook her head, closed her eyes, and was beginning to doze off again when she sensed something was wrong.

"You what!" Drake shouted into the phone. He sat straight up in his chair. "When?" he asked. Then a moment later, "How the hell did you let that happen!"

She sat up, too, alarmed by the desperation in his voice. "What is it?" she asked.

He glanced briefly at her, his eyes filled with turbulent emotion, then looked away again. "I'll be right there!" he barked into the phone. He flipped it shut and stood, shoving the chair backward in his haste.

"Drake, what is it?" Elizabeth asked again. The look he gave her frightened her even more. "It's Allison, isn't it?" Her heart hammered in her chest.

"It's probably nothing. I'll take care of it. You get some rest." He was already halfway to the door.

"Drake!"

"I'll check it out. I don't want you to worry."

"I'm going with you." She slid her feet over the side of the bed and started to stand.

"Shit!" he swore. He was at her side in a flash, hands gently urging her back into the bed. "No, you're not!"

She held her ground. "Tell me what's going on," she challenged him. He studied her for a long moment. Hurt akin to agony clouded his eyes. "You're right," he breathed. "It's Allison. She's missing."

twenty-one

"Oh, my God!" The room started to spin. "How? When?" Elizabeth gasped as Drake guided her back down, onto the bed.

"Marshall Field's. Your mother wanted to take her to lunch and buy her something pretty to take her mind off of things. Frank didn't think it would be a problem. She disappeared in the toy section."

"Disappeared?"

"She ran off, to look at some display, then disappeared between the aisles before they could catch up with her."

Elizabeth could imagine Allison doing just that, although she'd been warned at least a dozen times to stay close when they were shopping together.

She grasped at Drake's suitcoat. "You have to find her."

"That's the plan," he said. "Just as soon as I get you back in this bed."

"No, Drake, you really have to find her," she said, shaking her head.

"I just told you I intend to."

"But you don't understand." Her throat convulsed as she fought her panic. "She's your daughter."

He stilled. His gaze met hers again. His eyes flamed at her, dark and angry. "I know," he said evenly.

She removed her hand from his coat and clasped it to her chest. "Oh—then I told you." She was barely able to get the words out.

His lips turned up slightly. "No, it seems you hadn't gotten around to divulging that little fact yet." He drew back. "Why now, Elizabeth?" he asked, his voice hard as nails. "Why tell me now? Did you really think that knowing Allison is mine would make me search any harder for her? That I wouldn't bust my ass to find her anyway?"

"No, I—"

"God, you could give me *some* credit. Get some rest, you'll need it." He gave her one last caustic glance, then turned and stalked from the room.

Elizabeth sank back against the pillows. Tears stung her eyes. She glanced out the window where the clouds were gathering in the afternoon sky. The nurse had said something earlier about thunderstorm warnings. Closing her eyes, she said a prayer for Allison's safety, then said ten more, all the while cursing her own weakness.

Drake raced downtown. He called Andi and his FBI field contacts on the way. He was pissed as hell at Frank, but he realized he couldn't place all the blame on him. There was no reason to believe someone would go after Allison in a busy department store. Until now, the killer only seemed interested in Elizabeth. But what better way to get to Elizabeth than to kidnap her daughter—or worse.

Frank's response to the situation had been swift. He immediately ordered the security guards to close down the exits, but a thorough search of the store turned up nothing. Meanwhile, the police and FBI sent out an Amber Alert, notifying all authorities in the tristate area of Illinois, Indiana, and Wisconsin of Allison's abduction. They also set up a dragnet, fanning out from the store, going door to door, down State Street and the connecting streets showing Allison's picture and interrogating shop owners. But there were a million places in the Windy City where someone could hide a kid—that is, if they stayed in the city.

Now, as Drake paced back and forth in the security room of Marshall Field's State Street store, his heart turned over. He'd been pretty hard on Elizabeth. Truth was, maybe he *was* more concerned because Allison was his daughter. Maybe that knowledge made him even angrier.

Drake rubbed his hands across his face. A full two hours had passed since Allison's disappearance, and time was running short. In child abduction cases, every minute was crucial, and in this instance, with a killer on the loose, every second counted. All they had to go on was a description of Allison and a copy of the photo he had taken from her room.

He should call Elizabeth. She was probably going crazy, but he wanted to have something to tell her first.

"Key up those tapes one more time," he told the chief security guard. "There's got to be something there."

They ran through the surveillance videos again, first the toy section, then the clothing departments, then the exits and entrances.

"Stop!" They were looking at a portion of the tape Drake hadn't seen before. Something in the last two frames had caught his eye. "Where was this tape earlier!" he shouted.

"We just retrieved it from the camera."

"Great!" his displeasure was evident in his voice. "Wind it back. Okay, there! Run it forward again."

He stared at the image of a woman leaving the store by the State Street entrance. Her black hair bobbed against the shoulders of her beige raincoat. He thought it odd she was wearing a raincoat, as the day was warm and humid, but storms were predicted for later that evening. Although she was turned away from the camera, something about her jarred his memory. Even more significant, she was wheeling a medium-sized suitcase behind her, the tags still on it.

"Can you run that again—in real time?"

She was one of the last shoppers out the door before the security guard stepped in and locked the doors. Drake could swear he'd seen her before, but where?

His mind raced back to the videotapes taken at Julie's funeral. He remembered a dark-haired woman in the background, walking briefly into view of the camera in the street outside the funeral home, but her face had been obscured by a large hat at the time. He questioned Julie's parents about her, but they didn't know her and didn't remember her being at the funeral or the restaurant. No one seemed to remember her and he had to assume at the time that she was just a passerby.

Unless his mind was playing tricks on him, this was the same woman. Seeing her again in these tapes could not be a coincidence. "Run it again," he said. Then, after studying the brief glimpse of the woman's backside once more, the jaunty step, confident, brisk, efficient . . . "I've seen that walk, just recently. Did we get her face? Check the toy department tape again."

He waited an agonizing moment while the guard cued it up. "Yeah, there!" His adrenaline rose, kicking his heart into overdrive. It was the same woman. She seemed to know a security camera was trained on her, for she held her head down as she walked. The suitcase trailed behind her. They got a glimpse of her both coming, then going down the aisle, and he could swear that on the return trip her walk was not as easy, as if she were trying to act like the suitcase she was pulling was still lightweight when in fact something of substance had been added to it. The woman glanced sideways for just a second before hurrying out of the frame, but it was enough for him to catch a glimpse of her face. "Run it back," he said, "and stop on her face. . . . Yes, that's it."

He stared at her. Donny's words echoed in his head. "The yellow-haired lady is mean," he'd said. Yellow hair— blond hair. *Damn!* Donny had been trying to tell them the woman's identity all along. But they had all assumed he was talking about Julie.

"Get a printout of that frame!" he shouted to the security guard, then flipped open his cell phone and dialed Andi's number.

Elizabeth stared at the bedside phone, willing it to ring. She had wanted to dial Drake a hundred times in the last two hours, but realized she couldn't remember his number.

A sudden ringing from inside the bag Claire had set down on the table earlier made Elizabeth flinch. Thrashing though it she found a cell phone. She didn't recognize it as her own. She grasped it and pushed the receive button.

"Hello?" she asked tentatively.

"Dr. Iverson?" the raspy voice queried, sending chills up Elizabeth's spine.

"Yes?"

"Listen, and don't interrupt, if you want to see your daughter again."

Elizabeth tried desperately to place the caller's voice.

"There's a false bottom in the plant beside your bed," the caller said. "Dump the plant and you'll find two syringes. It'll be up to you to get your bodyguards into your room and administer the morphine.

"Then go to the supply room. On the second shelf, you'll find a set of scrubs. Wrapped inside them is a twenty-dollar bill. Put on the scrubs, then head down to the basement. A cab will be waiting for you at the supply dock. Take it to your apartment. You'll find a key to your car inside the left front wheel well."

"How—"

"I said don't interrupt! Get in your car and drive out to the corn maze. Your daughter will be waiting for you— she's looking forward to seeing how scared you get.

"And remember, don't tell anyone, especially not that FBI boyfriend of yours, or your pretty little girl will become fodder for the cows. Oh, and one more thing, bring the records and files you took from the center. I'm sure Dr. Benson will appreciate getting them back."

"Dr. Benson?" Elizabeth didn't have a clue as to what the caller was talking about.

"I said shut up! It's just after four o'clock now. Given the rush-hour traffic, I expect you no later than six. And Dr. Iverson, trust me, you *don't* want to be late."

"Wait!" Elizabeth cried. She needed to keep the caller on the line. She needed to hear Allison's voice, to make sure she was safe, but the loud click on the other end told her the caller had already hung up.

Elizabeth stared at the phone, knowing she should call someone, but who? The last thing she wanted to do was jeopardize Allison's life. Drake—she needed to call Drake, no matter what the caller said. He was FBI. They knew how to deal with these kinds of cases. She reached for the number pad, then remembered she didn't have his number, and the clock was ticking. Why hadn't she insisted on him leaving it with her?

Deciding she couldn't think about that right now, she flipped her feet over the bed and stood. Thankfully, the wave of dizziness was brief this time. She attacked the mum plant. Her first priority was to get to her car. She'd figure out how to reach Drake on the drive out to the farm. The caller had said something about Dr. Benson's files. As she dumped the dirt from the pot onto the floor, she racked her brain, trying to remember what on earth that was about. Frustrated at the empty spaces in her mind, she decided she couldn't worry about that, either. There was no time.

With the flowerpot clear of dirt, she scratched at the bottom with her good hand. Finally it came loose, revealing the two syringes filled with fluid. She grasped a syringe in her hand and turned toward the door, realizing she would have to lure one officer in at a time.

Exactly eighteen minutes later she was in the cab giving the driver directions to her apartment.

While Andi and O'Reilly headed for Claire Daniels's apartment, Drake made a beeline back to the center to check out Claire's office. Whatever was going on had to do with the center. He was sure of it now, and the answer lay with Claire, Dr. Benson's efficient but deadly blond secretary, who seemed to have developed a penchant for black wigs. He wondered what other little secrets she kept. Expertise with explosives? Knives? She certainly had access to surgical gloves and shoe covers, which explained why they weren't able to pick up any prints at Elizabeth's apartment and why the smeared trail had ended abruptly in the middle of the hallway. She must have taken the shoe covers off before she left the apartment.

Yeah, she was the one all right, but what he needed to know right now was where she had taken Allison. He prayed it wasn't too late as he burst into her office.

He started with her desk, thumbing through her calendar, then tearing through her drawers, one at a time, dumping their contents onto the carpeted floor before moving on to the next one. But he found nothing even remotely helpful. He flicked on her computer. He scanned her most recent files, scoured through documents, then swore when he had no luck there, either. Drake thought he might have at least found files containing the threatening letters, but Claire was either smarter than the average user, or there was nothing to find. He'd have the computer impounded, the hard drive searched by FBI technicians later, but that wouldn't help matters now.

Drake prayed Andi was having better luck in her search of Claire's apartment. Frustrated, he attacked the bookshelf behind the desk next, ripping out binders of supply house catalogs, telephone books, medical reference books, and the like, leafing through each one, then tossing them to the floor before moving on. By the time he was through, the office looked like a disaster area, but he was no further along.

He took a deep breath, then glanced toward Dr. Benson's office. Well, he'd gone this far, he reasoned, he might as well finish it. He should have a search warrant, but he wasn't about to wait for one.

Drake strode into the room and attacked Dr. Benson's desk, methodically searching through the small stack of papers there, then moved on to the desk drawers. He was able to open them all, except the center drawer. His pulse picked up a bit as he took his nifty lock-pick set out of his pocket. He told himself there were a hundred reasons why the drawer would be locked. He knew he shouldn't expect to find anything incriminating—that would be just too easy. But Drake's detective instincts were kicking in. He felt like a bloodhound on the scent.

The lock gave way within seconds under his competent hands, and he pulled the drawer open. A lone file folder lay inside. A key lay on top of it. Now his juices were really flowing.

Drake pulled out the folder and carefully slid the key onto the desk. There were three pieces of paper inside the folder. Two were letters addressed to Dr. Benson. The third was a black-and-white computer printout of a series of pictures of what appeared to be a heart and its surrounding arteries. He looked at the letters again. A quick scan told them he was staring at two blackmail letters.

"Bingo!" he said. His pulse quickened as he read the first letter. It demanded one million dollars from Dr. Benson. It also insisted, that along with the money, Dr. Benson—

. . . cease to perform unnecessary surgeries IMMEDI-ATELY, OR SUFFER THE CONSEQUENCES. If payment is not made within 48 hours, I will use the evidence I have to bring you down, along with your beloved center.

The letter went on to advise Dr. Benson to deposit the money in unmarked bills in a locker at Union Station, then mail the key to a central post office box.

Drake shook his head. His first impression was that the letter was the work of an amateur. There were much easier ways to get money in a blackmail scheme, specifically transferring it via the Internet to a numbered account in a foreign country. He flipped to the second letter, being careful to touch only the edges of the paper. This letter was even bolder, demanding another half-million dollars—

> . . . or I will go to the POLICE! Then everyone will know you for the fraud you really are. In case you don't believe I have the evidence, I have enclosed a copy of Mr. Babcock's heart scans. The ORIGINAL scans. The ones you planned to destroy!

Drake studied the images on the third sheet of paper. He assumed he was looking at pictures of a healthy heart and its arteries, but what did he know? The fact was, the images most likely had obvious implications for Dr. Benson.

Drake examined both letters again, noting that they were printed on plain ink-jet paper, probably twenty-pound weight, with no identifying marks. He studied the key. There was nothing remarkable about it, either, except that it had still been in the drawer, which meant it hadn't been used yet. Dr. Benson obviously hadn't paid off the blackmailer. Had he chosen another way to deal with it? Drake wondered. Could Dr. Benson really believe Elizabeth was the blackmailer? He remembered she had been questioning the doctor. He wondered how far back she had delved into his patients' files. There was no date on the letters and no envelopes accompanying them, although both had fold marks indicating they had arrived in envelopes.

Drake also wondered what Claire's involvement was in all of this. Was Claire working for Benson in more ways than one? Once again, he had more questions than answers and none of it helped him right now. He needed to know where Claire had taken Allison.

His cell phone rang. He flipped it open.

"Drake?" the caller asked.

"Shoot."

"It's Andi. We're at Claire Daniels's place. I've gotta tell you, it's kind of scary here, but unfortunately, no Ms. Daniels and no Allison. Sorry. Lot's of pyrotechnic stuff, though, and some creepy candid shots of Elizabeth—some outside her apartment, some in the parking lot of the center. Looks like Ms. Daniels was keeping her under surveillance. I have a guy checking her computer. She's got quite a setup. Looks like the girl led a double life."

"Any clues as to where she took Allison?"

"Not yet, but we'll keep checking."

"Listen, Andi, someone was blackmailing Dr. Benson. I'm not sure where that fits into all this right now, but I thought you should know."

"You think it was Elizabeth?"

"No. I know she's lied about some things, some *big* things, but she's not a blackmailer. Someone else might think she is, though."

"Ms. Daniels?"

"Could be."

"Well, we've got an APB out on her car, and—there's something else you need to know. Your FBI guy, Seavers, called. He finished running those background checks you were working on, the ones from the license-plate registrations from the expressway tapes. Some interesting info came through on one of the names, a certain Malcolm Clark. Turns out Malcolm Clark has been dead for three years. He died in a freak accident at a Fourth of July fireworks display he was setting up for the company he worked for. Seavers checked further. Malcolm was the son of James Clark."

"And? What does this have to do with this case?"

"James Clark shot himself in the head, just before the police broke down his door after he smashed his wife's head in with a baseball bat twenty-three years ago. When the police broke into the Clarks' apartment, they found a little girl huddled in a bedroom closet. She had a butcher knife clutched to her chest. The little girl's name was Danielle Clark. She was six years old and Malcolm's half sister. They never found Malcolm. Police records indicate a series of domestic disturbance calls before the incident. In the reports, the neighbors said Malcolm had run away a couple of months before the murder-suicide. He was fourteen at the time."

"And you're thinking Danielle Clark is now Claire Daniels."

"It's not a far stretch. She'd be the right age."

"That would explain why I had a hard time pinning down any info on her when I searched for records of the staff here. She must have changed her name when she became an adult. Did Seavers find anything else?"

"Only that she'd been in and out of institutions and foster homes until age sixteen, then she disappeared from any records. She was listed as a runaway then, too."

"Look's like our Miss Daniels decided to start a whole new life for herself. I wonder where the brother fits in and where she got his car."

"We'll keep searching here and see if we can figure that one out. It'll take us a couple of days to go through all this stuff. Meanwhile, we've got an APB out for Malcolm's Mazda, too."

"Great. Add Benson's car to the list," he said, his frustration working into his voice.

"Drake . . . we'll find her."

"Yeah, we will." But fear crawled higher up his gut as he clicked off the phone. It was time to check in with Elizabeth.

Drake was debating whether to leave the blackmail file and key for the police to guard until they got a search warrant, or to just take everything with him when Dr. Young breezed into the outer office.

"What the hell's going on in here!" Dr. Young shouted as he stepped over the pile of papers and books in Claire's office. Drake pocketed the key and grabbed the file just as Dr. Young entered Dr. Benson's inner sanctum.

"You!" the doctor accused, his pale blue eyes glaring at Drake. "I should have known." He scanned the room before returning his gaze to Drake. "What gives you the right to destroy these offices and go through Dr. Benson's files? Last I heard, you need a search warrant for that."

Drake eyed the doctor speculatively. As usual, Dr. Young was neatly dressed. His blond hair was combed up and back in a smooth, slick style. With his suave features, he looked like he could have stepped out of the pages of *Up-and-Coming Doctor* magazine—if there was one.

But there was something about the good doctor that didn't sit right with Drake. Although Dr. Young's words held just the right amount of arrogant effrontery, there was something odd about his cocky attitude. Again, Drake had the keen sense that this guy knew more than he let on.

"I was looking for your girlfriend," he said. "It seems there are some interesting secrets here at the center. Know anything about this?" He flipped open the file and held it under Dr. Young's nose.

Drake could swear he saw the doctor visibly pale under that tan of his as he stared at it.

"Jesus, no!" Dr. Young exclaimed, but it was a little too quick for Drake's taste. He couldn't possibly have had enough time to read the first letter.

"You can't think I had anything to do with that!" Dr. Young said.

"Oh, can't I now? Seems to me you're in a perfect position to know about this, or at least about Dr. Benson's activities. You *are* one of his chief cardiologists, aren't you?"

"So, what if I am? That doesn't prove anything."

"Listen," Drake said, his patience wearing thin. "My daughter is missing and your girlfriend Claire took her. My guess is that it has a lot to do with these letters and the attempts on Elizabeth's life. Whether or not Claire *is* the murderer, she has my daughter. If you know something, now would be a good time to spill it."

But instead of telling him anything about Claire, Dr. Young raised his chin defiantly and smirked. "Yeah, your *daughter*. I bet that was a kick in the head, huh?"

Something snapped inside Drake's head. "How did you know she was my daughter? When did Elizabeth confide in you?" Somehow he couldn't see Elizabeth telling this smug doctor her closest-held secret.

"Well, ah . . . she didn't. Not exactly," Dr. Young stammered, as if he realized he'd just made a fatal mistake.

Drake sensed the fear rise in him. He saw it in the slight twist in his features, in the way he suddenly avoided Drake's eye, and the bead of sweat that popped out on his brow. Yeah, fear came on suddenly, and it smelled. Dr. Young definitely knew more than he was letting on. Drake grabbed him by the collar and slammed him up against the wall.

"Listen to me, you smartass," he said, his voice low and deadly. "If you had something to do with this, you'd better come clean now. Because if I find out later that you did, you're gonna wish you were six feet under already."

He pressed his forearm against Dr. Young's throat, threatening to crush his windpipe.

The man's bravado collapsed almost instantly. His Adam's apple bobbed up and down against Drake's arm. Dr. Young's eyes bulged, and the beads of sweat joined together to form full-sized droplets that trickled down into his eyes.

Normally, Drake might enjoy watching the guy squirm, but there was no time now. He pressed harder. "Out with it."

"As soon . . . as you take your arm . . . off my . . . throat," Dr. Young croaked.

Drake eased the pressure, just enough to let him talk.

"I . . . tried to warn Elizabeth off," he gasped out, "but she wouldn't listen. She was on to Benson, too, or at least figuring it out. Benson's been opting for expensive surgeries for patients when less invasive, cheaper procedures would work. I suspected as much this summer. I got a few files together, confiscated some of the original x-rays and scan records . . ."

The light was beginning to glow in Drake's head. "You sent these letters."

Dr. Young nodded. "Yeah, I sent them. I wanted him to stop, but I also figured I could make the discovery worth my while. Benson made a lot of money on those surgeries. The more surgeries he did, the more money he made for

both himself and the center—and the more he looked like a
hero, saving patients and supposedly adding years to their
lives. He didn't seem to care that he also caused a few
deaths along the way. Percentage wise, he's considered
one of the best cardiac surgeons in the area. I figured he
owed me."

"He *owed* you? You sorry piece of shit. Why didn't you
just come forth with it?" The realization of what Dr. Young
was telling him made his stomach turn.

"Hey, it's not so easy to prove. If I'd gone to the police
and they prosecuted, he might have gotten off. I thought
this would be the best way to just make it stop. I didn't
want anyone else getting killed."

"You're just the Good Samaritan, aren't you?" Drake
eyed him with disgust. He'd love to break Dr. Young's
neck, but that wouldn't help him find Allison. "And what
does Claire Daniels have to do with all this? Was she your
accomplice?"

"Hell, no. She was just a way to get some additional
info on Benson, and one heck of a good lay, for a while.
But she got too possessive and became a liability, if you
know what I mean. I have no idea how or if she found out
about those letters, except she's pretty good at finding out
what goes on around here in general. Claire doesn't miss
much."

"Where did she take Allison?"

Dr. Young shook his head. "Like I said, I have no idea."

Drake glared at him. After a moment he decided Dr.
Young was telling the truth. But he wasn't done with him
yet. "You didn't answer my first question. How did you
know Allison was my daughter?"

Dr. Young smirked. "After Elizabeth was attacked on
the stairs, I went into her office before the police had a

chance to search it. I didn't want anyone getting their
hands on the files she'd been working on. I grabbed her
briefcase and got a little bonus for my efforts. Seems you
two were real hot in Atlanta some years back, huh? I knew
Elizabeth had it in her. She's got a hot little tail, that one,
although she'd never give me the time of day. You're a
lucky man."

Drake's eyes bore into Dr. Young for a long moment. Finally he released him. He turned as if he were returning to
the desk, then drew his arm back, fisted his hand, and
decked him—removing the smirk from the young doctor's
face.

twenty-two

Stepping over the unconscious Dr. Young, Drake spotted a piece of paper in Dr. Benson's printer. He grabbed it, then cursed when he discovered the sheet held no info, just the logo across the top that had caught his eye, and an incomplete Web address and the date at the bottom.

As he sat down and flicked on Dr. Benson's computer, his cell phone rang.

"Yes!" he barked into the phone.

"Mr. McGuire?" a tentative voice queried.

"Who's this?" he asked, making his way into Benson's Explorer program. Checking the recent history, he clicked on the MapQuest entry and held his breath. Within seconds a page popped up on the screen complete with address and driving directions.

"It's Mary—Mary Parisi. You asked me to call you if anything came up."

"Yes, Mrs. Parisi, what is it? I'm in a hurry. Has Donny told you anything more?"

One glance at the computer screen told Drake where Dr. Benson was. He could only pray Claire was with him. He remembered Allison telling Claire earlier this morning about their trip to the corn maze and how Elizabeth had feared it. Would Claire be sick enough to try to end it there?

"Well, not about that night," Mrs. Parisi said, interrupting his thoughts. "But I think I should tell you first, I wasn't totally honest with you the other day. I knew Donny saw something that night. He acted so strangely when he came in from sweeping the stairs—so angry. I was afraid if I told you, though, you would question him further and upset him even more. And now, well, I feel so ashamed, but I wasn't sure about what happened. I realize now I never should have doubted him. Donny would never hurt a flea, but sometimes I'm just not sure what goes on in his head."

Drake was heading toward the door. "Mrs. Parisi, please . . . now is not a good time."

"Right, well, of course, I know now that it couldn't have been Donny, especially after all these other attacks on Elizabeth's life, but I think he must have seen something when he was sweeping the stairs that night. Maybe even the murderer. He was so upset he went right to his room and then later . . . Anyway, I thought you'd want to know that Donny came in a little bit ago and told me Elizabeth was here. I thought he must be confused, but I went out and checked and her car is gone. He insists it was Elizabeth who took it. I thought that odd, since she's supposed to be in the hospital. I just thought you might want to know."

Drake felt his world tilt again. "Thanks Mrs. Parisi, you did right," he said between gritted teeth. "I've got to go."

He needed to see for himself that Elizabeth was really gone.

Elizabeth slammed on the brakes, missing the car in front of her by inches. Scanning the lanes on either side, she found no clear outlet. "Damn!" she swore, pounding her good hand against the steering wheel and trying not to panic. Traffic was completely stopped—again. A furtive glance at the clock told her it was almost half-past five. Just a half-mile more and she'd be at her exit.

When she stepped out of the Heartland Center earlier, she'd been surprised at the heat and humidity that engulfed her. The oppressive atmosphere had made her feel even more unnerved and breathless as she rushed to the waiting cab. Now the brewing storm was causing dusk to descend prematurely, sending an eerie light across the landscape. It sent shivers of foreboding snaking up her spine. *Please keep Allison safe!* she prayed for the umpteenth time. *And God, please let me get there on time!*

While she waited for traffic to move, she thought, guiltily, of the two policemen back at the hospital. It had been surprisingly easy to lure them in, one by one, like sheep to the slaughter. They believed her requests for help. She was very careful to give them only enough morphine to incapacitate them and not depress their respiratory systems, forcing them into a coma as the murderer had done to her bodyguard the morning she was attacked on the stairs.

But getting out of the center without being spotted wasn't so easy. She managed to slip into the supply room when the nurses were busy. The scrubs and money were exactly where the caller said they would be. Putting them on, though, proved quite a challenge with the cast on her right wrist that extended from her forearm to halfway down her fingers. Elizabeth had almost made it to the stairs when the elevator doors opened and Dr. Benson emerged, a grim expression on his face. She barely had time to pull the surgical mask up over her face and scoot into a patient's room before he turned and headed in her direction. She hid behind the doorway until he passed, then scurried across the hall and into the stairwell.

At the top of the stairs, dizziness assailed her once more. She grabbed for the railing and willed the disabling sensation aside. Although her conscious mind didn't remember the attack, she realized her subconscious did. It brought a cold sweat to her back as she negotiated her way down to the basement and out the loading gate door. Once in the cab, she closed her eyes and leaned back against the seat, gathering her reserves so she could carry out the rest of her mission.

When she reached her car, Elizabeth found the key in the wheel well, as promised. She wondered how the killer had been able to get hold of her keys to make copies. He must have had one made of her apartment key, too, she reasoned. It would explain how he managed to get to Julie the night of the murder.

A car honked behind her, pulling her back to the present. Elizabeth scanned the traffic again, but there was still no where to go. She picked up the cell phone again, knowing she needed to contact Drake. He would find a way to meet her at the maze. She was sure of it. She dialed 911, hoping they would patch her through to Chicago's Northside District headquarters where she could reach Detective Andi DeLuca. It was a long shot, but she had to try.

"Damn!" Elizabeth only heard the sound of dead air

when she held the phone up to her ear. Her phone wasn't getting any service.

A lane opened up and she dropped the phone into her lap. She grasped the steering wheel and veered sharply right, zooming into the lane and speeding forward, ignoring the throbbing in her head and her queasy stomach.

Lightning flashed against the darkening sky as Elizabeth raced up the farmhouse drive. She tried not to flinch at the pale corn leaves that flew in ghostly shapes across her headlights, torn from their stalks by the gusting wind. She no longer checked the clock. She only prayed that the caller would wait for her, that the killer didn't really want Allison, but herself—and some crazy files that she didn't have. Braking hard at the house, she jumped out of the car and ran for the back door.

Elizabeth was achingly aware that what she did in the next few minutes could mean life or death for herself and Allison. A rumble of thunder urged her on. She ran through the kitchen and into the living room. Trying the gun cabinet and finding it locked, as she knew it would be, she snatched a log from the fireplace bin and smashed the glass. She grabbed her father's shotgun and a box of shells, then, holding the shotgun awkwardly under her right arm, spilled the shells onto the floor and slid one into the chamber. She cocked it down, grabbed a handful of extra shells, then raced outside again, praying that the shotgun still fired after all these years.

Dusk was closing in fast. She flicked off the car's headlights and returned to the roadway. Driving to the field, she passed the lane that lead to the maze's parking lot, then pulled off the road. She decided to approach the entrance on foot, hopefully gaining the element of surprise. Alongside her, the cornstalks glowed a pale gold against the angry sky. She hurried on, panic threatening at the edges of her psyche. She wondered how in the world she was going to find Allison in the ten-acre maze. Planted in both directions, the maze was denser than a normal field and far less penetrable. She'd have to stick to the mowed corridors.

As Elizabeth neared the entrance, the rising wind filled the air with a violent rustling. It screamed in her ears like a banshee come to torment her. Only the occasional rumble of thunder, which grew louder with each lightning bolt that flashed across the sky, drowned out the sound.

At the edge of the deserted parking lot she slowed her steps. The awnings of the concession stands were battened down against the fury of the advancing storm. Ahead of her the entrance loomed. Strings of fake cobwebs stretched across the opening, leaving an empty, dark hole in the center like the entrance to some dark, forbidden womb. The sign above the entrance read WELCOME TO BOOVILLE: HAVE A SCARY GOOD TIME!

"Cute," she muttered as she clutched the shotgun tighter to her chest and stepped through. She moved quickly, knowing she needed to spot the killer and her daughter before they spotted her.

Drake braced himself as another gust of wind yanked the helicopter precariously to the right. Beside him, the pilot fought to keep the craft under control.

"I can't hold on to her much longer!" the pilot shouted into his mike. Drake could barely hear him through the static in his headphones. "I'm going to have to put her down," the pilot added, "or we'll all be lost souls tonight."

"No! Just a little farther," Drake urged. "We're almost there." He could see the angry waters of the Chain O'Lakes below, the whitecaps blown off by the wind, and the traffic lights on Route 12 where it snaked up through Fox Lake. A few more miles and they'd be over Richmond. The farm was just a minute or two past that by air.

Joey DeLuca tapped his shoulder from behind. "I think we should let him land!" he shouted as another lightning bolt lit the sky. "I'll call the local police. They'll get us a car and drive us the rest of the way."

Drake shook his head. That would take precious time— time he knew in his gut they didn't have. "Just a little longer . . . we're so close."

The pilot nodded. "Okay, but no promises. If this wind gusts any stronger, we're going down."

Drake strained his eyes, trying to see into the gathering darkness ahead, and prayed they weren't too late already.

Lightning flashed once more, illuminating the angry clouds and the thrashing cornstalks. The storm was almost upon them. Sensing that she was near the center of the maze, Elizabeth slowed her pace and tried to catch her breath, ignoring the pain that shot through her rib cage. Another flash of lightning told her she'd reached another dead end. Frustrated, she turned and headed in the other direction, all the time feeling as if the corn was closing in on her. She knew it was just a figment of her imagination, but it didn't make her feel any better. She tried not to think of how frightened Allison must me, held somewhere in this monstrous labyrinth by someone who was far worse than a monster.

Elizabeth stepped around another corner and was

stopped short by something soft and yielding slamming into her face. She jumped back, clamped a hand over her mouth to cut off her scream. Looking up, she spotted a small, dark figure dangling from a pole in front of her. The figure seemed to dance in the wind.

Her throat convulsed.

Not Allison! her heart screamed.

Fighting panic, she reached out a shaky hand to touch the figure, then fell to her knees in relief. It was only cloth, stuffed with hay and dressed as a witch. Her relief was shortlived, though. Seconds later another lightning bolt snaked across the sky, causing her heart to virtually stop.

A woman stood at the end of the path, not twenty feet away. Her tan raincoat flapped open at her sides. Her short blond ponytail flipped wildly in the wind at the top of her head. In front of her, a child stood, chin slumped on her chest, her own strawberry-blond ponytail held tightly in the woman's grasp. But it was what the woman held in her other hand that took Elizabeth's breath away. The knife glinted, cold and malevolent in the lightning flash. Its tip was pointed up, directly toward the little girl's throat.

The sky went dark again, but the image remained, emblazoned on Elizabeth's optic nerve, even as she darted back around the corn. She wanted to believe the woman was another hay figure, the scene just another macabre invention of the maze's designer, but she had recognized in an instant her daughter's strawberry-blond hair—and the woman who held her.

She shoved the panic down, forcing herself to think clearly and take deep breaths while all the while what she really wanted to do was rush the woman and murder her with her own bare hands! She couldn't think, couldn't understand why Claire Daniels would want to hurt her or Allison. She knew Claire was jealous of her, jealous of her relationship with Dr. Young, but that relationship was mostly in Dr. Young's head. She suspected Claire might also be jealous of her relationship with Dr. Benson. But was that jealousy enough to commit murder? On the surface, Claire had always acted friendly to her and had seemed to genuinely adore Allison.

So why was she now holding a knife to Allison's throat!

Elizabeth took one more deep breath, then darted into the corn. She pushed through, parallel to the path. If she could just stay quiet enough, the storm loud enough, she thought she might have a chance.

She had hoped to surprise Claire from behind. But moving through the tightly planted cornstalks with a shotgun in one hand and a cast on her other proved nearly impossible. She guessed she was only a few feet from Claire when a sudden lull in the wind caught her taking a step at the wrong moment. A cornstalk snapped under her foot. She held her breath, praying that Claire hadn't heard, but the woman's senses were on full alert.

"Who's there!" she shouted.

Elizabeth didn't dare breath.

"I said, who's there!"

Lightning flashed again. The wind picked up, howling even louder this time. Unfortunately, the dark green scrubs she wore did little to camouflage her against the drying cornstalks. In the flash of light Claire saw through the few stalks remaining between them.

"So, you've come!" she shouted above the wind. "I knew you would. Come out here where I can see you better!"

Elizabeth hesitated.

"I said, come out of that corn! I have a knife, the same one I used on your friend. I'd hate to use it on your little girl, but I will if you force me to!"

Elizabeth let the shotgun drop to the ground, hoping Claire hadn't seen it. Slowly she stepped out. In the last trembling light of dusk, she tried to examine Allison, searching for any signs that Claire had hurt her.

"Allison?" Elizabeth called out. Allison didn't look up. Elizabeth grew more alarmed. "What have you done to her?" she demanded.

"Relax. She's only drugged so she won't remember a thing. Nice place for our little chat, don't you think?"

Elizabeth sized up the distance between Claire and herself, wondering if she could rush her before the woman could do real harm to Allison.

"Dr. Elizabeth Iverson." Claire's voice scratched against Elizabeth's nerves. "I bet you don't feel so smart now, do you? Why don't you just hand over those files, then we'll talk."

"Honestly, Claire, I don't know what you're talking about!"

"Oh, please, spare me the act."

She tried another tactic. "Whatever it is," she said, trying to sound calm, "I'm sure we can work it out. Just let Allison go. She hasn't done anything to you." She put a hand to her own wildly blowing curls to keep them from flipping across her face and blocking her view.

"Of course I can't let her go," Claire snapped. "And don't tell me you don't know what I'm talking about, either. You think you fooled everyone with that amnesia act? I know you were just trying to take the focus off yourself, so you could hide the fact that you were blackmailing Dr. Benson."

Elizabeth's mouth fell open. "Why on earth would I do that?"

"Don't make me spell it out for you. We haven't got the time." As if to emphasize the point, lightning streaked across the sky again followed almost instantly by a loud clap of thunder. A raindrop splashed against Elizabeth's nose. In the garish flash, she marveled at how sharp Claire's features looked now, with her hair pulled back fiercely from her face, emphasizing her high, angular cheekbones, her long, thin nose, and her eyes which shone way too brightly. Elizabeth could clearly see the touch of madness in the woman's eyes and wondered why she never spotted it before.

"I know I made a mistake," Claire said, her tone rising with the frenzy of the approaching storm, "killing Julie instead of you, but it's your own fault. You were supposed to be home, changing for your party. How was I supposed to know you were called back to work?

"But fate allowed me another chance. I thought my pyrotechnic brilliant—a little trick I learned from my stepbrother. Too bad your boyfriend managed to control the car. I wanted the two of you plastered across the pavement. I bet it gave you a good scare, though, didn't it?"

"I hate to disappoint you, but I really don't remember."

"Right, amnesia. Then you don't remember the stairs, either! It was quite a scene, but once again you cheated death. Not this time, Dr. Iverson. You're going to give me those files, then we'll trade—Allison for you. They'll find her in the morning crying over your dead body. It's just too bad I won't be there to see it!"

"You'll never get away with it."

Claire laughed, high and shrill. "That's what your friend sputtered, just before she collapsed on the floor. Now give me those files, or I may have to change my plans. I wouldn't want to hurt your kid—but maybe just a nice slice down her tender little cheek."

Elizabeth stared in horror as Claire raised the tip of the knife. Lightning raked the sky again, accompanied instantly by a sharp clap of thunder, louder than any so far. It was enough to bring Allison out of her drugged stupor.

"Mommy?" she asked, raising her head.

Elizabeth's heart wrenched. "It's okay, baby. I'm here. Don't move!" Whatever Claire had given Allison, it was beginning to wear off. New fear tore through Elizabeth as she prayed Allison wouldn't do anything to imperil herself even more.

But Allison took a step forward, despite Elizabeth's warning. Claire tugged on her hair, pulling her back. Through the gloom, Elizabeth saw the knife graze Allison's cheek; droplets of blood formed on her face.

"Damn it!" Claire shouted. "Now look what you made me do!"

Elizabeth's mind raced. She needed a plan. If she ran back into the corn, would Claire actually hurt Allison? She couldn't chance it. Her only hope was to keep Claire talking and pray for an opportunity to rush her.

"All right, I admit it," she said quickly. "I blackmailed Dr. Benson. I needed the money. It's not easy raising a daughter on a single salary."

"I knew it! I knew it was you!" Claire shouted. "What do you think of your mommy now, Allison?" The girl looked up, confused. "She's not so smart now, is she? Hopefully, though, she was smart enough to bring the files with her."

"I don't have them. They're in the car." The raindrops came faster now, spattering in the dirt between them. The wind turned sharp.

"Jeez! I told Noel you were nothing but a stupid bitch!" Claire screamed. "I swear I don't know what he saw in you. Miss Cold Ass is what I called you, with your preppy ways. You managed to fool Carl, too, didn't you, and even that handsome FBI guy, but not me. I was the one who saw through you."

Again Elizabeth forced herself to act calmly, although she'd give anything to scratch Claire's eyes out.

"You're right. You were the one, you caught me. Now, if you'll bring Allison, I'll give you all the proof I have. And there will be no more blackmail, I promise. No one will have to know about this."

Claire cocked her head suspiciously. "You think I'm stupid?"

No, I think you're out of your mind, but that isn't going to help me. "What else do you want from me?"

"I want you to explain it all once more—to him!" Claire pointed the knife toward a point in the path behind Elizabeth.

She turned and saw Dr. Benson standing less than three feet behind her. He flicked on a flashlight and aimed its beam at Claire.

Elizabeth wondered how long he'd been there. In the glow of the flashlight, she spotted his salt-and-pepper hair in disarray, his tie loosened at his neck, his suitcoat open. It was the first time she'd seen him such a state, but when he spoke, he was all business, calm, as if speaking to a patient.

"Claire, what have you done?"

Claire ignored his question. "Go ahead," she ordered Elizabeth. "Tell him you were the one blackmailing him! I want him to know that I took care of it all."

"Claire?" Benson asked again.

"I took care of it!" Claire shouted, clearly proud of her

actions. "I knew she was blackmailing you. I found the letters. I knew you'd never believe it was your prissy protégée who sent them. But I knew it was her all along."

Dr. Benson shook his head. "Claire, you're insane," he said matter-of-factly. He moved past Elizabeth, the flashlight still trained on Claire.

Claire held up her arm to shield her eyes from the beam of light. The knife glinted in her hand, thankfully no longer pointed at Allison. "I did this for you, don't you see? I did it for you, Daddy."

Elizabeth wasn't sure she heard right. She stared at the two of them.

"I know, Claire," Dr. Benson said, his tone patient again. "I know."

"I did it for you," she repeated. Her face began to crumple, her confidence in her actions waning. Elizabeth had the odd sense she was watching the woman turn back into a child right before her eyes.

"Yes, I understand," Dr. Benson said, moving closer. "Now give me the knife, Claire, I'll take care of it from here."

"We have to get the files," Claire reminded him, not willing to give up the knife just yet. "And then we have to kill her. She knows too much." She looked up doubtfully at Dr. Benson.

"Yes, I know," Dr. Benson soothed. "That's a girl, now just give it here." Slowly he stepped forward and laid his hand over Claire's where she held the knife. Shivers raced up Elizabeth's spine as she watched Claire look up adoringly into Dr. Benson's eyes. Finally Claire relinquished the knife and Dr. Benson chucked it into the corn.

Relief poured through Elizabeth, but it was short-lived. A fiery blast burst from Dr. Benson's side and a loud percussion echoed through the corn maze. Claire's shocked expression mirrored Elizabeth's own as she watched Claire release Allison and slump to the ground.

Dr. Benson had shot Claire! Even as her mind processed this fact, Elizabeth was stepping forward, reaching for Allison. But Dr. Benson had his own agenda. Elizabeth stared in renewed horror as he grabbed Allison and pointed the gun at her head.

"Not so fast," he said. "Claire was right about one thing: I never pegged you for a blackmailer."

twenty-three

"Mommy!" Allison cried out.

Seeing her daughter held again, this time at gunpoint, when seconds before she thought she'd have her in her arms, brought Elizabeth's memory swirling back. A kaleidoscope of images danced in her mind—Julie lying in a pool of blood, Mrs. Beal bleeding out on the operating table, Drake in the ballroom of the Palmer House Hilton, Drake and Allison at the farm, she and Drake locked together in a passionate embrace in the shower, her hair on fire, a baseball bat flying toward her face . . . The torrent of images almost brought Elizabeth to her knees.

"I'm here, baby!" she shouted. "Everything's going to be okay!" But Elizabeth feared Dr. Benson was an even deadlier foe than Claire. If she rushed him, he would surely turn the gun on her. But that would give Allison time to run into the corn and hide until someone came looking for her.

Elizabeth cursed herself for not letting someone know where she was headed. Why hadn't she kept trying the phone? How could she have been so daft to think she could keep the situation under control? She glanced down again at Claire's limp form.

"She called you Daddy," Elizabeth breathed.

"The woman was mad. She had some harebrained idea she was my daughter, which I assure you, she was not."

"But why kill her? You already had the knife!"

"Why not? She killed your friend. You should thank me for getting rid of her. If nothing else, it spared the government the expense of a trial."

Elizabeth shook her head, finding it difficult to believe Dr. Carl Benson, world-renowned surgeon, could be so coldly calculating.

"Now the files," he said. "Where are they?"

"Let Allison go."

"Not a chance—not until I have those files in my hands. Don't worry, I'm not a monster, I won't hurt her, unless you force me to."

But Elizabeth didn't have the files. The last time she'd seen them they were on her desk. Did he really think she had blackmailed him? She realized it was the only pawn keeping her alive. She had to keep the game going.

"The files are in a safety-deposit box. Someone else has the key. They're supposed to hand it over to the police if anything happens to me."

"How cliché," Dr. Benson said, shaking his head. "You disappoint me, Elizabeth. I never guessed you would do this to me when I've given you every opportunity to grow in your career. When Claire called telling me to meet her here, I half-guessed it might be her. I would believe it of Claire, but not you."

Anger sparked within her. She welcomed its fire against the ice in her chest. "Let's just say, the disappointment's mutual. I never thought you capable of murdering your patients."

"Like I explained before, that's a matter of opinion. They would have needed the operations sooner or later, and most likely would have had complications then, also. I simply sped up the process. I guess we both had bills to pay."

Elizabeth didn't answer. The rain poured down harder. She swiped at her face, trying to keep the rain out of her eyes.

"Funny thing is, I was seriously considering making the payoff—can't allow my reputation to be ruined, you know. Now it seems we're at a stalemate," Benson said. "I suggest we figure it out quick before you and your little girl catch a chill."

Elizabeth felt the urge to laugh. The idea of him worrying about their health right now was ludicrous. "You're just as insane as she was!"

"Perhaps, but I've got the gun. Now, what are we going to do about this?"

"You're going to put down your gun, release the girl, and step aside!" Drake's voice drilled, hard and menacing beside her. Elizabeth's heart sang in wonder as he stepped out of the corn, his own gun pointed at Benson.

"Why don't you tell him the truth now, Elizabeth," Drake urged. "Tell him that it wasn't you who blackmailed him, but Dr. Young. Yes, that's right. We've got Dr. Young all neatly tied up at headquarters and he's singing like a bird. He's handed over a ton of evidence against you, Benson. Looks like your little scam is up, Doc."

"Ah, Special Agent McGuire. Too bad Claire was such

an imbecile and didn't do you both in while she had the chance."

"Yeah, too bad for you. Now drop it. I'm an excellent marksman. I won't miss."

Benson just laughed and jabbed his gun deeper against Allison's temple. Elizabeth gasped as Allison looked from her to Drake, alarm mixing now with the confusion in her face. "I'm not going down alone," Benson warned. "I'll take this sweet little girl with me if I have to."

But Allison had had enough. Elizabeth watched as her precocious little girl raised her elbow and jammed it back hard against Dr. Benson. He gasped in pain and the flash-light fell from his grasp.

"Son of a bitch!" he yelled.

Allison's short stature had caused her jab to hit directly where it would hurt the most—his privates. The light went out as the flashlight hit the ground, but not before Elizabeth saw Allison dart into the corn.

The wind drove the rain now in torrents, deepening the renewed darkness. Elizabeth scratched at the floor of the maze, searching for the shotgun. Grabbing it, she turned, realizing that Drake couldn't shoot now because if he missed Benson in the dark, he might hit Allison. Another quick flash of lightning found Benson pointing his gun now at Drake. Elizabeth raised the shotgun and swung at Benson with all her strength. The angry retort of Benson's gun tore once more through the maze just as she made contact.

She knelt, trying to catch her breath, and waited for the next flash of lightning. The illuminated sky revealed Benson's gun on the ground, but he was no longer in sight. Glancing toward Drake, she spotted the blood that darkened the shoulder of his shirt.

"I'll get Benson, you find Allison!" he yelled, ignoring

his wound as he picked up Benson's gun and dove into the rows of corn.

Elizabeth was already diving into the space where she'd last seen Allison, praying that she found her before Dr. Benson did.

Drake felt his way through the trodden corn, sensing Benson in front of him. He burst onto another corridor and scanned ahead. He thought he saw a slight movement through the blinding rain to his left. He followed and was rewarded when, in another flash of lightning, he spotted Benson diving into another wall of corn. He raced forward into the dense growth.

Despite the wind wailing above him and thunder rumbling at his feet, Drake was able to follow the sounds of the desperate man crashing through the brittle stalks. He came out on another corridor, and cursed as he lost him for a second time. A movement off to the right caught Drake's eye and he raced on, once more on the trail.

Suddenly he burst through the edge of the maze and into a neighboring cornfield. Up ahead, the driving rain shone against the headlights of a combine advancing toward him. The farmer was trying to harvest as much of the corn crop as he could before it became soaked by the storm. Benson was silhouetted in the combine's lights.

"Give it up, Benson!" Drake shouted. He spread his legs and took a shooting stance, his gun aimed at the fleeing doctors who was only a few yards ahead.

To Drake's surprise, Benson turned toward him, but his defiant stance sent a warning screaming through Drake.

The doctor laughed, the sound almost maniacal. "It doesn't really matter if I get away or not, now, does it!" he shouted back. "My reputation's already compromised. Tell

Elizabeth she's a damn good doctor and I was proud to have her on my staff!"

"No!" Drake shouted. He took a step forward, but was too late. He watched, helpless, as Dr. Benson turned and threw himself toward the combine. A bloodcurdling scream filled the night as the man disappeared beneath the machine's hungry blades.

"Mommmmy!"

Elizabeth's heart turned over at her daughter's scream. Allison must have heard that horrible sound, too.

"Allison, where are you!" she shouted. She had to take a chance that Benson was on the other side of the maze by now.

"Mommy, I'm over here!"

Elizabeth burst onto an open corridor. Brushing her wet curls aside with the back of her arm, she scanned the area ahead. Elizabeth ran toward the light at the end of the corridor. Her heart leaped when she discovered Allison standing in the pouring rain beside a man she now recognized as Drake's cousin, Joey DeLuca.

Her precious daughter was safe and sound.

Tears spilled from Elizabeth's eyes as she raced toward her. Lifting Allison into her arms, she ignored the pain in her ribs as she held her close.

"Mommy, where's Drake?"

"He'll be here," she whispered. "He'll be here, sweetheart," she repeated against Allison's ear and prayed for all the world that she was right.

A rustling interrupted Elizabeth's thoughts, and Joey DeLuca turned, illuminating the darkness up ahead with his flashlight. Drake's dark, wet hair clung to his forehead. His shirt was torn, his pants muddy and ragged. To Elizabeth, though, he was one of the best sights she'd ever seen.

The grim look of relief in his eyes as he spotted them told her all she needed to know.

As he started to walk toward her, Elizabeth stepped forward, still holding Allison, and met him halfway. He took them both into his arms and they collapsed together to the ground as the rain poured down around them.

twenty-four

. . . He's a liar and a drifter! I'm sure he just wants my money. Well, I don't have any! My parents didn't leave me any. They didn't have any because they worked in the Peace Corps. That's why I had to live in foster homes.

Elizabeth sat in an interrogation room at district headquarters reading one of the journals Andi had found at Claire's apartment. The date of the first entry in this particular journal was just over three and a half years ago, when Claire's half brother, Malcolm, came back into her life. According to the entry, Malcolm found Claire by locating one of the foster homes she'd stayed at as a child. Her foster mom revealed that Danielle kept insisting everyone call her Claire Daniels. He used that name to find her through the Internet.

I've been having nightmares. Terrible nightmares. A lot of screaming, dishes crashing against the kitchen wall. I wake up shaking. Someone's holding me. I'm huddled in the corner of my bed. He's trying to crack jokes, tell me everything's going to be all right. He's a kid, what does he know? But I look up to him. I try to believe him. I remember smiling cuz he smells funny, like he just shaved or something, but he doesn't really have to. Could it be Malcolm? God, what if he's right? What if he is my brother? Who am I?

Drake had filled Elizabeth in on Claire's background. Malcolm's version jibed with reality much better than Claire's. Claire insisted in her journal that she was the daughter of a doctor and a nurse, and that they had died in a plane crash when she was little, leaving her an orphan. As Elizabeth read on, though, she realized that with Malcolm's persistence, Claire eventually began to doubt her version.

The next entry was dated two months later.

Malcolm's dead. It happened at the fireworks show. Malcolm took me with him to watch while he set up. Something went terribly wrong! It was awful! Flaming rockets were flying everywhere. I screamed and ran. When I came back. Malcolm was bleeding everywhere, and burned. He's dead now.

The next entry chilled Elizabeth.

It's just as well that Malcolm is dead. He made up those stories. God punished him for his lying. I need to find my father. God told me he's still alive, he didn't die in the crash.

She skipped forward to another entry.

The nightmares came again last night. There was terrible screaming again and the sound of wood smashing, someone, my mother? Yelling, "She's not your daughter, you son of a bitch. Can't you tell? She's nothing like you!" . . . I'm sure, now, that my father was a doctor. That much must be right.

There were more entries, about Claire searching for her father, then:

I know who my father is now. He's Dr. Carl Benson. He was at Northwestern Hospital the same time my mother worked there. They worked on the same floor. I'm sure they had an affair. I have been working for Dr. Benson for six months now. Can you believe the coincidence? He doesn't know I know yet.

Then another entry, dated just a few months ago:

I told him today. He laughed at me! Said it was impossible, that he doesn't even remember who my mother was. But I know he's lying. It doesn't matter. He's an excellent doctor. I'm so proud of him. I'm happier than I've been in a long time because I'm able to be such a help to him every day. In time, he'll realize how valuable I am to him and welcome me into his arms.

A few months later:

There's a problem at the center. I need to take care of it, for Dr. Benson—my father.

Then another entry:

The nightmares are getting worse. I can't tell sometimes if what happens in them happened for real or if I'm just imagining them.

And the final entry:

SHE WON'T GET AWAY WITH IT!

Elizabeth closed the journal. Shivers raced through her as she realized just how demented Claire was. Still, she couldn't help but feel somewhat sorry for her, or rather for Danielle—for the frightened little girl she was, the woman she became. She was only six years old when she witnessed her mother's brutal murder at the hands of her father. It was no wonder she made up a fantasy past. Elizabeth could not imagine what might happen to Allison if she were to witness such violence.

Drake entered the room. "You okay?" he asked.

Elizabeth nodded. "Yes, but it's creepy. She was so messed up. I feel strangely sorry for her. Even though she killed my best friend, she didn't deserve to die at Benson's hand. Is there any way she could have been his daughter?"

"They certainly seemed to share the same streak of madness." Drake smiled wryly. "But it's highly unlikely, according to what we've dug up. We're running the DNA tests anyway, just to make sure. None of it really matters now, though, because all the principal players are dead, except for Dr. Young. Looks like he was just about to receive a big windfall. Seems Benson was getting to ready to make the payoff, like he said. Benson was amassing quite a fortune. We've scoured through his bank accounts, which were many, along with his stock and real estate holdings. He liquidated some assets recently and put them into a separate account, very nearly totaling the requested 1.5 million. Our suspicion is that he was not only profiting from his fees for the surgeries and his salary as director of the center, but skimming off the center's books as well. We're going over those, too. Dr. Young is cooperating fully with the investigation. Turns out he's not so dumb after all."

"I still can't believe Dr. Benson killed himself."

Drake shrugged. "Dr. Benson was a money-hungry egomaniac, drunk with power. The realization in the end that his reputation was about to be shattered sent him over the edge. I've seen it before—the higher someone is, the harder they fall. Now, are you ready to go?"

"Yes," Elizabeth said, pushing the journal aside. She was more than happy to put the whole awful business behind her.

epilogue

Allison studied Drake seriously for a long moment with those big blue eyes of hers, so much like Drake's. Finally she walked up to him where he sat on the sofa in their hotel suite. She climbed up beside him and wrapped her little arms around his neck. "You're gonna make a great daddy!" she said. Then she planted a big kiss on his cheek.

Elizabeth smiled to herself. As expected, her daughter had taken the news in stride.

Drake requested an extension on his leave from the FBI for another month, then put in for a transfer to the Chicago Field Office. Elizabeth thought of returning to the Heartland Cardiac Center for a short time, to follow up with her patients, but the center was shut down and the patients transferred elsewhere, pending a full investigation. It would probably reopen with new management, but Elizabeth decided she wouldn't go back. She was considering a fellowship in pediatric cardiology at the university hospital. It was another branch of cardiology she'd always been interested in.

That afternoon they went apartment-hunting, deciding they needed a larger space for the three of them. In the meantime, they moved into a bigger hotel suite, so Allison could stay with them and return to school. Elizabeth did not want to return to her apartment, not even for a brief time—the memory of Julie's death was still too strong. Although she would miss Donny and Mrs. Parisi, she knew it was time to move on.

Exactly two weeks from the night Elizabeth laid eyes on him in the ballroom of the Palmer House Hilton, Drake took her to the Cape Cod Room at the Drake Hotel on Michigan Avenue for a late dinner. They had the night to themselves because Allison was spending the night with Mary Parisi. Elizabeth knew that Mary and Donny wanted to visit with Allison before they moved out for good.

After the entrée, Drake set his napkin on the table and cleared his throat.

"This is something I should have done a long time ago," he said, reaching into his pocket. He pulled out a velvet box. "Elizabeth, I know life with me won't necessarily be smooth sailing. My job isn't always safe, but it's important, and I'm damn good at it. I can't give it up. But I can promise you that I won't take unnecessary chances. Also I can promise that our life together won't be boring. But the one thing I will not do is let you walk out of my life again."

The soulful strains of the pianist's rendition of "A New Day Has Come," made popular by Celine Dion, drifted across the restaurant. Drake took both of her hands in his.

Elizabeth gazed deep into his eyes. Emotion welled within her. The truth was, she couldn't fathom the thought of not having him in her life, either.

"Drake, I never should have run," she said. "I was scared, I admit it. And, as I've said a hundred times already, I'm so sorry I didn't let you know about Allison. I was afraid. I realize now, though, that we can't run away from our fears. We have to face them head on, no matter what happens."

He rubbed his thumb across her fingers, sending her heart beating strong and solid with her love for him.

"That's behind us now," he said. "Let's start fresh." He let go of her hand, opened the box, and pulled out a sapphire and diamond ring. The perfect jewels glistened brilliantly in the candlelight.

"This ring was my mother's," he went on. "My father proposed to her right here in this room."

Then he stood up and did something that took her breath away. He came around the table and knelt down beside her. "Dr. Elizabeth Iverson, will you marry me?"

Tears clouded her eyesight, but she didn't hesitate with her answer. "Special Agent Drake McGuire, I will. And, whatever life brings us, I promise you, neither you nor I will ever regret it."

He slid the ring onto her finger, then stood and pulled her up into his arms. While the restaurant lights twinkled out onto the rippling waters of Lake Michigan, he kissed her until her knees threatened to buckle beneath her.

They skipped dessert.

NATIONAL BESTSELLING AUTHOR
LINDA CASTILLO

There is a dark side to every passion...

The Shadow Side

Dr. Elizabeth Barnes has devoted her heart and soul
to medical research...at the expense of love. Then a
detective contacts her about a series of homicides,
which may have been caused by the anti-depressant
she developed. Now, this cop may be the only
person who can stop the killings—and save
Elizabeth from the dark side.

0-425-19102-8

ALSO AVAILABLE FROM LINDA CASTILLO
The Perfect Victim
0-515-13370-1

Depth Perception
0-425-20109-0

Available wherever books are sold or at
penguin.com

B682

The sizzling debut from
Nancy Herkness

A Bridge to Love

Kate Chilton thought she had it all. But shortly after her husband's death, she discovers a letter from another woman: his mistress.

Furious at his betrayal, Kate decides to get even and accepts a far-from-innocent invitation from a playboy millionare. And as one wild night quickly turns into another, what began as a fling becomes something else entirely.

"SIZZLING SEX, DAZZLING DIALOGUE,
UNFORGETTABLE CHARACTERS—
A BRIDGE TO LOVE IS A BOOK TO CHERISH."
—DEIRDRE MARTIN,
USA TODAY BESTSELLING AUTHOR OF *FAIR PLAY*

0-425-19126-5

Available wherever books are sold or at
penguin.com